TRACKING THE MIST

CLARICE MONTGOMERY

THM

ALSO BY THE AUTHOR

The Keepers of Men

Tracking the Mist

For Russell

PART I

THE HUNT

1

THE EVENING AIR near the ocean was cool and damp. Mist hung stagnant over the roads uninterrupted by vehicles or pedestrians. Along the sparsely lit residential streets, Erika walked side by side with her companion taking in the neighborhood.

"I've never seen a house on stilts in my life," she said.

Christina, walking next to her, turned her gaze towards the structures. "I suppose this would seem weird if you've never seen it before. It's for the hurricanes. All the houses on the island are built on frames like that to avoid flooding. Do you see that air conditioning unit attached to the wall there?"

Erika nodded.

"Same with those. They're either placed on some sort of platform or attached to the houses off the ground. Some hurricanes are so strong you can't avoid evacuations and mass damage, but these measures help tremendously most seasons."

Both of them walked with a light pace, something between a leisurely stroll and true cardio. There was no checking of watches or care for the time, just two women and the salty night air. Erika didn't know where they were going yet, but she figured Christina would reveal that when she was ready.

"How did you find me, by the way?" Christina asked.

Erika had arrived at Oak Island that morning. She rarely used a map, just drove between cities and towns until she felt the need to stop. That need could be internal, a pressure in her gut telling her to drive no farther, or it could be external, maybe a highway exit that spoke to her or a missing person's sign at a truck stop. "I have a sense about these things," Erika admitted. "I'm sorry this happened to you."

"Yeah. Me, too," the other woman replied. "Let's get this over with."

Christina turned at the next stop sign and headed closer to the water. As they walked, the sound of the ocean roared louder. Erika embraced the familiar noises, and she looked forward to the nights here. Rarely did she spend multiple days in any big metropolis, but it was always a blessing to be called to a place that wasn't littered with noise pollution. She missed sleeping near the water.

"Where did you say you were from?"

"That last place I lived full time was San Diego."

Christina smiled sadly. "Then you won't mind a little sand for our next stop. Did you bring a flashlight?"

"Sure did."

Christina pointed ahead of them, towards the water. "There's a pier near that lighthouse. We'll be going under there."

Erika moved the sleeves of her top up to her elbows and readied her flashlight. It was almost ten at night, but even for that hour the homes seemed too quiet, too dark. "Does anyone live out here?" House after house appeared completely closed with no open windows or cars in the ports.

"Of course, but most of the houses within walking distance are rentals and its hardly tourist season. Speaking of, do you have a place to stay?"

"Not yet."

This appeared to concern Christina. "Not that there's much competition but it's getting late."

"It wouldn't be the first time I've slept in my car," Erika conceded.

Christina looked thoughtful for a moment as they approached the pier. It extended across the marsh into the sand, giving visitors a direct path to the beach from where the homes were located. The lighthouse she mentioned stood out in the partial moonlight but wasn't in use. "We'll take the stairs on the other side to get there," she explained.

The lumber of the pier held steady as the women marched across. Halfway to the end, Christina spoke again. "You can stay at my place if you want."

Erika's stomach flipped at the thought. "I don't want to intrude on your space."

She shook her head in response. "You wouldn't be. I have a guest room, and it has its own attached bathroom and everything. There's no sense in you spending money when you don't have to."

"Sure." Erika relaxed her grip on the flashlight as they approached the end of the pier. "That works. I appreciate it."

At the steps, Christina began her descent onto the sand. "Don't worry about it."

The staircase was short, not even a full story, but when they hit the sand, Erika felt almost as though they'd been lowered into the ground. She believed that the sand was a normal color during the day, but without any sun, it moved beneath her feet like a dark, sinister lava. Before she could picture anything alive moving around her, she flicked on the flashlight.

The spotlight illuminated an area right in front of her, including the light-colored sand, the large wooden support beams, and a surprisingly unconcerned Christina.

"It was right over here." The woman shivered and wrapped her arms around herself. "I wish I'd brought a jacket."

Erika didn't have one either, but neither was she particularly cold. "Me, too."

"I just have to deal. I can't seem to get warm these days."

Erika carefully stepped towards her new friend, mindful not to use the pier's beams to steady herself. When she approached where the other woman had stopped, there was nothing about the space that differentiated it from other places covered by the wood structure. The sand wasn't disturbed in any unique way and there were no markings or stains on the wood.

"Is this the first time you've been back here since it happened?" Erika asked.

Christina shook her head. "It might sound perverse or obsessive, but I come back once a day, just trying to understand it. Like if I stare at this place long enough, I'll figure out why it happened, or I'll see something I missed on all my other visits that gives me proof it occurred the way it did."

"There's no 'why' to something like this, Christina. Or at least there's no reason you should feel responsible."

"I know that, like, intuitively. But emotions are hardly logical, especially when I have to consider my own rape."

Erika winced at the word. "It wasn't your fault."

"No, I know that. But getting justice will be an uphill battle," she admitted. "Do you really think you can help me?"

"This is sort of what I do," Erika replied. "And I understand your concerns about police involvement."

Christina nodded her head vigorously. "Thank you for that. What do you think we'll need? I'll help in any way I can, obviously."

"Well, sexual assaults are hard to prove. It's very 'he said, she said,' and rarely is there any tangible evidence of the act that would separate it from consensual sex in a court room, especially if you had a prior relationship with him."

"Not much of one, or for very long, but yeah, we did. I guess that makes sense."

"So, we'll need to focus on," Erika paused, looking at the other woman before continuing, "the rest of it. Is there anything tangible that could connect you and him to the event?"

The woman rubbed her left wrist, seemingly out of habit. "He stole my bracelet, after he was finished. I think as a memento or something."

"That gives me something to search for," Erika continued. "But if we can't find the evidence we're looking for, I'm thinking we need a confession of some kind, if we can get it."

Christina looked worried. "What if he doesn't think he did anything wrong?"

Erika raised an eyebrow. "Is he a psychopath?"

"I don't know. Maybe."

"Another avenue," she said, "is the fact that men like this are rarely single time offenders. There are probably other victims. Other pieces of jewelry wherever he stashed your bracelet."

Finding nothing she could use under the pier, Erika made her way back to the stairs expecting Christina to follow. The voice that spoke up from behind her confirmed it. "He had an ex-girlfriend from a while back. Maybe several months ago? We could ask her if she's findable. I don't think anyone has heard from her since she left town after their breakup."

"I'll be local until this gets sorted for you," Erika said. "Hopefully she'll be comfortable enough to reach out to me eventually."

They clomped up the steps in unison, finally making their way back to the car. "I really can't thank you enough for being here."

"Like I said, this is what I do. We'll find a way to make this airtight."

"It had better be airtight," Christina laughed, but the sound held no mirth. "There can't be any holes if I'm going to accuse the chief of police of rape."

2

RYAN GIBSON TWISTED THE DOWEL of the motel room blinds slowly, giving himself privacy. There was no paranoia to the action, just routine. His room was on the ground level with a door that led directly outside, though he wasn't worried about intruders or loiterers of any kind. The parking lot was mostly empty, his own truck in the company of only two sedans, one of which he knew belonged to the elderly man behind the front desk. It wasn't quite the pay by the hour type of establishment, but it wasn't luxury either. He usually stayed where his savings would stretch the furthest. Unpaid leave made a man learn quickly what he could and couldn't live without.

The room was old, but clean, and held a singular queen-sized bed in the center. It was dimly illuminated by the lamp on the bedside table while the rest of the small room still held onto its shadows. If he squinted just a bit, he could make the image of his residence for the night seem like an overlay of all the places he'd slept in for the last several months. Blur out the design of the comforter slightly, ignore the details of any wall art hung as an afterthought, and he could be staying anywhere. There was truly nothing about the room to differentiate it from any of the others.

Ryan left the shadowed corners of the room alone for a moment while he unpacked.

One of the motel's main draws was its communal laundry facilities. He'd been on the road for the better part of six months, and his four rotating outfits were beginning to show the stress of overuse. The other day, his wallet fell through his pant leg and landed on the ground next to his ankle because a hole had formed in his favorite pocket. He'd have to stop by Goodwill eventually to replace everything, but that wasn't something he had time for yet.

Arms full of clothing, he grabbed the small packet of detergent he'd purchased from the front desk and made his way outside. Laundry was just around the corner and not being used by other motel guests, so he took advantage and loaded everything inside. He had an hour and a half to kill while the combined washer-dryer did its best with his clothing, but he might not be there when it was done.

Hopefully, only honest folks stayed at this establishment, and his meager collection of outfits would be safe.

Unfazed at the idea of his garments being stolen, he returned to the room and opened his backpack. Inside, he removed an American road atlas, two notebooks, and six different fully used hotel branded notepads he'd taken from other places he had stayed. Ryan knew he needed to move the information they contained to a more secure place, maybe a third note-book, but he didn't have the inclination, nor did he have the time. There was a meeting he couldn't miss in the evening.

"Here we go again," he whispered to himself as he opened the atlas to its center map.

With it unfolded on top of the mattress, Ryan could see a two by three-foot road map of the United States, marked sporadically with red dots, forty-three to be exact, and his own notes following his trek. His finger tracked the first dot, over two thousand miles from his latest location, and moved south through several more stops, then north again and finally east.

Not all the dots were red. Some were blue and marked by nothing but an 'x'. Those weren't the ones he was focused on.

He grabbed the newest hotel pad and flipped to its first clean sheet. Then, with the red pen, he marked the town of London, Ohio, with a tiny, solid circle.

In a black pen, he wrote his notes as he muttered them to himself. "London. 'Accident' occurred November 12. Case solved December 29 via anonymous tip."

Ryan didn't know why he even made that note anymore. There was always an anonymous tip.

To a stranger's eye, the notes might seem bare, but they were all he needed to jog his memory about every case he had studied for six months. His original notes, if he wanted to reference them, stayed in the backpack during his travels.

Arms crossed, he stared at the map, the dates getting nearer to the present as he moved across the country searching them out. When he'd first started, he'd been over a year and half behind and had to visit several towns before he understood more of the pattern. Then his chase zeroed in on more recently solved cases in the hopes that all the evidence would eventually catch up to the present. He felt he was getting closer, both in space and time, to the man he was chasing.

"Where are you going next?" he asked the map.

His phone buzzed in his pocket, and he thought about ignoring it until he saw the name and swiped to answer. "Colleen," he said as a greeting.

"Hi, Ryan. Are you somewhere safe?" She knew better than to beg him to come home. Ryan made sure his friends and family had a general understanding of his whereabouts, that was the silent agreement he'd made with them. If they trusted that he was taking care of himself, they wouldn't insist he return to them.

Not that they could force him to, but he didn't like the idea of them worrying, so he maintained regular contact.

"Of course. Safe as I can be in this area." At that thought, he turned and made sure the deadbolt was secured, just in case.

"And where would that be?"

He glanced at the spot on the map, not yet marked in pen of any color, but naming his location, nonetheless. "Just outside Annapolis."

"Hmm. That feels really far away."

"You might be right about that," he smiled to himself. Colleen was a homebody, the kind of girl who would raise her kids in the town she was raised in, married to a boy she grew up with—it just wasn't the boy he thought it would be.

"Any leads?"

Ryan appreciated her indulgence. He didn't think she actually believed he would find the man he was looking for, but he was grateful she tried to act as if she did. It sure beat the antagonism and condescension from his parents who believed berating him was a viable plan for getting him home.

"There are always leads. Plenty of them end up being exactly what I'm looking for."

"But?"

"No sign of him yet. Just more solved cases. I know I'm getting closer, I feel it, but not having concrete evidence of that can be frustrating. It's hard to work blind like this."

She didn't say anything back, and Ryan pulled the phone away from his ear to make sure the call hadn't dropped. It was still connected. "Colleen?"

"I'm here," she said. "I think you're probably doing good work and if you feel you're getting closer, then I believe you."

"I appreciate that, Colleen."

She sighed and he could hear her shuffling papers in the background. "Do you think you'll have the answers you need, in say, three months?"

Ryan paused and his old friend spoke again before he could answer.

"It's just that Travis and I were hoping you'd be back in town for the wedding. You never RSVP'd."

He rolled his eyes since she couldn't see him. "I think I reserve the right to skip out when my ex-girlfriend is marrying my brother."

"It wasn't like that with us and you know it," she quipped back, not unfairly. It hadn't been serious, and it was manipulative of him to portray it that way. "We broke up years ago in high school, so you need to stop using that as an excuse to stay away."

"You're right," he sighed. "I just don't want to promise anything I can't deliver on. I doubt I'm going to be done with whatever this is by then. I need to find this guy."

"Well, at least it sounds like you're chasing a good guy for once instead of a bad one. Solved cases are a blessing. But what are you going to do if you find him? Slap him with a fine for being a good Samaritan?"

"No," he replied. "I guess I need to thank him for helping me. And I want to know how he does it."

Whoever this person was, it was someone brilliant and skilled, someone Ryan could learn from. His unsolved cases' rate could drop to zero.

Colleen was silent for a moment before replying. "You can't save everyone, Ryan."

Obviously, he thought. He knew that rationally, but it didn't stop the sleepless nights after a case had gone cold or standing over the body of someone who passed away too young doing something reckless. And, yeah, maybe he couldn't save everyone, but he could save as many people as possible or at least bring them justice. That's where the man he was chasing came in.

"I can keep trying though," he said with humor in his voice.

"Sure," Colleen agreed. "I'm just hoping some unsolvable crime happens near home so you can follow your vigilante evidence collector back here in time for the wedding."

Ryan winced. "Don't wish that on our community, Colleen. Seems like bad karma."

"Alright, I'll take it back if you promise to come home in three months."

"How about this," he said while shrugging on his jacket, "I will give you a firm yes or no to the wedding in less than six weeks."

"And a plus one?"

The hotel room door slammed shut behind him as he made his way to his truck in the parking lot. "I doubt I'll have anyone worth bringing in three months."

"A girl can dream. Stay safe, Ryan."

"You, too," he said before ending the call.

In the cab of his truck, he turned on the ignition and gave his windshield one swipe with the wipers to remove the drizzle that had accumulated while he was inside. The clock on the dash said he had plenty of time to get to the restaurant.

Good. He always wanted to be early for these meetings.

∾

"HERE'S YOUR BEER," the waitress sat a cold glass in front of Ryan and moved the pitcher over his empty cup, "and a refill on the water."

As she finished pouring, he looked up at her with a genuine smile. "Thank you."

She grinned back, appearing younger than she had before with a dimple in one cheek. Ryan originally thought she must have been in her early thirties, but now he wasn't sure.

"Do you need anything else?" Her voice was sweet and had the soft lyrical thing that he usually liked with women, but he had other business to deal with. She picked at one of the buttons on her shirt while she spoke, and Ryan couldn't decide if it was a nervous tick or some kind of unconscious signaling. Either way, he kept his eyes on her face.

"Not yet," he gestured to the empty booth across from him. "I'm still waiting on someone."

"Right," she said. "I'll just take another lap in a few minutes to see if they've arrived."

After she left, Ryan resisted the urge to stare at his phone while he waited. He had more discipline than that. It was a tempting way to pass time and avoid eye contact with anyone trying to offer empathy to a man they thought had been stood up. He could also convince himself that he was doing research, looking up new cases. Deciding to test his skills at waiting without distraction, he sipped conservatively from his beer while keeping his gaze forward, not focused on anything specific. The door to the restaurant was just ahead of him, right where he needed it.

"Stop glaring at everyone or he'll never approach," Sergeant Vincent, his former supervisor, had snapped at him one day when they were waiting in a park to meet one of their criminal informants. Well, the closest thing their town had to an informant. Kevin was a homeless man who kept them in the loop on what was being sold on the streets from high school weed smoking to harder stuff being cooked on the outskirts of town. If something deadlier arrived, like fentanyl, Kevin was the first to know and brought the new dealer's name directly to the police. In exchange, he avoided real charges for his harmless infractions and the reward of an occasional night out of the winter elements where he slept in a holding cell. It gave Kevin plausible deniability about his police connections with other criminals as well.

Ryan liked to think the man had good intentions, but Vincent was more skeptical. He thought the homeless man just wanted to get high on the streets without dying from a laced joint.

"If you don't unclench your ass," the sergeant had continued, "I'm making you wait in the car. Remind me never to put you undercover anywhere."

In the booth Ryan reached for his glass and saw crescent indents on his palm from where his nails had been resting a moment earlier. His knuckles, similarly, took a few flexes before they untensed from the fists he'd made, and he ignored the lingering stiffness in the joints on his right hand.

Maybe Sergeant Vincent had a point about him being more at ease in the field.

Wind followed the man who opened the front door of the restaurant before he was able to close it behind him. Dressed in uniform, he looked apprehensive as his eyes scanned the dining room, but Ryan recognized him from his head shot. He raised a hand to get the man's attention and stood to greet him.

"You must be Ryan," the man said as he offered a handshake. "I'm Jeff Carey."

"Jeff, thanks for meeting me. Have a seat," he said and slid back into his booth.

The friendly waitress returned for Jeff's order, still trying to make eye contact with Ryan which he avoided by taking out the free motel pen and pad to set on the table. If the person he was meeting with didn't mind, he might take some notes during the conversation. If they seemed uncomfortable with it, then he waited until they left and wrote everything he could recall right away. He couldn't get an immediate read which preference Jeff would have, as they stayed silent while they waited for her to bring his order. For those few minutes, neither spoke to each other nor sought out other distractions.

"Here's your drink." She set the glass down on the other side of the table and perked up again. "Will you guys be wanting food menus?"

Ryan looked at Jeff, waiting for his answer. "No, thank you," the other man said, and Ryan was relieved. Food was just a distraction and often came out when the conversation was already over anyway. He liked to have a quick exit if one of his meetings had emotional consequences for whoever he was talking to. A few months back, he'd been speaking with a detective about a case that affected her personally, as the victim had been close to her. She'd descended into violent sobbing towards the end of their meeting.

Ryan was surprised she'd been allowed to stay on the case, but her involvement hadn't created problems for the prosecution after the irrefutable evidence arrived from the vigilante.

Jeff took a swig of his drink and set it down. "It was...interesting to receive your call."

"I bet," Ryan agreed. "Have you ever had someone call and ask about the case?"

"A few pesky reporters here and there, but mostly no," he replied as he shook his head. "There was a week or so where it garnered some local attention, but we never really have a crime free day in these parts. There's always a full caseload."

Ryan had assumed as much. Annapolis was a huge city center, not as big or as dangerous as Baltimore, but with a crime rate that would have felt astronomical compared to what he was used to back home.

"I get it. Not all towns and cities are built the same."

"That wasn't meant to disparage your work. Hell, I fantasize about moving somewhere quieter, so I don't have to witness the worst parts of humanity on a daily basis. Where did you say you were from?"

"Cody, Wyoming. I was a detective out that way until I took leave about six months ago."

Jeff nodded and took another drink before continuing. "I have to admit, I'm a little in the dark. I'm happy to talk and answer questions, but I'm just confused as to why a detective so far from his home wants to talk to me about this."

"I was already coming to the East Coast for personal travel," Ryan lied, "when a friend mentioned your case. I thought it sounded very similar to something that happened in one of my cases last year."

Jeff's expression revealed a mild amount of surprise, but not enough for him to speak over Ryan.

"I could go first, if you want?"

"Sure," Jeff said. "I'd like that."

Ryan inhaled slowly, steeling himself for the conversation ahead. Plenty of time had passed, but there was no erasing the images and memories he had of the scene.

Jeff was right in his assessment of Ryan's caseload or lack thereof. He wasn't accustomed to that kind of violence.

"Eight months ago, we found the body of a local teenage girl. Her name was Sloane." Jeff's expression softened when Ryan began speaking, and he thought maybe his tone was revealing too much. "It's a small community, so when someone is murdered, it's unfortunately always someone you know."

"I'm sorry for your loss."

"Thank you." Ryan played down his relationship with Sloane for Jeff, but their families had been close enough to share holidays when he was growing up. Her father worked for the post office, and her sister graduated in the same class as him and owned a small bakery. The dispatchers at Ryan's precinct stopped by often for breakfast pastries to give to all the officers.

The bakery had since closed.

"It was a brutal scene. Her body was found in the early morning, on the edge of the Shoshone River. Perp probably thought she'd wash away, but we had a dry year. There wasn't enough water to pull her away completely and what was left of her clothes snagged on a bush. A local taking their morning jog found her just hours after she'd been killed.

"It was obvious there had been sexual violence involved, and the autopsy confirmed that for us later. Her shirt was torn, pants at her ankles. The water had washed away most of the DNA evidence, but the head wound was obvious enough that we saw it right when we arrived at the scene."

"Jesus," Jeff whispered under his breath.

"We knew from questioning her sister that a local nineteen-year-old had been harassing her lately. At first it was nothing terribly out of the ordinary, but the kid wasn't getting the hint. He'd call the house and hang up, he'd show up to homes where she was babysitting, stuff like that. Her sister officially filed a complaint, but nothing came of it."

"Why's that?" Jeff frowned at the news. Ryan didn't blame the man for his judgement. He'd feel the same way if he heard this story from the other side.

"The guy was the mayor's kid."

"Ah," was all Jeff said, but the disappointment left his face.

"So, basically, we know it's him, but it's his word against the justifiably angry sister's. His mom gave him an alibi for the night and there's nothing tangible tying him to the scene. The entire interview he's lawyered up to the gills, which we expect, but he's just so smug. Several times when I was recounting the violence Sloane must have experienced before her death, he grinned. At one point, he had the nerve to wink at me."

Jeff cursed quietly but didn't interrupt.

"It ate at me. We let him go, and he went back to his life while we pretended to investigate other avenues. I had to interrogate her dad, the neighbors, even the school janitor knowing they did nothing wrong. It made me feel dirty and useless. There were no good leads to follow because why would there be? The only place to go was that one kid."

"So, what changed?"

Ryan relaxed his jaw muscles enough to speak. "A month after we found her body, and probably two weeks after the mayor stopped pressuring us to find a fake criminal to pin it on, I got a package."

Across the table, Jeff sat up straighter and leaned forward.

"It was sent to the precinct but to my attention. We don't have the protocols of bigger cities, so no one flagged it as suspicious or anonymous. It just came to my desk, and no one thought anything about it."

"What was in it?"

Ryan finished his beer, then pulled his collar away from his neck. "Three items. First was a Ziplock with a used condom in it. When the labs came back, it was covered in Sloane's blood and our perp's DNA." The other man winced, but Ryan continued, "Second item was a brick. It was also covered in Sloane's blood and the kid's fingerprints. He also left skin flakes all over it."

"Those are compelling," Jeff interjected. "But also, still technically circumstantial. If you were going to take a case against someone with that kind of local political power, you'd still be at risk when it came to a jury."

"The last item," Ryan said, "was a cassette tape. It was a recorded conversation between the mayor's son and his best friend. It sounded like they didn't know they were being recorded. The idiot bragged, at length, about what he'd done to Sloane while his friend egged him on for more details."

"Hmm," Jeff appeared thoughtful. "Is there a chance the friend was trying to help? Maybe he was the one recording?"

"That was my first thought, but when we brought him in, he freaked. The kid burst into tears and begged for his parents," Ryan explained, leaving out any particulars about that interrogation. "Lucky for him, his dad is an attorney. They arrived and we gave them the interrogation room. At that point, I thought we were going to get locked out again, but this kid came from a good family. I think he was probably in more trouble with his parents than with us." Ryan laughed, but with limited authentic humor. "The dad negotiated for community service for his son, for not reporting his friend and withholding evidence from authorities, in exchange for an on the stand testimony from him to put the mayor's son away."

"Did it work?"

"The perp pled guilty, getting fifteen years before a chance at parole. It's not enough, but it's more than we would have had. And the mayor resigned in disgrace, which was just an added bonus."

"Let me guess," Jeff had a cynical lift to his brow, "you still don't know who the anonymous tip came from?"

Ryan shook his head. "The friend doing trash pick-up in our parks insists it wasn't him." If it had been him, admitting it probably would have kept him from facing as many consequences as he had, even if his father forced him to do community service anyway.

Jeff waved at the waitress, though Ryan was loath to be interrupted right when they were getting to the other man's turn to share. "You want another one?"

Ryan shrugged. "Sure."

The dimpled waitress poured two more beers out of the tap before walking them over to the table. Both detectives took a long swig before speaking again.

"I can see how you think our cases are similar," Jeff began.

Ryan put his elbows on the table, leaning forward and mirroring Jeff's stance when it was his turn to talk.

"My situation was a little different. Like I mentioned, our case load is always full. There's so much murder and robbery and violent crime that most days I don't even feel like showing up. I'm not trying to belittle your experience, but something like what happened to your Sloane would have been less jarring in our neck of the woods."

"I understand."

"That being said, I feel all of them. Not unlike you probably do, as well."

Ryan nodded and hoped he would come across as sympathetic. "I never thought you didn't."

Jeff seemed to accept this and continue, "Mine was a little bit different than yours, for a few reasons. We never had any real suspect. Honestly, we never expected to find one. Certain parts of our city don't trust or respect police, and this area was one of them.

"The victim was a thirteen-year-old kid. A gunshot to the neck, left in the street. It makes me sick just thinking about it, but I knew the area we were working with. No one who lived there was going to speak to us, and even if they wanted to, there would be, at best, social consequences for that person. Most likely the consequences would be violent or deadly. We didn't do much with the case at first because there was nothing to do. Even if I had a lead, most of the people I arrest for serious crimes get released on bail. If not for the information we got, this kid's murder would never have been solved."

"What kind of information?" Ryan had more access than the average person to evidence and cases that were usually closed to the public. He knew an anonymous tip had helped solve this case, but he didn't know in what capacity or how much of an impact it had.

"Similar package to yours, but not sent to me, submitted to basically our physical version of an anonymous tip hotline. It was different though."

"How so?"

"Well, like yours, we received the murder weapon. It was the gun used to kill our victim, covered in fingerprints and everything, but that wasn't enough. There was more than one set of prints, so it wouldn't have worked for us. Even if it was the murderer, he ended up being one of those guys I mentioned: in and out of courts with little to no repercussions. If you get out on bail, why show up to your hearing, you know?

"Anyway, the gun wasn't going to be enough, but we didn't necessarily care about that until after the forensics came back on it."

Ryan had his notepad out, ready for anything he might not remember, but he tried not to use it. Sometimes, note pads made people nervous. They added a paper trail, but Ryan had a feeling he might need it soon and it hadn't scared Jeff so far.

"Why not?" he asked.

"It also came with a note," Jeff continued. "Essentially, it said that this was the weapon that murdered our victim, the prints of the murderer are on it, as well as some others. The shooting had happened because of some gang related activity in the area that turned deadly. Our victim was just collateral damage because he was in the wrong place at the wrong time.

"The note then said that if we ran the forensics on the gun and every-thing matched what the tipper predicted, we should be at the abandoned shipping containers off 19th and Chesapeake at 3:15AM that Thursday morning."

"How did your supervisors handle that?"

"I didn't tell them," Jeff smiled. "I just scheduled a long overdue poker night with some other officers for that exact time and location. Turns out, there was a huge deal going down. The quantity of drugs these guys were trying to move was more than I'd ever seen, which is saying something. We got all of them arrested and questioned separately. It was the kind of move-ment that pulled the case into federal jurisdiction, which meant our judges weren't able to let them off easy this time."

"What about your perp?"

"One of his friends squealed, thinking it would get him reduced time. It didn't."

Ryan nodded and finished his second beer. "Happy endings all around then."

"The only ones people in our line of work can hope for, anyway," Jeff agreed and finished his drink as well. When he set his glass back on the table, Ryan watched a bead of condensation roll down the side until it pooled at the base, disappearing into the small puddle collected beneath it.

They sat for another moment before Ryan spoke. "I have to ask..."

Jeff looked apologetic. "Sorry, man," he said as he threw on his jacket and shuffled out of the booth. Once he was standing, he shook Ryan's hand again. "Nothing on my end about the anonymous tip either. No prints, no video, no voice, no nothing. I wish I had more information for you."

"Oh, I was just curious and wanting to connect—"

"Sure." Jeff gave a half smile as he put a hand on Ryan's shoulder. "You were just in town, I get it. I hope you find what you're looking for." The other detective walked towards the door, and over his shoulder, offered one last platitude. "Enjoy your extended leave."

Ryan wasn't surprised at being caught, and he didn't really care. He was disappointed at the lack of new direction. All he needed was one, just one story like his, that had a new lead. But unfortunately for him, this guy covered his tracks very, very well.

He threw a fifty-dollar bill on the table and left, hoping the waitress didn't confuse his generosity with interest.

3

FOR ALL THE RESEARCH HE DID trying to find the man who helped him solve Sloane's murder, Ryan didn't always have his next direction picked out when he hit the road after meeting with someone like Jeff. Every third interview or so, he liked to travel with no destination in mind for a couple hours before stopping to pick his next solved case. It made him feel as if he was in control of his voyage rather than following someone helplessly.

Annapolis had been industrial, cold, and dreary. He didn't mind that kind of weather since he'd grown up in a snowy, mountainous climate, but he figured it wouldn't hurt to drive south for a bit, maybe find a smaller town. He wasn't likely to get anything resembling spring or summer but maybe he could go somewhere that didn't require him to wear a jacket all the time.

At noon the day after his meeting with Detective Carey, Ryan checked the outside temp on his dash and was finally satisfied with what he saw before pulling into a truck stop off the interstate. He liked to be efficient with his stops, picking places where food, gas, a cleanish bathroom, and reliable Wi-Fi were available. This place had the first two and, hopefully, the two second as well.

It was a sunny day, which was good for travel, and Ryan was not the only one to take advantage. The parking lot was busy but not overcrowded, and he found a space to park before pulling his backpack from the passenger seat. The diner attached to the large gas station had two brightly lit signs, one advertising that it was open and the other declaring that the internet was for paying customers only.

Now all he would need eventually was the clean restroom.

He pushed the door open and was greeted by a bell ringing to alert his arrival. At that time of day, it felt superfluous since the dining room was well occupied and appeared to be fully staffed.

"Welcome in," the closest waitress greeted him while she reached for the menus and hand-rolled napkins and silverware. "How many will be eating with you today?"

"Just me," he said.

"Do you mind sitting at the counter?"

"Not at all."

She grabbed a single menu and silverware set before smiling and nodding him in the right direction. "Over this way, sir."

It was the first time in a while he'd been called 'sir' by anyone, much less someone a bit older than he was, and it warmed him. The sentiment reminded Ryan of home, and he thought to himself that he might like it in the South. The weather, people, and cuisine were all great selling points in his opinion.

When they arrived at the counter, she placed the items neatly over the laminated placemat before asking him if he'd like anything to drink besides water.

"A cup of coffee would be great, please."

After slinging his backpack on the chair behind him, he pulled out his laptop. The internet password was printed at the top of the menu, and he plugged it in to begin his research.

When he'd first started this personal investigation, he'd hit a lot of road-blocks. As it turns out, not every crime solved with an anonymous tip was the kind he was looking for. Many of the first ones he looked into ended up being disgruntled exes or bitter family members outing the people who wronged them in some way. They wanted to get their revenge without being implicated and calling police stations anonymously was an easy way to achieve that. Unfortunately for them, once the intended target was arrested or questioned, they usually tattled on everyone they knew in order to get out of whatever penalization was on the horizon and the person who anonymously tipped got caught up in that wave.

It was several weeks before Ryan trained himself to narrow down the cases into ones that matched the modus operandi of the man he was chasing.

The cases couldn't simply involve an anonymous tip. Those were plentiful and typically didn't go anywhere. Often, the tips were wrong or lies or inadmissible. Ryan threw those out right away when he saw them.

No, he wasn't just looking for the majority, he was looking for cases that were impossible, that were desperately unsolvable until evidence arrived from an unnamed stranger that busted the case wide open. Some were like his, where the perpetrator was known to the police, but proof was missing. Situations like those affected him the most since he could relate. The other cases were like Jeff's, basically uninvestigable until the package arrived.

Ryan did a couple of quick searches on different news websites before finding a story that interested him. An added benefit, even if unnecessary for his purposes, was that it was only a couple hours away.

"Are you getting food, sir?"

He grinned at the waitress before doing a quick scan of the menu. "Just the cheeseburger, please. No tomato."

She jotted down his request on a small order pad while she spoke. "Everything else on the burger okay with you? And it comes with fries, but you can upgrade to a side salad if you want."

"Fries are perfect. And everything else on the burger is fine, thank you."

Once she left, he pulled his phone out and dialed an old friend from work. As usual, he only had to hear the ring once.

"I should have blocked your number a long time ago," Loretta answered. Her consternation amused him, and he didn't hold back his chuckle.

"You love hearing from me."

"Maybe I would if you called every once in a while to ask how I was doing. I only ever hear from you when you need me to look something up because you don't have access to our databases anymore."

Ryan winced. She wasn't wrong, and he didn't like to think he was taking advantage of her. "I'm sorry, Loretta. How's David? Is he still playing baseball?"

"Just made the cut for varsity last week," she bragged. "And I appreciate you asking after my son, but I'm not on break, so why don't we just get around to why you really called?"

"Fair enough," he said. "I'm looking into a particularly nasty one, but it has our mystery man's name all over it. This is exactly the kind of case he works on."

Loretta hummed her excitement over the news. According to most people in Ryan's life, he was wasting his time chasing an apparition, an uncatchable man at best, and one that didn't exist at worst. They believed that he'd never find the person responsible for solving his case, and what proof did he have that all the other ones he investigated were even connected? What was his proof that it was the same person all over the country?

But for all her complaining that Ryan didn't call enough for personal reasons, Loretta was a true believer in his cause. The entire situation was one that hit her hard, from the murder to the inability to arrest the perp, up until the miracle of the evidence being delivered. She wanted to know who helped them as much as he did, maybe more. Sloane had been a close friend to David their entire lives, probably could have been more someday, and Loretta was out for scalps after her murder. She was likely planning an extravagant thank you gift for whenever Ryan found the guy.

Though, finding him was proving harder than expected since he clearly didn't want to be found. It really did feel like grasping at vapors on some days or chasing after fog.

"You got a city and dates for me?"

Ryan dutifully rattled off the town's name and when the crime had occurred. He could tell when she had the case pulled up because he heard her quiet gasp across the line.

"I swear, every day I see something so egregious it makes me want to give up on humanity entirely."

"If you wanted to maintain your faith in the goodness of mankind, you shouldn't have gone into law enforcement."

"You can say that again. Let's see if this has our hero's fingerprints on it," she replied. She often referred to the man as a hero or an angel. Loretta had a way of making things feel fantastical, like life was a movie and she was always looking for the next main character to romanticize. Her nature offered a reprieve from the darkness of their world, and Ryan loved her for it.

"I have a feeling it's him," he replied. While he listened to her click sporadically as she read over the case notes she had access to, the waitress dropped off his burger. He mouthed a silent *thank you* before shoving two fries in his mouth. They were pleasantly hot and crispy, and he reached for three more before Loretta spoke again.

"Oh yeah," she said over the line. "If this isn't our guy, then I don't bake the best bread in Park County."

"Your sourdough is fantastic," Ryan garbled out over another mouthful of food.

"Like your opinion is worth anything. You'd eat a roadkill possum if it was fried long enough."

He swallowed and took a long swig of water before speaking again. "You have a contact for me?"

Loretta rattled off a name and phone number while Ryan copied down the information in one of his notepads. "We're getting closer, Ryan. I can feel it. I think you're going to find our man soon."

"I hope so," he said. "I don't want this to be all for nothing, you know?"

"You can't think that way," she argued. "You're going to find him, and even if you don't or he's not who you thought he was, I think you've done well for yourself these past few months. You've grown up a lot, all things considered, and I think you're really refining your investigative skills."

"That's a positive too, I guess," he responded. If he was being honest, Ryan wasn't sure when or if he was going back to detective work. Even though Sloane's murderer was in jail, the whole case had made him feel impotent. If not for the tip, the murderer would still be walking around free and there would have been absolutely nothing Ryan could have done to change that. That kind of potential injustice made him want to scrap his whole career.

He still lost sleep about it sometimes.

"Let me know how this one goes," Loretta said. "And then I'll wait to hear from you until you need me again."

"You're the best."

"I know," she quipped before hanging up on him.

After closing and pocketing his phone, Ryan finished his lunch and left cash for the tab. He ripped the top sheet off his notepad and put away his laptop before making his way to the restroom. The other diners didn't pay him any consideration, keeping their eyes on their company or food, and Ryan was relieved. It wasn't that he drew much attention, bad or otherwise, but he wasn't in the mood to acknowledge anyone with a nod or a smile. His mind was someplace else.

The bell above the door signaled his departure, and his waitress spoke up from her spot behind the counter. "Travel safe, sir!"

He waved back at her and when the door closed behind him, he felt a brush of melancholy. Ryan didn't care for the feeling, but he decided it might be nice to stop here again if his traveling permitted. The food had been above average, and he liked the environment.

Finally, back in the cab of his truck, he held up the piece of paper with the name and phone number given to him by Loretta. Not everyone he sought out wanted to meet with him, but a surprising number had been receptive. They were also perpetually curious about the man who helped solve their cases. Ryan, after his experience with Sloane's murder and subsequent investigation, was alone in his single-minded obsession over finding him.

Without further delay, he typed the number into his phone and called.

THE RED ZONE, A SPORTS BAR IN A SMALL TOWN just south of Greensboro, North Carolina, where Ryan was meeting a man named Cornelius Benson—apparently friends called him Corn—would not have been his first choice for this conversation.

It was rowdy. Not that that was a problem for Ryan, he loved college basketball as much as anyone, but multiple games played across all the screens and the volume was on full blast for the NC State game. Large groups of young people crowded around high-top tables too small for their numbers, and they cheered with gusto anytime NC State made a basket. They also cheered whenever the other team missed one.

No, Ryan didn't choose the spot, but he never did. His mission took him to new places, towns where he didn't know anyone and he was a stranger. Strangers are almost universally ignored in cities, and while small towns can be relatively welcoming, they become less so if a newcomer trounces in asking questions about a local crime. He always found that the people he wanted information from were more open and talkative when they chose the venue. It had seemed to work so far, and Ryan hadn't had any reason to change that tactic yet.

The sports bar was making him rethink that strategy.

The main problem wasn't even the sound. As he walked through the packs of people, he didn't see a single open seat, at the bar or otherwise. He almost took his phone out to text Detective Benson about changing locations when a flailing arm caught his attention.

The arm belonged to a heavy-set man sitting by himself at a corner high-top with one unused stool. Ryan acknowledged the man and made his way to the table.

Before sitting, he verified his companion. "Detective Benson?"

The man had a wide smile that did nothing to slim his face. "You can call me Corn," he said.

"Right. Corn. Okay," was all he said back as he took his seat.

"And I can assume you're Ryan Gibson?"

"That's right."

"Well, welcome to Randleman. We're small, but you'll find we're as friendly as they come," he said.

"You guys aren't that much smaller than where I'm from."

Corn finished his drink, which appeared to be some kind of bourbon over ice. Normally, people drinking straight liquor made Ryan uncomfortable since he saw the devastating aftereffects of heavy drinking all the time in his work. In his opinion, the risks didn't outweigh the benefits, even if he was trying to forget something as ugly as Sloane's death. He tabled his discomfort for the moment since the other detective appeared to have the body mass index to handle several more drinks if he wanted. Once he set his glass back down, he spoke again.

"And where's that?"

"Cody, Wyoming."

"Ah," Corn replied, as he flagged down a waiter. "The misses and I went to Jackson once back in the day. It was pricey, and I'm not much of a skier but her family is really into that sort of thing. At least the kids had fun."

The waiter arrived with another low-ball glass of liquor for Detective Benson. He must have been a regular, as he hadn't even had to reorder.

"And for you?" The waiter turned to Ryan.

"Whatever light domestic you have on tap is fine."

Once the waiter left them alone, the other man spoke again. "What brings you out this way? I love this town, was born here and never plan on leaving, but from an objective standpoint, I don't see what would draw you all the way out here when you live somewhere as pretty as Wyoming."

Corn's southern accent became more pronounced as he made his way through a second drink. Or maybe it was only the second drink that Ryan had seen. "I've been traveling all over for a few months now. I took an extended leave of absence from work and have been making my way across the country."

"No shit? I should have done something like that back when I was young and single. Wouldn't trade my family for the world, but I married young, and Rosie had our first son nine months after the wedding. What's your favorite place you've seen so far?"

The trip wasn't for sightseeing, but the detective couldn't have known that. It was becoming apparent to Ryan that Corn did not want to bring up the real reason they were meeting, and it would be up to him to broach the topic.

"Mostly," he answered, as he sipped from his glass, "I haven't seen anything special. I've spent most of the last six months talking to other detectives, like you."

Detective Benson's expression sobered, and he nodded as his gaze turned downward into his glass. "Got it. You know, when you called, my first instinct was to avoid you or tell you to go to hell. I thought you might be one of those freaks from the media or some sicko who wants to hear a horror story. It was one of those cases you lose sleep over, especially since it could have so easily gone another way."

Ryan understood that better than most. "I could go first, if that helps."

"Sure. Thank you," Corn replied.

Amongst the raucous patrons at the bar celebrating NC State's win, Ryan recounted Sloane's murder and subsequent investigation. He detailed the mayoral corruption, as well as the evidence package and confession from the friend.

"Well," Detective Benson said when Ryan completed the story, "do you have any idea who the tip came from?"

"Not one clue," he replied. "No prints, no return address, no one calling for a reward. Not a single detective I've spoken to these past few months has any leads, either."

"Damn shame."

"Can you tell me about the Jordan case? I'll understand if you're uncomfortable or you've changed your mind."

"No, nothing like that. It's just a tough one. Always is when a kid that young gets killed."

"What happened?"

"At first, nothing criminal, or so we thought," Corn explained. "The Jordan family had one of those above ground hot tubs, something they used year-round but swore they were good about covering when it wasn't in use. The story we got from Juliet Jordan, the kid's mom, was that she'd accidentally left it uncovered and when she went inside to shower, four-year-old Tyler climbed inside and drowned.

"She was inconsolable, as we expected. And shit, we were going to leave it at that. It was a fucking tragedy, rare, but childhood drownings do happen. Every time, it's a fucking tragedy."

Ryan sipped his beer. "So, what changed?"

"On our end, nothing. The tub was so highly chlorinated, we didn't get any foreign DNA off the kid, and there were no other injuries, no broken bones or head trauma that would have explained it except that Juliet—Mrs. Jordan—told us that he never learned how to swim. We checked his blood-work, too, and there were no medicines or anything that would have caused loss of consciousness prior to submersion, nothing in his system that would impair his ability to try and break the surface. So, we chalked it up to drowning and started planning some city subsidized children's swim lessons in Tyler's honor. His mom was all on board about organizing it, too."

Corn then said something under his breath that sounded like *sick bitch,* but Ryan couldn't be sure.

"How long after Tyler's drowning did the tip come in?"

"Exactly three weeks," Detective Benson said. "It was right after Tyler's funeral. I was at the precinct late, just didn't want to go home and bring all that darkness on my family. Sometimes it takes an extra lap around the neighborhood in your car before you can go inside, you know what I mean?"

Ryan nodded as if he understood.

"This package gets dropped off to the precinct anonymously. All it has is one of those home burned DVDs. No note, no nothing. I actually had to find an older laptop with a slot for it before I could watch it."

"What was on the tape?"

Corn sighed, then his face paled as if he didn't want to remember what he saw. "There's about a three-inch gap between two of the fence panels in the Jordans' back yard. Past the fence, it's pretty open, but the next yard is quite a bit shorter, and there's another house whose yard backs up to the fence. The owners of that home—the Vons—are really into home security. Cameras and motion sensers all over the place, guns in the safe. You probably know the type.

"Anyway, not only do they have the camera doorbell, but they also have two different backyard cameras. One is on the backdoor, the other is hidden in a bird feeder towards the back of their yard of all places. On the afternoon that Tyler drowned, for whatever reason—I can only assume divine intervention or some kind of witchcraft—the bird feeder camera lined up perfectly with that three-inch gap in the fence with a clear shot of almost the entire hot tub in the Jordans' yard."

Ryan swallowed back some bile but didn't interrupt. It might be his only chance to get this whole story out of Corn.

"The video clip was about eight and a half minutes long. It showed Juliet lifting Tyler into the hot tub and holding his head under. He fought her, fought for air for maybe only two of those minutes, but she held him under for much longer. An entire life ended, and all it took was less than ten minutes."

Ryan felt pressure in his throat that he tamped down before speaking. "I'm so sorry."

"Well, so am I."

"And Mrs. Jordan?"

Corn scoffed into his glass before realizing it was empty again. "That whore is in jail. If everything goes as we hope it will during the trial, she'll get a lethal injection when this is all over."

"Justice is served then," Ryan replied.

"Damn right."

"Do you think the Von family submitted the footage? I mean, that makes the most sense."

"No," Detective Benson replied. "They were horrified when they found out. Had no idea until we asked them about it. I guess there was some kind of breach in their cloud, and the footage was pulled from an untraceable IP address."

"Damn. I was hoping you had something about the anonymous tip." If the man was using untraceable IPs, then there was no way he was sloppy enough to leave fingerprints on the package.

"Well, the precinct has security cameras."

Ryan put his glass down. "What do you mean?"

"It's like I said. I was there when it got delivered."

Ryan sat up straighter, hope flooding his chest in a way it hadn't yet on this mission. "I just assumed that your package arrived by mail or private delivery service like my evidence did." This changed everything.

Corn huffed and rolled his eyes. "No mail is getting delivered by someone on foot at ten o'clock at night."

"So, you have the delivery on tape and saw the package being dropped off? You saw him?"

Detective Benson's face grew serious as he shook his head.

"I saw *her*."

4

ERIKA EXITED THE COFFEE SHOP after her shift, pocketing her cash tips for the day. Finding employers who would pay her under the table wasn't always easy, but she'd never gone long without some kind of income. She'd really gotten lucky in Oak Island, though, not having to pay for housing. Christina didn't have to offer her home.

Her manager was more than okay with keeping her off the books, paying her cash after each shift and sending Erika on her way.

"Saves me the payroll taxes," she'd explained. Fiona, who owned and managed the shop, usually ran it herself during slow seasons but was happy to have the extra hands that year. Playing with her new grandbaby apparently held more appeal than designing lattes.

The arrangement worked just fine for Erika.

The sidewalk along the main road hardly made Oak Island a walking town, but the shop where she worked was so close to Christina's house that she felt silly driving there.

As she walked by a small consignment store, the owner was pulling sales racks of clothes inside. Erika had seen the store many times commuting to work on foot but hadn't ever visited.

"It's supposed to rain," the woman called out. "I hope you don't plan to walk far."

"Almost there," she called back without stopping.

In most of the towns and cities she visited, Erika could get lost in the populations. She liked to avoid large city centers—too much violence and pollution for her tastes—but she also kept the practice of not visiting places that would immediately recognize a stranger in their midst. These towns were small enough that locals never went anywhere without seeing someone they knew, but they also offered her the cover of polite anonymity. If someone saw a person they didn't know, there was a possibility they'd forgotten their meeting. No one wanted to risk the embarrassment of reintroducing themselves to someone they had already met.

Erika found that was especially true in the South. People were polite, but she wasn't exerting herself to make any new relationships.

Christina was an exception. There were no risks in trusting her while Erika stayed on the island.

"How was work?" Christina asked when she got back to the house. She was sitting on one of the lower steps that went to her second story front door. Like other houses close to the coastline, her eleven hundred square foot home was protected from flooding by giant stilts, though it was further inland than some of the more expensive homes.

They probably had a more specific architectural name, but Erika liked calling them stilts, as if the homes there were happy participants in a neighborhood carnival. The bright, beachy colors many people chose to paint the exteriors helped enliven that fantasy.

"Good. Not too busy, but the patrons were generous," she answered and sat on the step next to Christina.

They sat in companionable silence for a minute. While Erika waited for Christina to speak again, a man walking his bicycle home waved at her, and she waved back tentatively, glad when he kept moving without trying to speak to her.

"You hungry?" Christina asked.

"I could eat."

"Good. I need a change of scenery," she stood and dusted nonexistent debris off her pant legs.

"Do you think I need an umbrella?"

The other woman shrugged. "It rains a lot here. May as well get used to it," she responded before stepping out from under the home's cover.

Erika followed, and they walked in the direction of the pub. She didn't feel comfortable with how many times she'd already visited. If she continually showed her face in the same restaurants and bars, she ran the risk of becoming a "regular," and waiters and bartenders would try to befriend her, so she'd request one of their tables when she came to eat. It would make it harder to leave quietly without causing a stir later.

But it was Christina's favorite, so she didn't fight for new food options often.

"You seem down today," Erika said.

"Not down, just trying not to get discouraged," she conceded. "I guess when you arrived, I thought you'd swoop in and make everything better. I know that's not fair to you, and I'm grateful for your help, but it feels like we've made no progress."

Erika wasn't offended by the statement. In a lot of ways, Christina was generous in her assessment. "These things can take time, and I've only been here a couple of days."

"How long do you usually spend on a case like mine?"

"Yours is unique in more ways than one," Erika acknowledged. "Sometimes I can gather evidence quickly and move on, but most scenarios that require my help have sensitive aspects to them. Do you understand?"

"Yeah, I do." Christina smiled at her, but it didn't change the loneliness in her eyes.

Erika wished she could hug the other woman to comfort her. "We'll find it, so don't worry."

"I believe you. I'll just be relieved when this is all over and I can move on."

They arrived at the pub just as a light mist of rain began. Happy with their timing, Erika put a hand on the door but turned to speak before opening it. "That's all I want for you, too."

Christina offered her a real smile this time before they entered the restaurant.

It wasn't peak hours yet, so they could walk past the hostess stand without speaking to anyone and utilize the open seating in the bar area.

Erika always insisted on a corner table or a low traffic area so no one would hear her speaking.

It was mostly empty when they sat, but Erika kept her voice unnaturally low when she talked. "Maybe you could share some more about yourself?"

Christina looked surprised at this. "Do you think it would help?"

"Of course. Any information helps me," she explained. "If I know how you first met him, maybe places and things he knew you liked, it could help me find something on him."

"Ah. Right."

They quieted when the waitress arrived, and Erika spoke to her in a normal volume when ordering. Once she was gone, Christina began her story.

"Carter Cahill must be one of the youngest people to become chief of police around here. And it wasn't because he didn't earn it either. There was talk of that when he got the job since his dad is such a huge deal around here. The Cahills are big in local real estate."

This caught Erika's attention. "Do you know how many open properties they have right now?"

Christina shrugged. "I'm sure we could find out."

The waitress returned with the food, and Erika dug in as soon as she left. "What else can you tell me about him?"

"He wasn't the most romantic sort, but it's probably because he didn't need to be. When you're that good looking, and you've got a uniform? Forget about it. When he started giving me the time of day, I thought I was dreaming. Like why should he care anything about me? I was several years younger, with no degree, a crappy but well-paid job at the bank. What did I even bring to the table?"

Erika spoke around a mouthful of food. "I mean you're really pretty."

"Yeah," Christina scoffed. "I guess now I know what he was really after."

"Sorry," Erika whispered back after swallowing her food.

"Don't be," she replied, then wrapped her arms around herself while she shivered. "Anyway, like an idiot, I thought when he offered to buy me a drink that night it was the best thing that ever happened to me. Eventually that led to going home with him in the hopes that it would lead to a real date."

Erika didn't have much of a response to that. Christina wasn't a close girlfriend she could lecture about dating strategy. She was a victim and trying to rewrite the past was a futile exercise.

"I was infatuated with him, but I think also just tired of being alone," she continued.

"Being alone is hard," Erika agreed, without commitment.

"I guess you would understand," Christina said. "When you work with people like me, do you do everything yourself?"

"Yep," Erika replied. "One woman show."

"That sounds lonely."

Erika didn't answer right away. On paper, she didn't feel lonely. While she didn't have any female friends, there hadn't exactly been a shortage of attention from men with her age and appearance working in her favor. On more than one occasion, she went home with a guy simply because he had a bed and she didn't.

It saved money on hotels and rent, and she usually had fun.

In her travels, she spoke often with people like Christina and her cash-based jobs always required human interaction of some kind. The household in which she grew up allowed for independence and she spent much of her childhood alone by choice, needing very little time with friends. A family tragedy—one she didn't like to talk about—had only emphasized that isolation when she was a teenager.

But there was something missing, and she'd only made the mistake once of trying to fill that void. Her short-lived affair with a mechanic in Glenwood Springs, Colorado, several months back had made it too hard to leave when the time came, but she didn't let her mind wander back to that man with any regularity.

Erika changed the subject. "What else can you tell me about the Cahills?"

"Apparently, they're like huge gun nuts." Christina rolled her eyes. "Not like collectors or anything, but they're really into hunting. Carter and his dad, Robert, take time off for every kind of hunting season: turkey, bear, deer, you name it. They've got some fancy hunting lodge on the outskirts of the Croatan National Forest. I think they eat and store everything there."

"How sustainable," Erika said. "Did you ever see it?"

"No. I think he promised to take me once, but I never had the chance."

The meal was finished in silence, and Erika was about to ask for the bill when two men walked in, laughing loudly at a joke no one else had heard.

Christina looked over her shoulder then shrank into herself, and with the low lighting of the pub, it took Erika a minute to see why.

One of the men who entered was Chief Cahill. Erika didn't recognize the other guy, but he was in a police uniform, so they must have come in after a shift. "Let's get out of here," she said before throwing a wad of cash on the table.

"Thanks," Christina replied. "I don't even want to be in the same room as him."

Erika skirted the side of the restaurant quickly enough to avoid being seen by Carter or the other man as they left the pub. It was raining steadily by then, but it was not heavy enough for Erika to justify running. They'd get home soon enough, and she could take as long and hot of a shower as she wanted.

When the water gathered in her clothes enough to weigh her down, she thought about making a drenched rat joke until Christina spoke again.

"God, I am so pathetic."

"You're not pathetic. None of this is your fault."

"No, you don't understand," she said. "After everything he did, I still want him."

5

"I THINK WE NEED A NEW TACTIC," Ryan spoke into his truck's speaker phone. "I'm pretty sure I butted up against her latest work."

The latest visit with Detective Benson had been heartbreaking but revealing. He couldn't imagine how Corn was dealing with what he saw on the video, and he was grateful he hadn't had to see it.

Ryan would have liked to see the security footage of the woman who brought it to the station, but the other detective didn't bring it. He only supplied Ryan with a printed still of the woman, one he claimed was the best shot of her face.

Loretta paused her typing. "Her?"

"Yeah. That's the latest I got from Detective Benson," Ryan replied. He told her about the previous night's conversation, leaving out the disturbing details of the child's drowning.

"Wow. I guess that serves us right, assuming it was a man this whole time."

He had a hard time reconciling it as well. Not because he didn't think a woman was capable of doing investigative work, but because he'd so solidi-fied the image in his mind of a man, probably a man with a decade or two more experience than him, that it was going to take work to change his thinking. It was like following a favorite character through three novels, picturing him a certain way, only to find out in a footnote that you'd guessed their appearance completely wrong. The new information made Ryan feel unbalanced.

He looked down again at the photo from the security footage that had the clearest image of the package being dropped off at the Randleman station. The face of the woman wasn't discernable since it was covered in shadows except for her nose and the curve of her left cheek bone, and her stature was too small to be masculine. Her dark brown ponytail also alluded to her gender. Despite these details, she looked like she could be anybody.

"Well, it could still technically be a man. He might have had someone else drop the package." A girlfriend, perhaps? No, with his movements and constant travel he wouldn't have someone that close to him. He might have used a local, though Corn mentioned not recognizing her in the slightest.

"Nope," Loretta popped the rebuttal. "I like the idea of it being a woman. I'm sticking with that. Now, what's all this about a new tactic?"

Ryan had the road atlas unfolded on his dash as he sat parked in his truck. Across the map, the red dots collected with greater frequency, and closer in time, culminating in his stop in Randleman. "I think the Jordan case was the last one she helped solve," he explained. "She was only there two weeks ago. If I keep going after solved cases, it'll set me back, pull me further away."

"What did you have in mind?"

"Well," he winced at how broad his search was about to get, "I think I need to start following unsolved cases." Loretta was quiet on the other end. "Loretta?"

"I'm here," she said. "Do you have any idea what that looks like? Are you insane? You know the statistics. Something like forty percent of murders go unsolved. Seventy-three percent of violent robberies are unsolved. Ninety-one percent of motor vehicle thefts go unsolved. You might as well open your search to the whole goddamn planet."

"I know how that sounds—"

"And those are just the ones that get reported! People don't even call in violent crimes anymore because they think it won't change anything."

"Loretta—"

"Don't 'Loretta' me when I'm being perfectly reasonable."

"I'm not saying that this plan isn't unreasonable. I'm just saying that it might be our only shot. She solved the Jordan case less than two weeks ago. This is the closest I'll ever get to catching her unless I change tactics."

Loretta quieted for a moment, and Ryan listened to the clacking of her keyboard. "Okay, I understand what you're saying. What do you need from me?"

He relaxed in his seat, glad to have his friend back on board. It was easier to work with her than against her in almost all scenarios. "I'm not looking for all unsolved cases. I think I have a grasp on the kinds of things she looks for now. I'll send you a list of the specific categories of unsolved crimes we should focus on moving forward. We'll focus on violent crimes, obviously. We should also limit our victims to young people. Not all her investigations are into minors per se, but let's keep the age to thirty and under. First, though, I'd like your perspective on something."

"You want advice? Guidance?"

"Both," he admitted. "I guess in widening the scope here, we lose a little focus directionally. She was here thirteen days ago, which is as close as we've been, but that also means she could be anywhere now." The idea of it made him physically ill. He wouldn't be able to handle going from almost having her within his grasp to losing her entirely.

"Hmm," Loretta hummed. "You're worried she's already across a border into another country or something?"

"You can admit it's more than possible."

She clacked a little more on the keys. "It is. But let's save both of us from worrying and you from traveling and keep you in North Carolina for a couple days. There's no reason to believe she's still there more than she's anywhere else, but you're there, so that's where we'll start."

"Good call." Ryan felt relieved that the decision had been made for him. "I'll get the list of possible unsolved crime categories for you and then hit the road as soon as we pick one."

Once his call with Loretta ended, he exhaled. The visor on his truck was pulled down since the sun wasn't quite above him yet and glare on his windshield was brutal. He hoped whatever case they chose didn't involve his driving directly into its light.

Ignoring his growing headache, Ryan rummaged around in his backpack for the red pen, drawing a dot on Randleman. This was it. He was finally, after all these months, catching up with the person who helped him solve the devastating murder case back in Wyoming.

In hindsight, he didn't start this task with any true confidence that he would get answers. For Ryan, his curiosity about the man—woman—who gave him the evidence was more about running away. It gave him the excuse he needed to get away from Travis and Colleen's wedding and his own completely obliterated trust in the local institutions that had almost failed Sloane.

Almost.

As he traveled, got closer to his target, Ryan could almost discern a physical reaction to his own excitement. It felt like electricity in his limbs.

He understood that he had developed an unhealthy parasocial relationship with the stranger. His self-awareness extended at least that far. At night, he dreamed of meeting the person, confronting them about how they learned what they did, how they stayed hidden. While he drove, he imagined conversations with them in his head. More than once, one of these fake back and forth verbal tussles helped him pick the next location to investigate. At times, it was as if his prey was guiding him along in a spiritual partnership. The more he learned, the thirstier he became for any information, any scrap left behind by the pursued.

"I'm going to find you," he said aloud, continuing the one-sided communication. "Soon."

～

RYAN PACED HIS HOTEL ROOM back and forth in front of the map. He had no new towns to mark, no notes to add. All he had after another week on the road were dead ends and disappointment.

He felt further from his goal than he had in months, making him edgy. He'd been careful not to stir up trouble, but every hour that came and went with no new leads wore on his nerves. Ryan could feel himself getting sloppy, walking too closely behind every brunette woman he saw, letting himself sound too desperate when he spoke to other police officers.

Most recently, he stopped in the town of Sanford to speak with one of the local detectives. Loretta had found him a kidnapping case out of the local elementary school, only a day old. This was the new kind of case he sought out, ones with no answer yet. Ryan arrived in a town with a somewhat public, usually violent unsolved crime.

"Seems right up her alley," Loretta said about his elusive case solver. "It's a young person for one, and also so far Matthew Ellis hasn't been found."

That had been true up until that morning, but not before Detective Hunter had a chance to cancel their meeting.

"Sorry to waste your time," the older man said to Ryan over a cup of coffee. "But as it usually is with these cases, it was a custody dispute between divorcing parents. His dad picked him up from school and tried to flee the state."

"So, Matthew was found safe?" It was obviously good news, but Ryan had a hard time keeping the disappointment out of his voice.

Is this what he'd been reduced to? Had his mission to find this person turned him into someone who celebrated tragedy?

For his own sanity, he prayed that wasn't true.

"Safe and sound with his mom now. His dad seemed to have freaked out and didn't really think it through. Hard not to feel for the guy, cause now he's for sure going to lose any shot he had at partial custody. Kids these days all have smart phones, and his mom sent us his location with that Find My iPhone app," Detective Hunter confirmed, before standing up to leave Ryan alone at the table. "But I wish you luck with this and I hope you find this person soon. I get the feeling you won't rest much until you do."

He was closer to the truth than Ryan wanted to admit, but rest was hardly a priority even before he began this chase.

As was standard when he was feeling lost, Ryan's mind often sought out Sergeant Vincent. "You've got a relentless nature," he'd said once. "It's one of the things I respect most about you. Your guiding force is the truth and a genuine desire to help people. That's the kind of thing I look for in the colleagues I surround myself with professionally.

"But you have to understand that not everyone wants help, and not everyone can be saved. If you can't learn to live with that duality, this job will drive you mad."

Ryan snorted at the memory. On that, they could agree, but that didn't mean he was giving up anytime soon. He would just have to deal with losing his mind.

Pulling one of his oldest notebooks from his bag, he flipped to the first pages. Within them were his earliest notes on Sloane's attack. The details of her murder still activated the bite of his grief, and he might never get over the brutality of it. He reread the passages about her wounds and the clear ways she'd fought against her attacker before dying.

As was his routine, Ryan forced himself to picture every moment as punishment. Sloane may have been alone when she died, but at least he could join her in her suffering.

He swallowed the nausea-inducing regret and moved on.

He flipped further into the pages, where he'd entered notes belonging to crimes against people he didn't know. These were easier to read, but no less disturbing in their content. His eyes moved over notes about violated children, missing persons, murdered innocents. It was enough to turn the stomach of any veteran police officer, the kind of content they pledged to suffer so the general population didn't have to worry about it themselves.

"You look to bring justice to the weak, the powerless," he whispered into the pages. "But how do you do it? Is anyone helping you? Where are you now?"

No one answered, and he didn't bother giving a voice to his final question.

Why Sloane's case, and why give the evidence to me?

6

THE NUMBER OF HOUSES FOR SALE on Oak Island was astounding. They ranged in price from what Erika would consider entry level starter homes to vacation houses for the ultra-wealthy. Dozens and dozens of listings offered complete remodels, cozy comfort, or beach walk access. If this had been her search pool, she would be stuck for a long time.

Happily, only thirty-four listings belonged to the Cahill Group. They tended to favor the luxury side of pricing, but there were still a variety of places that were more accessible financially. Six of those listings were within a mile of Christina's home.

"I don't see why I can't go with you," she complained.

"I can't do this with any distractions," Erika replied as she tied her running shoes. "Please just stay here, and I promise to give you a full recap when I get back."

"Fine, fine. Just please, for the love of God, don't get caught. I won't be able to bail you out of jail."

Under other circumstances, the phrase would have made Erika giggle, but she was too focused on her task. For all the different skills she'd developed over the years, she'd never been caught collecting evidence, even when using more questionable methods. Erika didn't like to think of herself as a criminal. Surely no one did, but she saw her role in the world as one that brought justice to truly evil people. She was an enemy of the worst society had to offer.

But she did know how to pick locks and wander self-invited into places she shouldn't be. For research and evidence gathering, of course.

"My sister used to say things like that," Erika said, trapped in a long-forgotten memory. "If I skated the rules too much, she'd threaten to leave me in jail."

Christina's expression softened and she sat up on the couch and crossed her legs. "Do you think we would have gotten along? Me and your sister."

"Yeah. I think she would have loved you." Christina looked as if she wanted to say something nice but was coming up blank, which suited Erika just fine. She didn't want to talk about it.

She stood up and cleared her throat from the painful emotions she'd inadvertently drawn up. "If I'm not back in time for my coffee shift tomorrow, then I give you permission to start worrying."

Christina nodded her agreement, then stood up from the couch. "I'm going to go lie down then. Good luck out there."

With that conversation out of the way, Erika closed and locked the front door to Christina's house behind her before taking the stairs. With her tight ponytail, running gear, and fanny pack, she would appear to anyone watching her to be taking a late-night jog. Not advisable, if one was offering her safety advice, but she posed no threat. Anyone who approached her would arguably be the more hostile one in the interaction, at least to the casual observer.

Within the fanny pack, instead of a snack or water, she had the means to break into almost any lock, short of a police grade bypass tool. She was ready for a self-guided tour of Oak Island's for-sale homes.

Erika began her jog down the street to the first house of the Cahill Group listings that she'd chosen for the night. If Carter was hiding evidence of his crimes, however numerous they ended up being when her time on the island was done, an excellent option might be to stash anything incriminating in vacant houses. Even if a house had no owner, police would still need a warrant to search and collect from it, unlike with trash cans and public dumping, which are fair game. Carter could hide and subsequently destroy anything that would tie him to Christina very easily.

As she picked up her pace, Erika didn't let herself linger on the fact that the evidence she needed could already be gone, that he'd tossed Christina's bracelet, among other things, into the sea. She was confident she could find something in one of these houses.

Tactics varied for breaking into different houses. She was perfectly capable of jailbreaking a standard alarm system, so she didn't worry about those. Most traditional locks were pickable, and smart locks had their weaknesses as well. She knew how to keep the space clean, and if the home was lived in, she took pictures before searching so she knew how to put everything back where it had been before.

Obviously, she waited for homes to be empty before she went inside. That wasn't an issue with these houses on the market for as long as they had been.

For this errand, and many others before it, she tried to get into the head of the person who committed the crime. It was an unpleasant exercise, but a necessary one.

If I was Carter Cahill, she thought to herself as her breathing picked up, *where would be the best place for me to hide something I stole from a victim?*

It would need to be a low traffic place, somewhere people were unlikely to stumble upon it. This eliminated the more affordable homes, which the Cahills would likely host open houses for, as well as personal walk throughs multiple times a week.

When the first house on her list came up on her right, it was the one listed for $350 thousand. She jogged past it without a second glance.

The homes listed with prices in the millions had more potential. They were shown less often, and realtors would limit open house attendance to those who could actually afford the property. Foot traffic in those places would be much lower.

They represented their own challenges as hiding places. Homes with that kind of sale value would have fewer showings, but sellers would be concerned about wear and tear or environmental effects on the property.

They'd also have advanced security measures, but Erika knew all about those.

Fifteen minutes into her jog, she arrived at the third house on her list. It was listed for $2.95 million and had been on the market for the better part of the past calendar year. The location was also compelling, as the lot sat directly on the coastline and was only a five-minute walk from the pier Christina showed her the night she arrived.

If Carter had needed to dump something after he attacked Christina— clothing, condom, jewelry—this house would be the perfect stop.

Erika slowed her jog to a power walk. She didn't need to be worried about sound as she strolled the street. The home was close enough to the ocean that high tide meant the sound of the waves covered her footsteps more than adequately.

On her first pass of the large three-story home, she confirmed a few of her expectations. A small sign in the yard announced that the property was protected by a well-known security firm, and the empty car ports meant no one was staying in the house that night. A second pass of the street confirmed the surrounding houses were empty as well.

Opposite the beach-side mansion were undeveloped lots, filled with shrubbery and other plants that thrived along coastlines.

"Perfect," she whispered. The absence of homes directly across from the place she was scoping out meant there wouldn't be any doorbell camera footage of her entering. Erika saw no cameras on the sides of the house next to this one either, so she approached quietly with growing confidence.

Swiftly, she made her way up the steps to the first level.

She paused for another glance over her shoulder before kneeling in front of the door's hardware. For the price of the home, she was surprised it was a traditional lock and not a smart one. The digital, coded smart locks made it more difficult to remove evidence that someone had tampered with it. They usually required a battery override and passcode reset, which would be immediately noticed by the seller the next time they tried to enter and their password failed.

Erika pulled on gloves before removing her pick set and working diligently on the lock. It might not have been digital, but it was still expensive, and she spent more time out there vulnerable to any passing cars than she would have liked.

Once inside, she heard the repetitive, familiar beep of an activated alarm. The screen next to the door promised her thirty seconds before it fully triggered and called the local police station.

"Nice try," she said. Quickly replacing her pick set in the fanny pack, she then removed a small device of dubious legality for civilians.

Sometimes it paid to be a military brat.

Placing the device flush against the wall-mounted screen, she pressed a small button and watched as the alarm ceased its beeping and subsequently rearmed itself. If no one was watching the house remotely on any of their devices while she'd worked, then it would appear as if the security system had never even been disabled.

Safely inside the darkened home, she turned and surveyed her surroundings.

Enough light filtered in through the windows that she knew she would only need her flashlight sparingly, which was good. A beam inside an empty home at night may as well be a beacon telling the world someone was robbing the place.

The first floor consisted of an open concept kitchen and living room with a walkout back deck and a pool. Erika ran her gloved hand along the top of the couch, checking for dust. When none came away on her hand, she assumed that a cleaning crew likely came in at least once a week.

"That eliminates any areas that would see a maid," she muttered out loud. She turned toward the stairs to check some of the obvious hiding places first.

A house on stilts next to the beach in a hurricane zone obviously had no basement, but perhaps it had an attic. That space would likely not be toured by most potential buyers during a first pass visit, only to be combed through at the time of inspection after an offer was made.

She marched quietly up the stairs to the second level, bypassing it for the third.

The living room furniture must have been for show, as the other floors were conspicuously empty. Maybe on her way back down to the first level, she'd check some of the closets.

Finally on the third floor, she entered an open area. Not the attic, but a space that looked as if it could be used as a large playroom or family area. The entire room was surrounded by large windows that extended visibility to the neighborhood, the height enabling Erika's vision to see miles away, both of the island and the sea.

A touch of vertigo pulsed over her in waves as she looked downward. Stepping backwards slowly, she scanned the ceiling for an attic.

Erika increased her speed, as the completely uncovered windows left her feeling exposed. A standard pull-down trap door style attic was positioned in the back left corner of the room.

"Let's get this over with."

She pulled the door down and made quick work unfolding the wooden ladder. Once the joints clicked into place, she pushed her left foot down on the first rung, testing it against her weight. "Here goes nothing."

She climbed each rung with hesitation. Moving upward into the pitch black of the attic went against all her instincts. It reminded her of being a kid and having to turn off the lights at the base of a stairwell, only to try to out run the darkness by racing up the steps. She had to truly fight to move into the void above her.

Once her upper body was inside, she took a moment to breathe through her nose to avoid coughing. Whoever sold this house wasn't going to get the full asking price if the buyers had any pesky qualms about mold.

Erika took the collar of her long-sleeved running top and pulled it over her nose before taking her penlight out of the fanny pack.

The brightness was jarring at first, but she adjusted to the small light quickly. The attic was open, and no structures interrupted her line of sight to each corner. Puffs of fiberglass rose up in between each framing beam, but there was no place for storage or even a safe landing to stand on and enter the room fully. After a quick sweep, she abandoned any hope that she would find something up there. There wasn't even a lone box waiting to be picked through. Perhaps she could dig deeper into the insulation, but she couldn't risk tracking any dirt or grime back with her through the house.

It seemed that the only secret the Cahills were hiding in the attic of this home was some aggressive attic mold.

She descended the ladder steps quickly and folded it back into itself before pushing it closed. After cringing when it shut louder than she anticipated, she cursed herself for being so cowardly.

"Stop it. You're the only one here."

She moved down the stairs to the second floor, where she opened each closet to check the box of searching through the whole house. As expected, they were all empty, but she didn't let that discourage her from continuing. There were still other houses to search, including wherever Carter currently lived. Erika just needed to learn his schedule before attempting that search.

Headlights filled the living area just as she was passing through the kitchen, followed by the crunching of gravel under wheels, but it wasn't until she heard the unmistakable clomp of boots on the stairs leading up to the front door that she panicked.

"Shit," she hissed. Her eyes darted towards the cabinets in the kitchen, and she hurried to the ones under the granite island.

As she suspected, the cupboards were completely empty. She crawled inside the one farthest from the home's entrance and curled into a ball, closing the cabinet behind her just as the front door opened and the alarm started its countdown.

"I told you to get rid of the silent trip alarm years ago, Dad. It gets set off by animals all the time," a deep, masculine voice spoke from the front of the house. He sounded like he was on the phone with someone since no one replied while he disabled the alarm.

"Of course, I'm going to look around, but this is a waste of my time, so don't count on any future visits to your properties. I have my own job to think about. It happens to be a pretty important one, by the way, not that you've ever cared."

As the voice drew closer to the kitchen, Erika pressed a hand over her mouth, trying to completely stifle the sounds of her breathing. Her heart thumped with a powerful rhythm that seemed to perfectly pair with the man's footsteps.

Beneath her, the pressure of the wood base was hard against her backside, and her weight directly on that one area was causing her left leg to fall asleep, but she didn't dare move for fear of any creaking.

She'd just have to pray she wasn't found since she wouldn't be able to run until she got feeling back. Instead of worrying about that pain, she tried to hear more of the man's voice.

"Well, I just got here, so no, I haven't found anything yet. I'll check all the rooms then I'm going home," he said.

A few moments passed while whoever was on the other side of the phone call spoke. "Are you drunk or something? No, I'm not going to clean the house for you right now so you can show it to a last-minute buyer tomorrow. Jesus Christ," the man said. "I'm not obligated to help you just because you feel like I abandoned the family by going into law enforcement."

Erika's terror spiked when she realized who she was sharing the space with.

Nice to meet you, Carter.

"No, you're right, I don't want to have this fight right now either. We've both made our decisions. I'll just finish up my search around here and head home." Another pause floated through the kitchen while the other caller, presumably Robert Cahill, spoke to his son. "Obviously I'm still coming to family dinner. I wouldn't do that to Mom."

A few more heavy steps brought Carter to what Erika could only assume was right outside her cabinet door, and she didn't dare exhale when he was so close.

A bead of sweat trickled down her nose, followed by an infuriated tickling sensation, and it took all of her will power not to shift her arms and wipe it away. Eventually, it passed across her right nostril, and she was able to remove the salty menace with her tongue.

"Yeah, see you Sunday," Carter said, then hung up.

He seemed to stay in that one place for a full minute. He was so quiet and unmoving while he stood right outside of where she was hiding, Erika thought she may have gone insane from a lack of oxygen and imagined the whole episode. She worried that the brief, quiet puffs of air she pulled in to stay conscious weren't enough.

There was no force on earth that could get her to leave her hiding place, though.

Then, out of nowhere, he laughed, short and sharp, almost like the humor surprised him as well. "Yeah, fuck this," he said, and Erika listened as his steps moved farther away, until they reached the entryway of the home. She heard the door open, then slam behind him.

Erika wasn't stupid. She waited long enough in that cabinet to be absolutely sure Carter had left the property, but she didn't allow her fear to keep her there any longer than necessary. There was always the possibility that

Robert Cahill understood his son's tendencies and would drive to the house for his own search, or maybe just arrive in the early morning hours to prepare for that showing. Either way, she would be long gone.

Tentatively, she pushed open the cupboard and looked around, seeing nothing different than when she'd entered. Before she could stand fully, she wriggled her left toes around in their shoe and bent her knee repeatedly to bring sensation back to the limb. Once the tingling had turned into pain, she was able to get upright. She quickly unfurled herself from the cramped position and stood. The rush from standing too fast dizzied her, and Erika grabbed the counter to stop herself from falling.

The light from the moon sat at an almost unnoticeable new angle, the only indication of the time that had passed since she entered the house.

"Yep. Time to get the hell out of here."

She tip-toed with more care than when she first got to the building, mostly out of paranoia. She didn't want to be trapped inside a cupboard again in case someone else decided to show up. As she advanced towards the door, she reached for her fanny pack. It wasn't ideal to have to disarm the security system another time when there were clearly eyes on the property, but she stopped when she read the alarm screen. Erika could have cried happy tears at what she saw.

In his haste to leave, Carter had forgotten to reset the alarm.

7

TWO DAYS LATER, Erika still hadn't recovered from her sleepless night. She thought when she got back to Christina's place, she'd pass out immediately, but she was too keyed up after almost getting caught by Carter.

"You could have just called off," Christina said to her from a chair in the corner of the shop.

"Some of us like to eat," Erika quipped back, though the other woman wasn't wrong. There had been almost no foot traffic into the store the whole morning and being paid exclusively in tips, that meant she might be working for free that day.

So much for being able to buy dinner.

From her seat, Christina shivered and burrowed further into the chair while she glanced aimlessly at the covers of magazines that littered the top of a coffee table.

Erika felt guilty for being short with her. "I can turn up the heat, if you want?"

Christina shook her head. "It's not going to help, and I don't want to make it harder for you to work. You're the one that has to be on your feet all day."

She nodded and decided to take inventory for Fiona. Erika couldn't actually order anything as an under-the-table employee, but she could make lists for her manager since it was so slow. Customers always acted like it was a personal affront to them when something like oat milk ran low, and like all customer service employees, Erika liked to keep unpleasant interactions to a minimum.

"I was able to pull footage from traffic cams the night it all happened," Erika spoke while she went through the coolers.After visiting the empty house, she'd decided to dig up any city footage she could find from the privacy of her locked bedroom. Almost getting caught had made her realize that illegally searching multiple houses on the market was too high risk with little hope of finding anything useful. She wanted to narrow her search drastically before she attempted something like that again.

In her peripheral vision, she could see Christina tense slightly before she spoke. "Did you see anything new?"

"Honestly? Not really," she admitted. "It shows you both walking hand in hand, headed towards the pier. We probably couldn't even use it to prove you were too intoxicated to consent."

"Because I wasn't. It wasn't that kind of rape."

Erika wrote the final item for Fiona's shopping list and pinned it on the cork board for employee announcements and hours. The board probably got more use during busy seasons, but for the time being it was just for notes between the two of them.

"Do you remember anything else from that night? Anything we can use?" Erika didn't like pushing, and Christina was always extremely reluctant to talk about it, but she needed more if she was going to help.

"Mostly I remember a lot of pain," the other woman whispered.

Neither of them said anything after that, and Erika let the guilt collect in her gut for mentioning the whole ordeal before she had any good news to offer.

She straightened up when a car pulled into the small lot out front. The shop was only open for one more hour, and her entire day's wages rested on this customer being extremely generous.

That hope drained from her when she saw Chief Cahill walking towards the glass doors. "Incoming," she whispered to Christina before he opened them. Her friend looked over, then shuddered before walking towards the storage room. "Thank you," she called back before disappearing.

Erika tapped her fingers one at a time on her thigh to ground herself.

He's just here for coffee, she reasoned. *Carter doesn't even think anything happened the other night. You're not a suspect.*

He pushed his sunglasses to the top of his head after he entered the shop and grinned widely at her. "Good afternoon," he greeted. She could see the appeal if she tamped down her disgust with him long enough. Rarely did one see a man as good looking as Carter outside of a movie theater screen.

"You, too," she offered back. "What can I get started for you?"

"Six lattes, to go, please." At her raised eyebrow, he laughed and continued, "Not just for me. I'm just grabbing something for the station's evening shift. I think everyone has had a long week."

"How generous," she said tightly before ringing up his total then flipping the tablet towards him so he could pay. "It'll be just a minute."

As she turned on the steamer for the milk, she felt his presence like a hum against her skin. Erika could see why he got away with so much. Not only was he traditionally handsome, but he also had an all-over golden coloring that made him seem at home by the ocean. His smile was friendly with seemingly no ulterior motive behind it. With his family ties and civil service, it would be hard to find anyone willing to condemn him.

It would take more than a witness's testimony to get him.

"How long have you been here?"

Erika had been distracted by her task. "What was that?"

"Here." He pointed at the light-up sign displaying Fiona's name behind the counter. "To save time, I'm usually partial to the drive through but I still walk in on occasion. I haven't seen you in here yet."

"I've been with Fiona about three weeks."

"Ah. Well, then, welcome," he said, smiling again.

Finishing the final shot of espresso, Erika hurried through the last of the drinks. She wanted him out of there, but she had no public excuse for being nervous around him. Carter didn't know she'd heard about the violence he was capable of, and she wanted to keep it that way for as long as possible.

Maybe he'd chalk up her jitteriness to attraction. He seemed like the type that assumed all women wanted him.

"Where are you staying?"

If Erika hadn't already been operating under maximum tension, she would have spilled everything she was working on.

"I have family in the area," she lied.

Carter raised an eyebrow. "Who is your family?"

"I doubt you know them," she said. "They're a transplant, like me."

Before he could inquire further, she finalized his order. "There you go." She pushed the drink carries towards him and smiled.

If Chief Cahill could tell that she wanted him to leave, he didn't show it. Instead, he reached his hand across the counter. "Carter Cahill."

"Erika Willett," she replied and shook his hand. Despite its clean warmth and strength, her forearm erupted in goosebumps. Again, hopefully he interpreted that as an attraction to him and not overwhelming fear.

"Well, Erika Willett," he replied and pulled out his wallet. "I'm going to leave you with my card. I work with the police here, so if you get any trouble around the shop or otherwise, feel free to call me."

Seriously?

"I'll be sure to do that," she said and waited until he left before releasing her breath.

To her right, she felt Christina approach before she saw her. "Glad that's over," she said as she walked to the counter. "What's this?" She looked down at Chief Cahill's card like it was a live fungus on something she was about to eat.

"Nothing you need to worry about." Erika picked the card off the counter by its corners, trying not to touch it too much. She could potentially match his fingers prints from the card to Christina's bracelet later, though it was a long shot.

Christina wrinkled her nose. "I feel like police officers having cards is weird. Like, isn't that what 911 is for?"

Erika took off her apron and put everything on the counter back in its spot before flipping the open sign to closed. "Personally, I like to avoid police all together."

"Seems weird with what you do."

"Not at all," Erika said as they left, making sure the shop's door was locked before they walked home. "The less they know about me and my methods, the more useful I am to them."

RYAN HAD ONE MORE HOUR on the road before his next destination. He had to routinely remind himself not to grip the steering wheel to the point of cramping. The wheel itself had been well worn at the ten and two hand positions over the years, and the discoloration he caused could almost serve as a driving aid for teenagers.

"I need you to simmer down." He could hear Sergeant Vincent lecturing him in his memory. "We get called to go into tense situations, often violent ones. We need to be a calming force when we arrive, not an aggravating one."

"They can't tell I'm nervous," Ryan had argued.

Vincent had snorted, not bothering to engage in such an obviously untrue statement.

Heck, Ryan hadn't even believed it himself when he said it.

He was, by his records, over three weeks behind the woman. He'd lost several days in towns with open cases that involved violent crimes against young people. It was a much different endeavor than speaking with officials about closed cases. Those detectives could be withholding or secretive, but nothing like the men and women working on open cases. Ryan knew this and tried to approach the investigating officers with humility and an air of helpfulness, but it didn't always work out that way. Instead, he would study local papers that talked about the crimes and retraced the steps of anyone who took interviews. He would try to communicate that he wasn't looking to take credit away from anyone.

He was looking for a brunette ponytail.

The trees of a national forest towered over both sides of the two-lane road, and had he not been rushing toward the next goal, he would have pulled over. The Ryan Gibson who grew up in Wyoming would have taken his time on a trip like that. He and Travis spent much of their summer breaks in the forest camping together before he graduated high school, and he missed that connection with his brother.

If this trip had been an honest vacation, he would have stopped at every park, taken a picture next to every random "World's Largest" item sprinkled across the Midwest. There was a part of him that mourned the loss of that young man, the one he'd once been, but he wasn't going to do anything to get him back until it was time.

"I just want to say thank you," he said to the stranger he'd followed across thousands of miles of road. "I want to ask you how you do it."

The voice responding in his mind had taken on a feminine, almost flirty lilt since his stop in Randleman. *You'll have to catch me first!*

The ringing of his phone through the truck's speakers interrupted his spiraling thoughts.

"Hi, Loretta." It was more of a grunt than a greeting.

"Someone's in a mood today."

"I'm fine," he muttered. "I'm just trying not to lose hope here. I feel like she's slipping away and there's nothing I can do."

Loretta's keyboard clicking was like a comforting white noise that worked as a salve on Ryan's nerves as he drove. "I think you need a new plan this time. You've spent the last week and a half mooning after random women, making me run the plates of everyone you see with a ponytail. At this rate, you're definitely going to lose her."

"Thanks. You have any helpful advice or just criticisms?"

"Well," she clicked a few more times before giving him her full attention. "Up until now, you've been following. Following solved cases, following people in towns with unsolved cases. You had the right idea to change tactics and be more proactive, but it seems like you're actually doing the same thing. I think you need to be a participant."

"How so?"

"I think on your next stop, you should go straight to the investigating officers. Tell them your story and offer your services."

Ryan glared at his dashboard as if it had been the one speaking and not his friend. "And what? Tell them I'm chasing a ghost and I need their help? Maybe I should promise them a solved case in exchange for finding this person who might not exist."

"No, I think you tell them the truth. It's worked best for you so far," she retorted. "Tread carefully, unsolved violent crimes are a sore spot for many public officials. But make it clear that you're not trying to encroach on their territory. You're there to help."

"I'm there to help," Ryan repeated.

"Sure. You've been chasing this girl for almost seven months. What if you're the one solving a crime and she comes to you?"

Ryan sighed and used his signal to turn off the road towards his destination. "I wish I believed in God like you do, Loretta."

"You'd be much better off, believe me," she said. "I've scheduled you a meeting with the local investigating officer. I'll text you the details. After this one, maybe you take a vacation?"

"I'm not taking a vacation," he said instead of what he was thinking.

I will let this mission kill me before I give up on it.

Loretta sighed, and Ryan could feel her eyes roll across the line. "I thought you might say that," she said. "At least at this next stop, you can stick your feet in a sandy beach for five minutes and pretend it's some place foreign."

He thanked her before hanging up and checked his messages. When he saw the meeting time, he cursed.

She really hadn't given him an opportunity to think his way out of that one.

While Ryan appreciated not having any time to second guess himself, he would have liked to clean up some before meeting other officers. He was overdue for a shave, and he was pretty sure the shirt he was wearing needed a wash soon.

At a stoplight, he sniffed his underarms and decided he was passable.

Closer to town, he could see the brightly colored homes and businesses. It seemed like the kind of place that should have had more foot traffic, but the sidewalks were quiet. His truck windows were rolled down so he could feel the fresh air, and he thought it was the perfect temperature, but maybe this weather was considered cold in the South and that's why no one was outside. He kept his left elbow folded at an angle out the window, letting the salty breeze relax his standard driving position.

After a couple minutes driving through the town, he even found himself humming.

Any freedom from anxiety fell away as his GPS announced that he'd arrived at his destination. The police station was clean but small, not unlike the one he worked at back in Cody. He pulled into a visitor parking space and grabbed his backpack. There was no way of knowing how his story was going to be received by someone who hadn't had the same experience, but he wanted to be prepared with his maps and notes just in case.

Ryan walked into the precinct. He saw the standard front desk behind protective glass, but no one at the moment was manning it.

"Sorry about that," a man's voice called from his right. "Amy is on her break. Are you my two pm meeting?"

"I think so," Ryan replied to the slightly taller, slightly broader fair-featured man walking up to him. "Detective Ryan Gibson."

"Chief Cahill, but you can call me Carter. My office is right this way," he smiled brightly, and Ryan followed him farther into the building.

8

THE TWO MEN STARED ACROSS A DESK at each other without saying anything as an analogue clock on the wall ticked away the seconds.

Carter Cahill took in the other guy sitting in his office. If he was a betting man—and he did like to gamble on sports occasionally—he would wager that Detective Gibson was no more than two or three years younger than he was, but his appearance told him that the weight of his time traveling had consequences. Ryan needed a shave and a hairbrush, and probably a sleeping pill and a dark room to pass out in.

There was also something about him that wouldn't calm down. He slouched to the side, with a pretense of social leisure, but his grip on the armrest of his chair betrayed his nervousness. His gaze darted from Carter to the map laid out on his desk.

The skittishness made him want to kick the chair out from underneath Ryan.

Carter decided to put him out of his misery instead. "That's quite the story."

Ryan laughed, but his voice broke in the middle, so he coughed to cover it. "Yeah, I know how it all sounds."

Chief Cahill leaned forward and looked closer at the map. It was a fascinating investigation, what Ryan had uncovered, and he found himself truly impressed with the work. "I'm sorry about the girl back in your hometown. That's terrible business."

"Yeah, thanks," Ryan replied. "I guess we can be grateful to have justice for her at least."

"I understand your need to chase this," Carter conceded. "If some vigilante angel came out of nowhere and helped solve the violent assault and murder of someone I knew personally, I'd probably do the same thing."

Ryan sat forward in his chair, his left leg jiggling. "So, you believe me?"

"I believe that you're not lying to me," he compromised. There was still the extremely obvious chance that Ryan had lost his mind, and this person wasn't real and a figment of his imagination, but Carter could admit that the man seemed like a true believer. "And I think there's a possibility some of these other cases are connected to the same person you're looking for. But I'm not sure how I can help you. I've never had a case resolved like this, as much as I would love to have free anonymous help with crimes."

"What kind of crimes do you get around here? What are the rates?"

Carter smiled proudly, though he was irked the other man didn't know already. For all his research into the person who helped him solve the case, he could have run Oak Island crimes rates through a search engine. "Some of the lowest in the state. We have almost no violent crime, and most of our citations are associated with tourists. We'll get some public intoxications, and we will for sure see a rise in minors in possession when spring break rolls around in a couple of weeks. Other than that, it's mostly the occasional robbery."

Before Ryan could follow up with any questions about open cases, he continued, "I tell you what. I'm as curious about this as you are. Why don't you stay a few days, shadow some of us if you want while we go on calls. Maybe your mystery solver will show up and surprise us with something."

Detective Gibson sat up straighter. "Sure, I'd love that." He stood quickly and packed his maps and notebooks back into his backpack. "Can I come in tomorrow?"

"Give me a day to get the rest of the crew on board and then we can talk." Carter got out of his seat to walk Ryan out of the precinct. The rubber on the soles of their shoes squeaked across the tile as they stepped in tandem towards the exit, a cacophony of sound that always drove Carter up the wall.

"You have any dinner plans tomorrow?"

The detective appeared confused by the question. "I guess whatever is walking distance from the Seaside Motel."

"I wouldn't want to interrupt that," Carter joked. "Why don't you join me and my family? We eat dinner together every Sunday, and you'll get a true Southern welcome to the town."

Ryan, apparently unused to hospitality by strangers, stood still for a moment. "Yeah, uh, that would be nice."

"I'll pick you up at four," he said, then handed him a card. "Just shoot me a text with your name in it so I know how to get ahold of you."

He waved after the detective as the door closed behind him. Before returning to his office, he watched the man walk, and he had a gait that betrayed his anxiety. It was twitchy, and his focus seemed to be trying to be everywhere at once.

Ryan Gibson was a smart guy. Really smart. He also had a natural tenacity and obsession with certain crimes that made him pick at them until he found the perpetrator. His focus was commendable, and his talents were wasted on small towns in Wyoming. Carter's hometown wasn't high crime, but he would be stupid to turn away good talent like that if he had a shot at making the detective stay, as long as he understood that not every crime reported to the station deserved an equal amount of attention.

But before he could consider recruiting Gibson to his force, he needed to run an errand.

CARTER TRULY HADN'T MEANT TO FOLLOW Erika home from the coffee shop after he left. She had closed the shop and began walking in the same direction Carter took driving back to the precinct.

He told himself he was just making sure she arrived home safely, ensuring a new member of his community wasn't harmed in her first weeks on Oak Island.

His curiosity about Erika increased tenfold when he saw which home she entered.

Carter was already cutting it close on timing for his meeting with Ryan, so unfortunately, he'd have to wait before he could confront her.

As he parked across the street from Christina Higgins's house, he noted the two cars parked beneath the home in their stalls. It was still midafternoon, and he hoped Erika would be home after her shift resting and not out somewhere else.

He didn't really want to delay this conversation.

Carter's heavy steps on the stairs that brought him to the second story front door were the only warning he could offer to the house's occupants before he approached the entrance and banged on the wood three times.

A flutter from the draperies in the window preceded Erika's answer to the door.

"Chief Cahill," she spoke through the few inches of opening she created, hiding everything behind her inside the home, though her smile didn't betray any nervousness. "What can I do for you?"

Carter activated a genial expression meant to disarm her of any anxiety. "You must have underestimated how well I know the people of my town."

"How's that?"

"You said you were staying with family," he explained, "and that I wouldn't know them. I happen to be pretty well acquainted with Christina. How are you guys related?"

Erika nibbled on her bottom lip before relaxing her features. "I'm her cousin. Our family thought it would be a good idea for me to visit, and just, you know, check up on things."

"Ah. Well, it's good she has people that care about her. She might have mentioned me to you at some point."

"If she did, I don't remember it."

Carter didn't let the comment faze him. "She wouldn't happen to be back there somewhere with you, would she?"

"Nope," she said. "I'm sorry."

"It was worth a try," he smiled. "You still have my card?"

Erika acknowledged him with a nod.

"Good," he replied. "Can you promise me something, Erika?"

"What's that?"

"The next time you see or hear from Christina," he said, "will you promise to call me?"

"Sure," Erika shrugged. "I can do that."

"I really appreciate it. You take care of yourself, Miss Willett."

She lifted one side of her mouth in a half-hearted attempt to smile back at him. "You, too, Chief," she said, then closed the door quietly in his face.

Carter dropped his own expression once the door closed, then turned to walk down the stairs back to his car.

Erika Willett was someone he wanted to keep an eye on.

9

ERIKA ACTIVATED THE DEADBOLT and placed her head against the door. She needed to slow her heart rate, or she would put herself in an early grave.

Once she calmed down, she turned towards the living room, where Christina leaned against the frame of her bedroom entrance.

"What are the chances of Carter getting in touch with your family to verify my story?"

"Slim," the woman said. "He doesn't actually want to find me or speak to me. It's checking a box for him out of obligation."

Erika nodded and wandered farther into the house. Christina's comment didn't ease her anxiety, mostly because she knew she wouldn't relax fully until the entire case was resolved. "He must have seen me walk back here. I'll have to be more careful."

Christina just shrugged before moving to the couch. "It's a small community. The longer you're here, the more people will find out about you. You're staying here is a pretty safe thing for him to find out compared to the other stuff."

"Right," Erika agreed, though she didn't sit down.

When a full minute passed and she still hadn't left her position standing in the middle of the floor, Christina noticed.

"We should get dinner, some place noisy," she said.

Erika withheld an eyeroll. "That just means you want to eat dinner at the pub again." She wasn't opposed to the pub, per se, but her interactions with Chief Cahill had fried her nerves. She'd feel better ordering in or simply going to bed without food. To be honest, she was surprised Christina wanted to be anywhere near where they'd seen Carter before, but she wasn't any kind of shrink. Maybe her friend wanted to gain some power back, and she wasn't going to let him chase her away from her favorite spot.

Erika really had no idea how she would react if she was in Christina's shoes, but she thought about it often. "I should probably stay away from places we know he frequents."

Christina waved her off. "He'll be on duty tonight, so we're safe as long as a fight doesn't break out," she said. "Plus, you clearly need a distraction and I'm tired of being cooped up in here. I think we'd both benefit from doing something normal."

Erika shuffled towards the entry way where her shoes and jacket were kept. Christina's case was unique and, therefore, taking her longer to resolve than she usually would, which meant getting closer to her. Dinner while she stayed in the woman's home was the least she could do.

She pulled on her coat and smiled at Christina. "You make some compelling points. Let's walk to the pub."

After a gleeful dance from Christina, they made the chilly yet refreshing walk to the pub. The clouds had been a constant companion with the earlier week's rains, but it wasn't late enough in the spring for it to be humid. "It's a Saturday," she mentioned. "Maybe you'll meet someone."

"Someone to what?" Erika scoffed. "Have a short fling with before I shove off someplace else?"

"Well, it's that or spend all your nights with me," Christina said.

Erika sobered her expression. "I don't mind spending time with you," she replied.

The other woman scoffed. "Right. Because being around me is such a huge party."

"It's not like that," Erika insisted. "Think of us as a team. We have a shared goal now, and I'm here to see it through."

Christina didn't reply, but Erika understood her reticence and didn't begrudge her for it.

As they walked to the pub, the overcast weather made the afternoon seem darker than it was, triggering the early illumination of streetlights along their path, telling children to go home after their bike rides to the beach. To Erika, Oak Island felt like it was lost in time, not a distant one, but one like her childhood, where there was a high trust among the community and kids could run around without constant supervision. She could admit, maybe only to herself, that she would be sad to leave when the time came.

While they were helpful in alerting those outside to the darkening hour, the streetlights did little to light the two women's way. Not a terrible problem, since they knew the walk to the pub by heart.

As they entered the restaurant, Christina spoke over Erika's shoulder. "At least one of us should have fun."

Talking was almost impossible after they walked inside. The place was crowded with locals, pushed inside due to the chilliness on an early Saturday evening with the promise of live music. As the band set up, Erika led Christina to a small high-top in the back corner of the bar area, a place she knew she hadn't sat before.

Service would be slow with the crowd, but that suited them just fine. Both women were there for the atmosphere rather than the food and libations. It was nice, Erika could concede to be surrounded by the noises of happy people. As long as no one tried to draw her into their circle or force her to talk about herself, she could see the benefit of getting out of the house and having a night to escape.

She liked places like this, where she could get lost in the racket without participating. Whenever she was in a new town, she sought out loud, crowded places rather than quiet ones. It allowed her to get away from restless thoughts and kept her from being the subject of anyone's scrutiny.

Women alone at bars tended to draw lots of attention.

The other patrons in the packed room turned their bodies toward the stage when the band walked out.

"Hi, everyone," a man with a guitar spoke into the microphone. "You're about to get an earful of Oak Island's favorite volunteer fire department rock band: Sinister Candles."

The crowd erupted in cheers, and Christina leaned across the table to whisper to Erika, "They're actually really good. They were basically a band who didn't get booked enough and took jobs as firefighters on the side."

"Why 'Sinister Candles?'"

"They started calling themselves that after they joined the OIFD," she explained. "They said it was to raise awareness about the causes of residential fires, but I'm pretty sure candles don't even account for a large percentage of them. I think the real reason was their original name wasn't family friendly enough."

"I'm afraid to ask," Erika said.

"Seriously. I remember it being something about necrophilia."

"Eww," she replied, shoving the menu away. "Maybe I don't need dinner anymore."

Christina backtracked. "Don't let that scare you off! They're seriously good."

Erika chuckled, enjoying the lore behind the men performing on stage. "I can't wait to hear them."

As a smooth melody came from the speakers, she relaxed in her seat. This was easy. This could be nice, a meal after work, not entirely alone. If she wanted to change, she could. It wouldn't hurt to take a break between cases, would it? Stay in one place for a few months and make it feel like home?

She was even enjoying the band's songs, which surprised her seeing as they had formerly branded themselves as people who had sex with dead humans, or at least people who thought such activities were funny or intriguing. The sound wasn't too hard for her tastes, and the lyrics were thoughtful, if occasionally trite and cliched. It was easy beach music, and they suited the pub's atmosphere perfectly. After a drink and three songs, Erika had apparently relaxed too much.

"I was sort of joking when I said you could meet someone here tonight," Christina whispered, "but there's a guy at the bar staring right at you."

Lost in the moment, Erika didn't think twice about looking over to the bar to see who it was. When she saw his identity, she spat out her mouthful of drink back into her cup.

"What's wrong? He looks normal," Christina reasoned.

"Obviously, he's normal," Erika spat. She turned her body, so it was fully blocking out the man at the bar. "Don't look at him."

"Why not?"

"Because," she hissed, "he's one of the people I've helped before."

"Oh." Christina perked up at this and looked closer at the man. "That's fantastic! Is he like me? Can we go talk to him?"

"No, not like you," Erika said quietly, feeling bad for shutting Christina down. "Sorry. No, he was the one I gave evidence to back on an old case. I don't know why he's here."

Christina deflated slightly at the loss of a potential new friend. "Well, it could be a coincidence. You always work anonymously, so there's a strong possibility he doesn't know who you are at all. I mean, what really are the odds that he's looking for you here on the island, specifically? Maybe he's just staring at you because he finds you attractive."

"I don't think I believe in coincidences as glaring as this one. Can we just go home? I promise I'll make it up to you by taking you to something equally loud and social another time."

Christina pouted but stood up obediently. "Fine, we can go home."

Erika slapped some cash on the table and followed her, trying to look as inconspicuous as possible. This kind of complication was the last thing she needed.

WELL, FUCK.

It's not like Ryan got rejected exactly. They would have had to be speaking for that to happen.

The meeting with Chief Cahill had gone better than expected, and he'd called Loretta right away to tell her. She'd been happy for him, but she'd also been on the way to her son's baseball practice.

"You know I love you, but it wouldn't hurt to make a few new friends along the way," she chastised kindly.

And Ryan agreed, to a point. He had at least a few days to kill in a new town, and he was going to get to shadow other officers this week, a task that would resemble his old job. It made him feel grounded in a way he hadn't been while traveling to different cities as rapidly as he had been. The routine nature of Oak Island's potential relaxed him, and he felt that it wouldn't hurt to form some connections in town while he was there. If he was going to be in Oak Island for a few days, living an almost normal life, could that include talking to a beautiful woman at a bar?

Apparently not.

The woman a few tables over who caught his eye took one look at him and immediately tried to hide. It was so abrupt of an avoidance that he thought he might have imagined it. He'd like to think it was a result of a personal problem on her end, some kind of intense social anxiety, but he didn't lack enough self-awareness to come to that conclusion.

Another glance at his unwashed shirt and the feel of his stubble explained her reaction just fine.

Ryan wouldn't let it ruin his night, though. The food was decent and the band playing had plenty of talent, which was more than he could say for many of his nights on the road. He could be grateful with just what he had.

He listened to a few more songs before paying his tab and making the short walk back to the Seaside Motel.

10

RYAN GIBSON WAS IN Oak Island.

The more Erika thought about it, the worse her conclusions became. There was no reasonable explanation for him being there that didn't involve her. Plenty of beach towns lined the West Coast that were closer to his home, so she ruled out vacation travel. He was local law enforcement back in Cody, meaning he had no professional excuse for being on the East Coast. She could think of nothing—besides her and Sloane's case—that would compel him to travel that far from Wyoming.

"You know, when you pace and pick your nails like that, it makes you seem guilty," Christina said from her spot sitting on the coffee shop counter. It was a slow day again, so Erika didn't bother asking her to move.

"I am guilty. Or I did the thing he probably thinks I did. It's why he's here."

"So?"

Erika stopped pacing. "What do you mean, 'so?' So, I've been discovered. I don't exactly work within the confines of the law when I dig up evidence for these things. Did you think I was looking for your bracelet in pawn shops?"

Christina sighed, as if Erika's puritanism was exhausting to her. "Yeah, but you aren't some hardened, violent criminal, running away from lives you've upended due to selfishness. You helped him catch a really bad guy. It's not like he's going to arrest you for that."

"He might," Erika admitted.

"How well do you know this Ryan guy, anyway?"

The long answer to that question was more complicated, as Erika had never directly spoken to him, but the short answer was that she knew him very well, as well as one could without spending time with them openly.

The decision of where to place the evidence was often harder to make than the process of finding the evidence itself. Uncovering video footage, bloody clothes, or a confession was a direct path. You need it, you look for it, you have it. Finding a person to trust with that information was more subjective, and she wasn't always sure she had mastered it.

On the surface, there's a multitude of different ways a police force can be corrupted. Sometimes it's an obvious money game, people who stole or lied before and would do it again for the right price. But often it's corruption of cowardice as well. A nice guy hiding behind a gun and a badge can be bullied into losing the incriminating information she delivered.

If she had to choose between them, she preferred the old-fashioned corruption rather than the spineless weasel. At least she knew she could pay for results with the first type.

It was certainly no exact science. Part of Erika's research was following the investigation of the open cases, and all its participants, to find a perfect recipient of information.

In Amarillo, Texas, she'd given the evidence to a detective related to the victim. Risky, since she was obviously close to the case in a personal way, but she would ensure that it wasn't destroyed. If someone tried to get between her and justice, then she would have gone public in a way that would make it impossible to bury.

In Annapolis, she'd chosen Detective Cary not because he was unfailingly ethical or a bleeding heart, but because he had ambition. He wanted to move up in the force, possibly enter political life later, and he never would have passed up the opportunity to put his name on a drug bust that large.

Corn Benson was an extremely involved and devoted father. Erika knew that Juliet Jordan's actions would have disgusted him, and no force on earth could have stopped his righteous crusade against the woman.

And then there was Ryan Gibson, loved by his town so much that not a single soul could say a bad thing about him. He was a man with an insatiable hunger for the truth, one that didn't let him rest until he found it, and a loyalty to honest communication that would actually prove detrimental in many aspects. He didn't have the gladhanding nature required to climb his way into power by either corporation or local government.

Erika knew, based on her research when she was in Cody, that he'd been passed over for well-earned promotion several years back for a man with a worse detective record but a better relationship with the corrupt mayor.

She watched him interview suspects, ones that weren't Craig, with frustrated impotence. She watched him sit, stoically, as he was brow beaten relentlessly by Sloane's angry father. The grieving man called Ryan every name in the book and the young detective took it without fighting.

"You know whose fault this is," the man said before leaving Ryan alone on the coffee shop patio.

Erika could hear his response, said only to himself, since her back faced his, her seat mere inches from where he met with the other man in the small restaurant.

"Of course, I know whose fault this is," Ryan had said.

Ryan loved the truth, and he loved solving puzzles to find it. He also had a brush of idealism to him, something that made him think he could save everyone who needed his help.

She didn't think his anticorruption stance that kept him from success in local politics boded well for her chronic use of outside-the-law means of uncovering evidence.

"I know enough to know I need to keep my guard up," was all Erika said in explanation.

She poured herself a cup of coffee and tried to think of ways to keep herself awake during the last three hours of her shift. A few customers walked in, and Christina moved to her favorite chair, but it wasn't hard to see why Fiona cut hours during the slow seasons.

"Incoming," Christina called from behind the arm of the chair. Erika saw a scheming look on her face but didn't have time to ask before a new customer walked in.

She was almost unsurprised to see Ryan Gibson walking towards her. In fact, she'd expected him to come in earlier.

When he got to the counter, it occurred to her that this was the closest he'd ever been. It was unnerving enough that she forgot to speak.

"Erika?"

She tensed. "Do I know you?"

He smiled, then pointed to the pocket on her button down. "Not yet, but you have a name tag, so I decided to start with that."

"Right." She shook off the interaction. "What can I get for you?"

"Double Americano."

She lit up the espresso machine and tried to appear antisocial, but Ryan was apparently in a talkative mood. "Aren't you going to ask for my name?"

"Maybe you should just tell me," she said, hoping she sounded flirty instead of terrified.

"Ryan," he replied. "I just got to town yesterday."

"Are you visiting for fun? Or work?"

"Maybe both," he said. "I've been traveling a bit recently and I'm thinking of settling somewhere for a few months. I'm a police officer by trade, and the chief here is going to show me around and see if I'm a good fit."

Erika's face drained of color as she handed him his drink. "Well, then the incoming spring breakers should keep you too busy for fun," she replied, all her social pretenses gone. "We're closing early today, so you should be on your way."

He smiled, like he knew a secret, but didn't fight her about it. Without another word, he turned and left, then Erika hurried behind him to lock the door.

"I can't believe he's working with Chief Cahill," she said.

Christina was being unnervingly reasonable about it. "There's no way for Ryan to know what he did. Carter is really good at winning people over and it's not like I've been blasting his name from the rooftops."

Erika turned to her. "How can you be alright with this? If he reveals who I am, it could unravel everything we're working on. He could destroy any chance of you getting justice!"

"For the record," Christina replied, not falling for Erika's rage bait, "I get a good vibe from him. I think we can trust Ryan, and if he does call you out, it probably wouldn't be the worst thing in the world to tell him the truth. If he gets close to Carter, then he can help you look for my bracelet."

Erika turned and leaned her back against the door. "I'll think about it," she said, but didn't voice what she was really thinking.

You have no idea what you're asking me to give up.

RYAN SAT IN HIS TRUCK parked two lots perpendicular to the coffee shop. The sign never returned to open, and he waited patiently for Erika to leave work.

While he waited, he dialed Loretta.

She answered after the first ring. "Are you getting along with all your new friends?"

"You know I could never replace you."

"Obviously," she said. "You caught me at a good time, what can I do for you?"

Ryan paused, wanting to be careful about how he delivered this. "I found someone. I don't know what it means yet."

"Ryan, I am not your illegal dating service."

"That's not—"

"I can't run the information for every pretty brunette lady you come across. You have to give me more than that."

"I would if you'd let me," he insisted.

"She's pretty, isn't she?" Loretta asked, an unwelcome smugness to her voice.

"She's fine," he lied. She was better than fine, but he wasn't about to admit that. "I've only had some limited interactions with her so far, but she seems skittish."

"Skittish how? Not everyone is a social butterfly."

He explained her running away at the bar, and the clear terror in her eyes when he read her name off the tag. "She also had a really poor reaction to my working with local police." That could have a multitude of interpretations, but Ryan didn't like to assume causality without evidence.

"Hmm. Where does your mind go with this one?"

"It could be a couple things. She might be running from something, either a danger to herself or something that put her on the wrong side of the law," he began. As he spoke, he spotted Erika walking down the sidewalk and started his truck. He waited until she turned onto a side street before following her.

"That's a fair guess," Loretta agreed. "Anything else?"

"Yeah," Ryan said. "I got the sense that she recognized me."

Loretta's key clacking stopped. "You think this could be our girl?"

"I think it's possible," he admitted out loud for the first time. The hope he felt would be tough to bury, and if he ended up disappointed that nothing came of it, he would have a hard time resuming his chase.

This Erika lady had something going on he needed to uncover.

"Alright, you get me plates, and I'll run them," she said. "But be careful. There's no need to scare this girl or get your hopes up over nothing. Tread carefully."

"I always do."

"I'm serious. You've been at this for a long time with very little progress. Don't screw it up because you get too excited."

Ryan swallowed before responding. "You're right," he admitted. "I'll be careful. By the book."

Loretta hummed her approval before ending the call.

From the end of the street, Ryan parked his truck and watched Erika disappear up the stairs of a small pink home on stilts approximately seven houses away. He waited fifteen minutes before driving by slowly and taking a photo of the license plates on the two cars parked in the port.

11

CARTER ARRIVED IN HIS station-issued vehicle at the Seaside Motel five minutes early. He'd been relieved when Ryan agreed to go to his family dinner. Honestly, he had no idea why he still bothered going. His financial independence meant he had the freedom to cut everyone off, but since they all still lived in town, it was better to just keep the peace.

Plus, if he really tried to leave, Robert Cahill would probably fund the campaign of whoever ran for mayor in the next election promising to remove Carter as police chief. It was a confrontation that simply wasn't worth it, so there he was, preparing for another Sunday dinner.

When Ryan came outside, Carter unlocked the car and waited for him to get settled. The detective had an improved appearance from the day before, much cleaner and well-rested. He had clearly shaved and put some kind of product in his hair, and the result was that Ryan appeared more his age. The time on the road associated with an investigation that had no end in sight had to have drained him, and the promise of a temporary home must have been a relief to him.

"Thanks for coming tonight," Carter said and backed the car out of the motel parking lot.

"Nah, thanks for the invite," Ryan replied. "You have no idea how long it's been since I've had a home cooked meal."

Carter winced but didn't take his eyes off the road. "I'm afraid you'll be disappointed then. The food will be delicious, no doubt, but my mom doesn't cook. She'll have catered the whole thing."

Ryan was quiet for a moment. "Your family dinners are catered?"

"Don't feel bad for thinking it's weird because it is," Carter explained. The dynamics of the Cahill family were unorthodox, and he had a lot of practice preparing visitors for the worst without scaring them off.

"So, are there a lot of people in your family?"

"Tonight, there will be my parents and my younger sister and her husband. My father likely invited additional guests of some kind, maybe a wealthy potential property buyer or whatever politician he's backing next."

"Interesting," was Ryan's response. "Will they be expecting me?"

"Don't worry, there will be plenty of food for everyone," Carter said instead of answering.

They rode without speaking for a few miles, enjoying the soft sounds coming from the radio. A local station was playing the Beach Boys and Carter let the happy sounds fill his car until he turned into a private neighborhood.

"I have to be honest with you before we go in," he confessed.

"Oh really? About what?"

"I invited you to be nice, welcome you to town and all that," Carter continued, "but also as a buffer."

"A buffer," Ryan repeated plainly.

"Yeah." Carter adjusted the seatbelt to give himself more space as he navigated the private road. "There's a very good chance that my dad brought some kind of woman here for me."

The other man looked confused. "Like, to date?"

"Yeah, something like that."

"Oh, I thought you had someone," Ryan said, pointing to a small Polaroid on the dashboard, a selfie Carter had taken, his arm around a stunning blonde woman. "That must be you and your sister then?"

"No, that's Lindsey. My ex."

It had been five months, but Carter could swear it was yesterday he read the letter breaking up with him, saying she needed to see more of the world. She said she'd always love him, but that if he ever loved her, he should let her go. The letter said not to look for her, that he should date other people when the time was right. After two years together, she hadn't even broken up with him in person.

Her note had sent him into a rage that later required him to replace all his glassware.

"I just haven't bothered cleaning out my car in a while," he said to explain the photo's lingering presence.

"You might plan on doing that before you have another woman in here," Ryan joked.

Carter parked in the circular drive of his parents' house without responding.

"HOLY SHIT." RYAN STEPPED out of the car and looked up at the massive estate in front of him. "This is where your parents live? Did you get to grow up here?"

"Yes and no," Carter replied. "My parents moved in here well after I left the house."

"This is insane." Ryan was having trouble moving past his awe. The huge white house was surrounded by well-manicured flower beds and a picturesque green lawn, while tall Grecian pillars stood in front of a two storied porch. Large windows with matching shutters framed each room inside. Mossy trees surrounded the structure, though they seemed shorter than they should be.

"Do you know when this was built?"

"Yeah. 2014."

Ryan did a double take. "Seriously?"

Carter sighed then shoved his hands in his pockets. "Yes, really. My dad built the Cahill Group real estate empire from the ground up. His story could be really inspiring if he told it honestly, but he's embarrassed about his childhood, I think. I guess they didn't have much. The fact that he's 'new money' is a huge point of contention for him. He has this obsession with old Southern culture and antebellum architecture. I would have given you more of a heads up, but there's really no warning that could prepare you.

"Just," he sighed, "get ready for a whole lot of weird."

Ryan looked closer at the home and, with his untrained eye, wasn't able to pinpoint anything about the house that proved it wasn't built in the time it mimicked.

"It's fine," was all he said. "Families all have their quirks."

Carter shook his head. "Not like this."

Ryan shrugged then tried to smile, but it probably came across off putting. "My younger brother is about to marry my ex-girlfriend," he offered. He wasn't sure why he shared that except to make Carter feel better.

It did remind him, though, that he needed to text Colleen. If he said *no* right away, it would start a fight between himself and the couple, which he didn't have the time or energy for. If he RSVP'd *yes* to the wedding, then he could push off their irritation until after they were married when he most likely wouldn't show up.

"No shit," Carter laughed. "That sucks, man. I'm sorry to hear that."

"It's okay. I'm mostly over it."

The chief looked as though he didn't believe a word out of Ryan's mouth, which was fair. He wasn't positive he believed himself. "Sure," he replied. "Let's get this over with."

Ryan followed Chief Cahill up the front stairs towards the door. He was curious, really, to see this family dynamic. Carter was so clearly reluctant to see these people at all, but Ryan was confused as to the reason.

He was relatively young for his position on the police force in town. Surely, that was a point of pride for any family.

Maybe the elder Cahills were angry that they hadn't gotten grandchildren from Carter yet. For a man obsessed with tradition, that would make the most sense.

They walked through the heavy front door and Ryan almost squealed when a man in a white button down appeared out of nowhere to his right. His hands were crossed in front of him, and he stood tall, but had his eyes lowered, refusing to make any visual contact with either of the men.

"May I take your coat, Mr. Cahill?"

Carter had not even lost so much as a step as he moved past the entryway into the house. "It's sixty degrees outside, Gerald. No one is using a coat."

Ryan sped up to follow him, barely catching the "very well, sir" spoken softly from the man in the button down.

As they walked farther into the home, Ryan could finally see cracks in the antebellum façade. The home's walls were white and covered with portraits of people he didn't recognize, but they were clearly prints and not actual paintings. The brass accessories on the candelabra lights were worn out in an artistic way instead of an authentic one. He bet if he tapped on any of the walls, he'd get a cheap, hollow, drywall sound, rather than the robust density of a historic structure.

When they got to the end of the hallway, the space opened up into a parlor room with six people standing around holding cocktails while an actual server moved amongst them with a tray, which felt to Ryan to be more than a touch indulgent.

Ryan leaned in and whispered to Carter, "Are we under dressed?" Looking around, he saw everyone in at least business casual if not their Sunday best when it came to attire. The women wore modest cocktail dresses in dark colors while the men wore sport coats with open button downs.

He looked down at his own flannel and jeans, then to Carter's similar clothing next to him.

"Who gives a shit?"

They didn't have to wait long before someone noticed them. "Ashley, darling! Thank you for joining us." An older woman with Carter's coloring walked over with her arms wide, clearly aiming for a hug. "And you brought a friend!"

Before either of them could speak, she pulled the chief into an embrace that would have strangled a lesser man. While holding Carter, she whispered loudly enough into his ear that Ryan could hear her, "I'm so happy for you," she said. "It's your father that has all the hang ups. I don't care who you love."

"Just a friend, Mom," Carter corrected. "This is Ryan. He's a detective from Wyoming, and he's going to shadow some of my officers this week to see if this precinct is the kind of place he'd like to transfer." It was a good story, and Ryan appreciated the chief's quick thinking. He hadn't even considered needing an explanation for his presence in town and he wasn't about to share Sloane's story with all these strangers.

"Oh, magnificent." She clapped her hands together as if the excitement of Ryan's arrival in Oak Island rivaled that of a former President. The woman appeared to almost be a cartoon of Southern hospitality come to life.

"Nice to meet you, Mrs. Cahill," he said.

"Please, call me Margaret Mae. Let's get you both a mint julip." And the slip of a woman was off on her mission to retrieve beverages for the men.

"Hey, Carter?"

"Yeah?"

"Who is Ashley?"

"Carter is my middle name," he explained.

"Oh," Ryan acknowledged.

"And to satiate your curiosity," Carter continued, "my sister's name is Scarlett."

Ryan raised an eyebrow. "Is that supposed to explain everything for me?"

"Both our names are from *Gone with the Wind*."

"Ah. I think I get it now."

"Yep," was the other man's only response before they walked farther into the parlor.

RYAN WAS NOT ENTIRELY POSITIVE he hadn't been slipped a hallucinogen at some point during the day leading up to his dinner with the Cahills.

He knew families could be eccentric, but this was just...odd.

First, he'd been introduced to Scarlett and her peculiar husband, Clive. The man was apparently some third son of a governor, but Ryan couldn't remember what state. His teeth were too big for his mouth, and he wore a napkin tucked into his collar like Winnie the Pooh while he ate. He had an advanced degree in botany, which could have been interesting, but throughout the night, he was constantly distracted by all plant life, from the mint leaf in his cocktail to arugula in the salad.

Scarlett lived up to her namesake based on Ryan's limited cultural exposure to classic Southern literature. Clearly spoiled, she exhibited impatience in every movement she made from the way she handled the servers to her interactions with Clive. She was often short with her husband, though the overly academic man didn't seem to notice or care. Ryan also saw how much jewelry she wore, though he had no expertise in that area and from his seat across the table could not tell if any of it was real.

The way she'd been raised was not all downside, though. Unlike her husband, Scarlett had obvious trained in the way she ate and spoke to guests.

"What's the most exciting thing you've ever seen in your work? Carter is always bragging about low crime rates, and he should be proud of that, but it makes for boring police stories, in my opinion," Scarlett spoke to Ryan.

"Well." He gulped down a piece of chicken, trying to squash the memory of Sloane's body. "I've had to give more than one DUI to men on horses. You'd be surprised how often it happens."

"Oh, that's funny." She giggled girlishly behind her drink. "What's always the excuse, though? That the horse isn't drinking?"

"That's true. Or, well, we hope the horse isn't drinking, but the rider drinking becomes a problem if he's steering the horse into vehicle traffic."

"I suppose that's true," she conceded. "We don't get anything that exciting around here. Our DUIs always happen in cars, unfortunately."

Ryan chewed his food quickly, trying not to speak with a full mouth in front of people who would clearly notice and care about such a social sin. "Those, I'll say, and I think Carter would agree, are much more dangerous than horse DUIs."

Silverware clinked for a few moments before she spoke again.

"What made you want to leave Wyoming?"

"It wasn't so much a desire to leave than to see new places," he replied. "I'd like to maybe get somewhere warmer, meet new people."

"I think I understand," Scarlett replied. "Though I've never had the inclination myself. I was born and raised here."

"There's merit to that kind of loyalty, of course."

She leaned across the table, her expression conspiratorial. "How does Oak Island rank against Cody?"

"I like them both, but that would be like asking me to rank a hot choco-late against an ice cream cone," he said.

Scarlett grinned at that before settling back in her seat. "Very clever," she said, and he couldn't help but blush under her compliment.

From across the table, Clive's vaguely hurt expression caused guilt to pool in Ryan's gut, marking the end of his interactions with Scarlett.

Besides Ryan, the two other guests were a man who owned a lumber yard chain that Ryan had never heard of and his nineteen-year-old daugh-ter, Alexia.

After they had all been introduced, Ryan leaned towards Carter to confer. "Was your dad thinking of her for...?"

"Marriage to me? Yeah."

"But it's—"

"A sixteen-year age difference? Apparently, not a problem for him."

Ryan noticed when they were all choosing seats for dinner, Carter had strategized himself away from the poor girl, who looked relieved when she didn't have to sit next to him. She appeared to have the same etiquette training as Scarlett, though with far less confidence and experience, the combination of which meant that she was utterly silent. She didn't seem to make any noise at all, speaking or otherwise.

Mrs. Cahill—Margaret Mae—possessed Scarlett's charm and monopo-lized conversation on her side of the table, covering politely for Alexia.

Lastly, there was Robert Cahill. He was the only man in the group wearing a bowtie, which Ryan thought made most people appear silly, but it somehow made the elder gentleman look more intimidating. It didn't help that he rarely spoke, yet everyone could feel his assessing eyes on them during dinner.

Like a cliché, he sat at the head of the table, glaring at everyone, waiting for someone to make a mistake.

"Ashley," Margeret Mae spoke, addressing Carter. "What kind of work will you be subjecting poor Ryan to on his vacation here?"

"Nothing he can't handle," Carter smiled back. "He'll just be riding along with some of my officers this week to see if he's a good fit. I'll make sure he only gets to see the scenic areas, so he'll want to stay with us."

"Excellent!" Margaret Mae seemed to have no shortage of joy to spread to anyone who needed it, contrasting her sharply with her stern husband.

"If you stay, Mr. Gibson," Robert interjected with his first sentence since everyone sat at the dinner table, "you must visit some of the Cahill Group properties. There's no sense in renting if you want to make a home here."

Ryan looked to Carter for any sign of how he should respond, but the chief was eating dinner, ignoring his father.

"I'll be sure to do that, sir. Thank you for the offer."

"No more business talk, darling, you can sell Ryan a house once he has a job here," Margaret Mae said. "Ashley, I heard all about your new shift protocols for handling tourist season. It sounds like it's going to make everyone safer and take a lot of stress away from your officers. That's brilliant work, sweets!"

"Thanks, Mom," Carter replied.

"You told me about that," Scarlett interjected. "It has some kind of new rotation, right? To keep everyone filtering through the busy areas without overusing certain officers?"

"Yes," Carter sat up, ready to explain. "It—"

"Anyone could have come up with it," Robert interrupted.

Everyone at the table quieted and returned to their meal.

Silverware clinked against plates and ice cubes rattled in their glassware until Carter said something again. "There's nothing wrong with public service, Dad."

It was an obvious sentiment, but one that was backed up by no one else at the table. The lot of cowards all stared at their food, abandoning Carter to his father's words.

"I agree," Robert replied. "That's what the mayor's office is for. If you want to depart from the family legacy, you could have aimed higher, Ashley."

"Well," Carter stood, shoving his chair with enough force that it almost spilled over behind him. "Ryan and I have an early morning. I'll see some of you next week. Scarlett, you and Clive enjoy newlywed life. Alexia, good luck with your freshman year at UNC and that communications degree. Goodnight, everyone."

Ryan uttered a few apologies to everyone at the table as he got up and raced after Carter through the dining room and the parlor. He caught up with the chief in time to see him land his fist through one of the walls. The sight should have alarmed him, but he suspected that kind of physical over-reaction was not foreign to Carter or anyone who knew him well.

And Ryan had been right about the house. They had used the cheap drywall when building their estate, as was proven by the gaping hole where Carter's fist had been.

Ryan attempted levity but failed when he opened his mouth. "How early are we talking for tomorrow?"

Carter shook his hand, grimacing at the pain. When he'd inspected his hand and apparently found nothing wrong with it, he addressed Ryan.

"Let's plan on meeting at eleven or so."

"That early? I'm used to sleeping in," Ryan quipped back.

Carter rolled his eyes and walked toward the exit. "Let's get out of here."

12

ERIKA, CLAD ONCE AGAIN in her fanny pack and exercise gear, decided to do something foolish.

Things were different before Detective Gibson arrived. She could pretend that she and Christina had time, that she could leisurely work in the coffee shop, listening to locals' gossip, while she collected evidence for Christina's case as it fell into her lap. She would have taken her time avoiding Carter while digging through his personal effects for something incriminating.

With Ryan here, everything had an expiration date.

She wasn't used to being followed, if that's what this was. She was used to working in the dark, where no one could see her, where she didn't feel rushed to complete a task before it had matured.

Erika jogged lightly, watching the houses pass her in the night like she had before. The evening she'd almost been caught by Chief Cahill, she had been worried about discovery in one direction. If she moved too quickly, too sloppily, someone could find her.

It was a frightening prospect, then, to also be afraid of being caught because she worked too slowly. Two sides were closing in on her, and she felt no closer to helping Christina than when she arrived on Oak Island.

Well, maybe Erika was helping her emotionally, but that was hardly comparable to seeing her attacker be arrested, though Christina had expressed gratitude at her presence.

Soon, she would need new running clothes. As winter ended and spring arrived at the beach town, even the nights weren't going to stay cold enough to justify her gear. It was a hazard of her occupation that she had to travel light. She only carried with her the clothes needed for exactly the climate she was visiting, meaning that her winter outfits from Maryland didn't have a long shelf life as spring encroached on North Carolina.

Erika's feet pounded the asphalt on her way to another empty house managed by the Cahill Group. This time, she was trying one of the more affordable properties with a blind and foolish assumption that Robert Cahill didn't have a silent trip alarm on any of those.

She just needed a small break, one piece of evidence to let her know she was on the right track.

A bloody t-shirt, a photograph, Christina's bracelet, anything.

Like the first house she tried, this one was on the water and within eyesight of the pier where Christina was attacked. It was a single story, leading Erika to believe it would be a relatively quick search.

She really needed a win.

As she closed in on her destination, all the thoughts tumbling in her head distracted her long enough for her to run directly into another pedestrian.

Her velocity was about to propel her to the ground before two hands held her upper arms, halting her descent. "Woah, easy. Are you okay?"

Erika refused to look into the eyes of the man who caught her. If he hadn't seen her face, he wouldn't recognize her and maybe he would leave her alone. "I'm fine."

Ryan Gibson stepped back to get a better look at her, not releasing her arms. If she hadn't already known his character, the action would have been alarming. Anyone else, any other stranger holding her like this would have gotten a swift kick in the nuts.

He should know better than to make a woman feel trapped when she's alone at night.

"Erika? From the coffee shop?"

Shit.

"Yeah, that's me."

He looked around them and then back at her, concern creasing his forehead. "You're just running around here alone at night?"

"Last time I checked, there wasn't a law saying I couldn't," she quipped.

"Doesn't seem safe," he replied.

"You're the one holding me captive." And with that, he finally dropped his hands. Erika moved around him to get back on track. Maybe if she tried to leave, he would let her.

No such luck. She moved less than four paces before he spoke to her. "Do you want to grab a drink with me?"

"What?"

"A drink. With me," he overenunciated. "I had a weird day, and I could use the company."

Erika stared at Ryan. She wasn't expecting this invitation.

She tried to decide what a normal woman would do in this interaction since that was what she was pretending. She had to operate under the optimism that his only exposure to her was the night before and the coffee shop that morning. How could she honestly interpret those interactions?

On the one hand, he was a stranger talking to her alone at night, so she could reasonably bow out, claiming to feel unsafe.

On the other hand, they were both single or hadn't announced aloud any alternative. Ryan was nice to look at in an approachable way, with an openness to his expressions that made him seem trustworthy. He also wasn't as physically intimidating as someone like Carter Cahill, with Ryan standing just half a foot taller than Erika's five-foot four frame.

If I wasn't Erika Willett, and he wasn't Ryan Gibson, what would I choose?

"I can do one drink," Erika said, "but that's it."

He smiled back, very pleased. "That's all I asked for," he said.

"But I get to pick the spot."

"I'll just follow you, then," he replied, and gestured with his arm for her to lead the way.

As they walked farther away from Erika's original destination, she tried to think of running into Ryan as a blessing. Blindly entering another empty house could have gotten her caught, and she knew she had to reevaluate more strategically if she was going to find justice for Christina.

Letting Ryan get to know her better also had its benefits. It may have seemed counterintuitive, but if she revealed enough about herself, it would reduce his curiosity. Right then, she was a mystery, but if she became just some woman he got drinks with, if she became banal and solipsistic and uninteresting, he would walk away thinking her incapable of the work she did.

If he was in Oak Island trying to find the person who helped him solve Sloane's murder, Erika needed to become a known entity. Nobody suspected their friends to operate behind the scenes as crime solving masterminds.

"Is it always this loud?" Ryan spoke, pulling her away from her scheming.

"Is what loud?"

"The ocean," he said. "It sounds like its right next to us."

"Oh," Erika smiled. One thing she missed whenever she was working inland was being near a body of salt water. While she wasn't overly spiritual or a crystal collecting hippie type, she knew there were certain geographies that felt to her as if they had healing properties. She loved oceans and mountains, though she didn't care for flat plains or deserts.

She particularly hated lakes for some reason, though she'd never been able to pinpoint why that was. Perhaps it was just too stagnant for her soul.

"It's just high tide. The water line is as close as it ever gets right now, but it quiets down drastically when the ocean pulls out for low tide. If you're here for a few days," she continued, and pointed down the street to the north, "the high tide is loudest towards the small cliffs. The caverns around the island's rock formations fill up entirely. It really is something."

"Maybe I'll check it out if you go with me," he smiled.

"Why don't we start with drinks," she countered.

He seemed to be standing deliberately close to her, though not so close they were touching. She thought she could even feel the heat coming off his body, but it must have been her imagination. It wasn't possible through their layered clothing.

"Have you lived here long?"

Erika looked at him before answering. He was staring ahead, almost to give her emotional space rather than physical. "What makes you think I live here?"

He smiled before holding the door to a seafood restaurant open for her. "Unless your days at the coffee shop are volunteer work, then you've got to be staying a while."

"Fair enough," she said, annoyed at her blunder, and wondering if she should lie. She didn't want him to connect her to the other cities, but it would be too easy to verify her arrival with anyone who'd seen her start working for Fiona.

"It's been a few weeks. I'm hoping to make it permanent once I've saved enough for a down payment."

"I just got here, too, but you knew that," he said as they approached the bar.

"Right. Some sort of cross-country police station wife swap, where you work here for free," she joked, and he gave her an obligatory laugh.

"Well, I'm not getting paid," he confirmed.

The space was nearly empty, though one couple in a corner booth mooned at each other over their drinks and it appeared the man tending bar was the only one working. A vague savory scent washed out of the kitchen, but otherwise everyone in the dining room remained unbothered by anything too fishy. A dimly lit bar with six open seats and no current patrons awaited them.

They sat in the middle, facing each other before the bartender approached them. Once they ordered, a quiet fell over them that was not altogether comfortable, at least for Erika. She was having a hard time getting a read on Ryan and his silence felt deliberate, like he was waiting for her to say something embarrassing.

"Aren't you going to ask what brought me here?"

Erika uncrossed and recrossed her legs before speaking. "I assume you're sick of the cold. Or maybe you've gone through a break-up and need some place new," she said. She knew neither of these things were true. Ryan had been born and raised in Cody, and with her research on him during her time there several months ago, she'd found no recent girlfriend.

"Not entirely wrong," he grinned and reached for the drink that appeared in front of him. "Winters where I'm from are brutal. And there may be some personal reasons I have for leaving."

Erika did the same, leaning in, mirroring his actions. "What kind of personal reasons?"

He answered quickly, "My brother is getting married in a few months."

"Most people would find that to be good news," she replied. "Is there some kind of drama that requires you not be happy for him? Are you jealous? Do you hate your brother?" Erika lowered her voice conspiratorially. "Does he have alternative preferences that you disapprove of?"

Ryan laughed, and its genuine nature surprised her. "Nothing like that," he smiled. "I certainly don't hate him, and I think I'm happy for him. He's just getting married to an ex-girlfriend of mine," he said.

Erika played with the condensation on her glass of wine. "And that bothers you?"

"Obviously," he scoffed.

Hearing his quick answer, she paused. As she sipped her wine, she looked at him over the glass, seeing his refusal to meet her eye.

"No, it doesn't."

Ryan stopped his glass halfway to his mouth. "Excuse me?"

"Your brother's marriage to a former flame of yours doesn't bother you," she repeated.

"You don't know what you're talking about," he replied, all pretense of relaxing gone. "How could you know what's upsetting to me?"

"I think you want to be upset about it more than you really are," she said, leaning in closer. His expression was paused, unmoving, and contained a mixture of bewilderment and respect. He might have been acting angry at her observation, but it was all for show.

Erika continued, "You believe that you're supposed to be distraught about it and the fact that you aren't worries you. It makes you wonder if there's something wrong with you, so you pretend to be bitter about it so you can participate."

He seemed invested, then, at her analysis and lifted one corner of his mouth in a conspiratorial smirk. "What am I trying to participate in?"

She grinned at him. "Normal people shit."

A quick laugh burst out of him before he replied, "Maybe I like normal people shit."

"Sure, you do," she said, the sarcasm in her voice strong.

He finished his drink and signaled for another. "Is it my turn now?"

For a moment, she was confused. She'd found a rhythm to their conversation, and he was changing it. "Your turn?"

"Yeah," he smiled. "It's my turn to hear a personal story from you then criticize your response to it."

Erika blushed under his attention, despite her wariness. Instead of thinking of something clever to say, she had a sip of her drink.

"Why don't we start with something easy," he asked, and she was grateful for his backtracking. "Where are you from?"

"All over," she said honestly. "My dad was in the Navy."

"I can't imagine what that was like. I've spent my entire life in Wyoming. I'll probably spend the rest of it there, too, eventually," he replied in a somewhat self-deprecating tone.

"Nothing wrong with that. Sometimes I wish I had a place to call home, or even somewhere I cared to return to once in a while." This statement was perhaps as honest as she could get with him, and the longer this conversation continued, the more she resented that reality.

"Home can be people," Ryan said.

Erika swallowed hard, pushing down her reaction to his statement. "It's just my parents and me. They live in Southern California, if you want to call that my home." She picked up her glass of wine and finished it, then set it on the table.

"I should go," she said, though it sounded like a question, even to her own ears.

"One more," he insisted. "We just got here, and I still don't have your number."

"Maybe I haven't decided if I want you to have it," she replied. "And I have work early in the morning."

He stood with her, as if to leave, too. "Can I walk you home?"

She laughed. "Absolutely not."

"Alright, that one was a stretch," he admitted, laughing along with her.

When she moved to leave, he grasped her wrist without urgency, and she was so surprised by his touch that she didn't pull away.

"When can I see you again?"

Erika slipped her arm out of his hand before answering. "You know where to find me during the day," she said.

A few steps away, she spoke over her shoulder, almost as an afterthought. "You should go to your brother's wedding. Be thankful you have him in your life."

She left the restaurant, hoping he would have no interest in caffeine anytime soon.

~

RYAN WATCHED ERIKA make her way towards the restaurant's exit, wishing he could get even a coy glance over her shoulder as she walked away, but she didn't look back.

He hadn't planned on seeing her that night but running into her on the street like that was an opportunity he couldn't pass up.

All he wanted was more information about her and he got a psychological evaluation instead. Most people's reaction to hearing about Travis and Colleen was some variation of *shit, that sucks, man* and then a desperate subject change, which he enjoyed.

Erika had pinned him with something he had no interest in thinking further about and he wasn't sure how that made him feel about her. Frankly, she saw too much.

After Carter had dropped him off at the motel, he'd thought about going inside but changed his mind before he got to the door. How could he sleep after that evening with the Cahills? He'd taken the walk alone to decompress after the bizarre dinner he experienced with the chief's family. Ryan's minor drama surrounding his brother's marriage had nothing on Carter's home life, and he was still reeling from the evening's interactions.

Robert Cahill was a piece of work. It was no wonder Carter had chosen a career far away from his influence, but Ryan worried for his sake that it wasn't quite far enough.

That became background noise when he ran into Erika. It was truly an accident, pure happenstance, but he'd been planning on going back to the coffee shop and asking to see her or finding a way to be around her again.

"You'll hear about coincidences a lot in our line of work," Sergeant Vincent's voice echoed in his mind. "Most people will say they don't believe in them, but that's a fool's religion. Coincidences happen everywhere, hundreds of times a day. You should trust your instinct, but don't let make believe patterns distract you from the real evidence."

Could the interaction he had with Erika that night be considered evidence? In his mind, their conversation had all but confirmed his assumption that she was the one he'd been searching for, the one who helped him with Sloane.

Loretta hadn't run the license plates yet, but that would only get him so far. Ryan needed a little bit more before he could push for the truth.

13

UP UNTIL SLOANE'S DEATH, Ryan had never been prone to nightmares. He still wasn't, as his dreams were usually happy memories, ones he had cherished before her murder. Prior to last year, he would have remembered those moments willingly and happily. These were the kinds of stories he would have recounted to her friends and family at her birthdays or future high school graduation.

The real nightmare was waking up to his new reality.

Sitting in his motel bed in the early hours before he was supposed to arrive at the Oak Island police station, Ryan rubbed his eyes and pretended they were dry. He hadn't turned on the lights yet, allowing the dream to leave him naturally rather than chasing it away with a fluorescent.

"Faster!" A four-year-old Sloane had cried.

"You're getting too big for this," Ryan fibbed to her. In this memory, he was twenty and dragging the little girl around her parents' yard while they finished dinner on the patio. She sat on his shoe, with her arms wrapped around his calf as he limped around the yard, pretending that she held him back more than she did. It was a regular game for them. Ryan often played with her after dinners, helping wear out her energy to make bedtime easier on everyone.

"Soon, you're going to be all grown up and have to carry me around," he continued.

"Never!" She countered before descending into a fit of giggles.

Ryan finally flicked on the light and headed to the motel shower to start his day. He no longer wanted to wallow in the dark premonition of Sloane's childhood exclamations.

RYAN ARRIVED AT THE STATION promptly at 10:45 in the morning. He didn't realize how much he'd missed having a routine, a schedule. He could almost pretend he was back to working his normal hours before he spent six months chasing a faceless vigilante.

A woman behind the plexiglass told him Chief Cahill would be out to see him shortly and he thanked her.

While he was invigorated at the idea of getting back to work in a somewhat official capacity, he didn't know what to expect from his day. He spent those minutes pacing the small room, unwilling to sit down.

Thankfully, he didn't have to wait long.

"Gibson, thanks for being here," Carter called out from behind the door, motioning him to follow. He obeyed, feeling like a loner on the playground that didn't socialize much, finally getting invited to play kickball with the older kids.

Ryan did not consider himself to be a quiet or completely unimposing man but compared to Chief Cahill he may as well be a mouse. The chief was huge, his presence demanded attention, and his footsteps completely blocked out any sounds Ryan's own shoes might have been making. It didn't matter much as they passed through the station, but if he had been following Carter somewhere in public, he imagined the result would be his own complete invisibility compared to the other man.

Carter's presence was godlike with his only fallibility appearing to be the dark circles under his eyes.

"I've got some boring stuff that's keeping me tied to the desk today," Carter explained, "so I'm going to send you out with one of my more veteran officers. You'll be riding along with Tanner Pratt for the afternoon."

"Sounds good," Ryan said.

They moved beyond the spaces Ryan had seen during his first trip to the station into a large open space filled with desks facing one another. Maybe half the seats were occupied, but everyone looked toward Carter as he entered, either in anticipation of a command or simply because it was impossible not to acknowledge someone like him.

"Pratt," the chief called out, and a man about ten years older than Ryan stood up from his desk in the back and walked their way.

"How much does he know?" Ryan asked.

"He's been briefed on the basics. All he knows is that you're looking for someone in a professional capacity that might be here. Whether or not you share more is up to you."

Ryan nodded. "I appreciate your discretion."

Carter chuckled to himself before responding. "Not my first day on the job," he said. "Your search also seemed like it was personal to you in a way I couldn't understand, and I wanted to be delicate with the information."

Before Ryan could say anything else, Officer Pratt was in front of them, holding a hand to him in greeting. "I'm Tanner. You must be Detective Gibson?"

"Yes, sir."

"Well, it'll be nice to have an extra set of eyes. Anything you need from me, Chief?"

"Take him on one of your normal routes," Cahill advised. "But make sure to focus on the best our island offers. We want Gibson to be tempted to move here," he continued with a wink.

Ryan didn't know what to think of that, other than to be somewhat flattered.

Tanner led him to where the squad cars were parked, unlocking the closest one. When they were settled in the front seats, he started the engine and turned to face Ryan. "Chief Cahill said you're searching for someone?"

"Yeah. It's a long shot, but I'm still looking."

Tanner pulled into the road, driving five miles an hour below the speed limit, and all the surrounding cars fell into a similar rhythm. Ryan didn't miss this aspect of being law enforcement: everyone around you drove on edge, and unless the emergency lights were flashing, every drive took at least an extra ten minutes.

No one wanted to be the one to pass a squad car, even if they were legitimately going the speed limit.

"How long have you been searching, if you don't mind my asking?"

The day was overcast, but as palm bushes moved by his window on their trip, Ryan felt the slow mood of the beach town seeping into his body. Against his own will, he relaxed a bit into the passenger seat.

"Over six months. I guess seven now."

"Damn," was Officer Pratt's response. "What exactly are you hoping to find here, riding along with all of us?"

Ryan almost told him a fib, that he was giving up and just wanted to do police work in a new town. It would shut down future questions and make his day easier, but he didn't want to lie. Part of him was still at the bar with Erika, hearing her observations, accidentally connecting himself to her. He didn't relish the idea of someone else seeing right through him again so soon after the fact.

"A reason to keep searching," he said instead.

14

WHEN RYAN WAS TRAINING for his first role with the Cody department, riding along with another officer was part of standard onboarding. He'd spent hours in the passenger seat, watching while a more tenured person from the station issued parking tickets or pulled someone over for driving under the influence.

He learned much during that time, not necessarily about the laws, which he had mostly memorized, but of the different ways an enforcer of those laws could behave and impose them. As a young man, he'd seen the law as black and white, right and wrong.

If a law is broken, the person who broke it should face consequences. To him, it was that straight forward.

Ryan quickly learned that was not the case, and he had both positive and negative examples to pull from in his memory.

The first time he rode with Sergeant Vincent, his supervisor pulled over a woman in her mid-fifties whose car had one missing brake light. Ryan had been preparing the ticket when the older man turned to face him with a disgusted look on his face.

"What the ever-loving fuck do you think you're doing?"

Ryan was legitimately stumped by the question. "Uh, I'm issuing an equipment violation."

Vincent stared at Ryan with obvious disdain before unbuckling his seatbelt. "You just stay in the car for this one, kid."

From the passenger seat, Ryan watched a very informative and humbling silent movie through the windshield of the sergeant's vehicle. Vincent approached the front driver's window of the small sedan, a wide smile on his face. He appeared to be speaking genially with the lady driving. His gestures were all reassuring, and his manner was relaxed and friendly. After some chatting, he returned to the car and pulled a small bag out of his trunk.

Ryan was smart enough to know not to ask what was going on until it was over.

While the sergeant walked back towards the sedan, the woman stepped out of her car, her arms tightening her sweater while she moved to meet him at the back bumper.

Leaning forward in his seat, Ryan continued watching the scene as Vincent changed the woman's brake light. They seemed to be speaking casually, the woman apologetic but happy, and the sergeant assuring in his confidence.

When the light was changed, Vincent waited for the woman to turn on her car and test its efficacy, then with a friendly wave he sent her off on her way, with no ticket to speak of.

When the older man strutted towards the driver's side, Ryan knew he was going to hear about it.

"Gibson," Vincent began as he buckled his seatbelt. "What is our job here?"

Somehow, Ryan knew answering correctly would only anger the man, as then he wouldn't have an excuse to offer a life lesson, which he loved doing. So, he stuck with what he would have answered that morning before he witnessed his sergeant change a woman's brake light for free.

"Our job is to enforce the law, sir."

"Our job, as law enforcement officers," Vincent enunciated each syllable for emphasis, "is to keep the people of Cody, Wyoming, safe. Most of the time, that means punishing people who break the law appropriately. In that sense, you're not entirely wrong."

Ryan gulped, waiting for a harsh delivery of wisdom.

"But please tell me, if we were to do things your way, how the hell the people of Cody are safer after issuing Mrs. Clark an equipment violation she can't afford then putting her back on the road with a still nonfunctioning brake light?"

They were already back on the street, driving to the station, so Ryan knew Vincent wasn't exactly looking for a response, but he gave one anyway.

"You're right, sir. They wouldn't be."

That was the day Ryan decided he wanted to be like Sergeant Vincent, and not like the other man he routinely rode along with during his training, Officer Lewis.

Kurt Lewis also applied the law pliably, but his leniency often deferred in the direction of women he found attractive.

"Perk of the job, Gibson, perk of the job," Lewis had said once after letting a college aged girl off with a warning for throwing a brick through the window of her step-father's house in exchange for her number.

With his experience, Ryan was excited to work with Cahill's men and women. He knew one could tell a lot about a person during a full workday, and he wanted to see how the Oak Island force operated.

Based on his time in the car, Ryan could tell Officer Pratt was a decent man, close with the locals and possessing a strong desire to keep them safe, but utterly without ambition. His casual approach to his job bordered on laziness.

At one point, when he was given a tour of the area rather than doing any police work, they'd driven past the caverns Erika mentioned.

"Those, back there," Ryan pointed behind them when Tanner drove by without stopping, "are those the caverns?"

"Caverns? Yeah, that's the spot," Officer Pratt replied.

"Well, uh, I heard they fill up, you know? During high tide and all that."

"Right," Tanner replied, not showing any concern. "They do fill up all the way. It can be a problem, for teenagers, you know?"

"Why teenagers?" Maybe visiting the caverns at high tide was a dare, some kind of coming-of-age thing that boys forced each other to do as they became men. Ryan's own version of that had been a rope swing over the Shoshone River.

Kids growing up in Cody might need to find a new dare, as Sloane's murder had poisoned the body of water.

Officer Pratt's mind was elsewhere, though. "Parking, man, I miss it. You take a girl to the movies, then maybe a frozen yogurt, and you go hide somewhere her parents won't find you making out. Do they still call it 'parking'? Anyway, no one would dare go down there right now. Not 'til early April at the soonest."

He only caught the last of his visuals in the rearview mirror before they turned a corner and Ryan could no longer see the rock formations. "Why's that?"

"Too fucking cold," Pratt said, before turning into a parking lot.

Ryan confirmed his assumption about his temporary partner's laziness when Tanner stopped for his third refreshment in as many hours.

Tanner parked and unbuckled his seat. "You want anything? They got a cute new thing in there making the drinks."

This normally wouldn't have bothered Ryan, but they were parked in front of the coffee shop where Erika worked, and he was feeling covetous after their one drink together.

Instead of chastising, he raised an eyebrow, then looked pointedly at Officer Pratt's left hand.

Tanner lifted his arms in mock surrender. "Hey, I'm happily married, so nothing like that. My Beth is plenty of woman for me. But there's something good for a man's soul when a pretty woman smiles at him. Nothing wrong with enjoying her laugh while she makes my coffee and asks about my kids."

Ryan was saved both from responding to that sentiment and from figuring out what to say to Erika when he saw Loretta's name light up his phone screen. "You go ahead. I gotta grab this."

When the other man finally slammed his driver's side door, Ryan swiped his screen to answer the call. "Good morning, Loretta."

"Morning, sunshine," she replied. "You have a second for me?"

"For you? I have whole entire minutes," he said. Through the windshield of the car and glass door of the coffee house, he could see Tanner interacting with Erika. She was loose and happy with the officer in a way she wasn't around Ryan.

So, it's not police, in general, that you're afraid of—just me.

Were he inclined to vanity, he might be flattered and assume her nervousness was born of sexual origins. However, depending on what Loretta shared, he leaned toward believing that Erika had known him previously somehow and didn't want to be found out.

It was a novel experience, hoping a beautiful woman wasn't attracted to him.

"The first plate, the North Carolina one, is registered to Christina Higgins, age twenty-eight, under the address where it's parked."

Ryan pulled the phone away from his ear and stared at it incredulously. "*The* Christina Higgins?"

"The one and only," she confirmed.

Interesting development. "She must own the house," he said.

"That's what I thought too, and it sure validates your idea to start following unsolved crimes."

"Let's not celebrate before we know more."

"The other plate, all the way from California, is registered to an Erika Willett, age twenty-three. That ring any bells?"

Holy shit! She's so young.

He knew after seeing her close up that he had a few years on her, but he hadn't realized it was an entire decade. Ryan thought back on some of the solved cases he investigated and counted backwards in his head to the oldest ones. Was it possible that Erika had been doing this since she was a teenager?

It seemed unlikely, but she'd proven multiple times across the country that she was an expert at achieving the impossible.

Ryan looked at Tanner paying though the window and willed Loretta to speak faster. "I may have run into an Erika."

"Well, you'll want to do more than run into her," she explained. "The car is registered in California but received a moving violation in Amarillo four months ago."

Ryan did some quick math in his head. "That's exactly when the Peterson case was solved with anonymous help."

"Bingo," she said. "I think we've found our guy, Ryan."

"It's too soon. We need more before I can confront her."

Loretta paused her typing on the other end of the line. "What if you just asked her? If you confronted her honestly, she might tell you."

Ryan shook his head, then remembered she couldn't see him. "I need more than a coincidence," he said. "I've been chasing this for too long to just throw all my research at someone if we're not sure."

"This is as sure as I think we're going to get, Ryan."

"Just," Ryan took a deep breath. "Find something else for me on her. Literally anything."

"And I'm supposed to just ignore what an insane invasion of privacy this is? You want me rummaging around in her life so you don't have to feel an ounce of embarrassment?"

From inside the coffee shop, Tanner pushed open the door with his hip holding two steaming cups in his hands.

"I gotta go," he said. "Thank you, as always."

He could feel Loretta's eyes roll when she said, "You are so not welcome."

15

"I HAVE AN IDEA," Erika said to Christina.

"If it involves rewatching *Clueless*, then count me out," the other woman countered.

Erika was sitting cross legged on the floor in front of the coffee table eating her frozen microwave dinner. This was a tentative routine they'd developed since Erika arrived in Oak Island. She worked during the day, got a dinner at the pub or at the house, then she would investigate either an empty home or hack the Cloud storage security cameras near the beach. Both forms of searching for evidence had been fruitless thus far, but Erika was confident she was on the edge of a breakthrough.

On nights when she worked from her laptop, Erika and Christina would watch a movie together before retiring to their sperate spaces. They usually alternated on movie preferences, with Erika's clear preference for romantic comedies and films with happy endings being negatively received by Christina.

The woman hosting had an undeniable draw to horror films that Erika did not understand or endorse. There was enough evil in the world, why would she want to entertain herself with it? What was so wrong with a happily ever after?

"I'm not really in the headspace to enjoy romantic story lines,"

Christina added before Erika could reply. "And it feels like we spend more time at the coffee shop and watching movies than we do working on my case."

"Sorry," Erika muttered. "But that's actually not what I'm talking about."

The woman sat up so fast that Erika almost got an empathy headache watching the motion. "Well, what are you talking about then?"

"I don't think Carter would have stashed anything in an empty house," she explained. This wasn't entirely truthful. In a perfect world, if she had time and safety on her side, Erika would have searched the remaining twenty-eight homes for sale under the Cahill Group. She was nothing if not thorough when it came to her investigations.

But she no longer had time or safety guaranteed to her, if they had ever been, so now she had to be bold and creative.

"Do you think it's possible he brought something to the hunting lodge or his primary residence?"

"Duh," Christina sat back down. "Obviously he would keep anything incriminating closer to him. I don't know why you didn't start there."

"Breaking into an occupied residence is a lot more dangerous than breaking into empty homes," Erika argued.

"Then I would focus on the lodge. It's so remote, most people would never think to look there unless there was a warrant or he was publicly accused."

Erika nodded. "Which you don't want to do," she said.

Which you refuse to allow.

"I don't know much about the lodge, though," Christina admitted. "If you're going to search it outside the law, then I don't think I can help you much."

"I wasn't expecting you to," Erika said.

The other woman seemed to take this personally and shrunk back into herself. "You know that I want to help," she whispered.

This was always the hard part with what Erika did. Cold hard evidence was easy to handle. It didn't get its feelings hurt, it didn't wrestle with the problems of good and evil, it didn't cry. All the evidence did was tell a story without embellishment, hopefully a true story, one that led to justice.

But Erika struggled consistently with the human component every single time she stopped in a new town to help someone who needed it. She had the skills to read people, analyze them, and catalogue whether or not they were honest, but supporting them in their pain was always much harder.

Christina was no exception.

"You are helping," Erika lied with a smile as she picked up her dinner plate to wash it.

RYAN COUNTED TO FIFTY, then pushed back on his knees after a round of push-ups.

He wasn't married to any kind of workout culture, but his mind was always more settled after physical activity. There was no need for a fancy hotel gym, just enough space on the floor for him to move and a suitcase for compound lifts. His habits of exercise were also a result of Sergeant Vincent's advice, though the older man didn't implement it for himself.

"No, I'm not going on a run with you, goddamn it, boy," Vincent said. "I'm telling you that you need to expel some of whatever it is that makes you so wound up, so you don't get us both killed at a bad traffic stop."

It was a far from unfair assessment, and Ryan had made physical exertion part of his routine ever since.

In his motel room, he shifted onto his backside and shoved his feet under the bed before beginning his sit-ups.

Earlier, he'd spent another unproductive day with Officer Pratt, speaking to any friends and family they happened to run into and snacking at every food joint they came across. It wasn't altogether a waste of time since these trips helped him understand the town's geography and culture, but Ryan couldn't ask any real questions. There were times when he was tempted to engage Tanner about why he was really in Oak Island, but those times were short lived.

Eventually, the officer would say something that reminded Ryan he wasn't a valuable wellspring of wisdom or information.

It was a good thing that Tanner Pratt worked as law enforcement in a town with such low crime statistics. In a big city, he wouldn't have been able to function as dog catcher.

After he completed sit-up thirty-seven, Ryan's phone rang.

He swiped to answer as he pushed off the ground and walked toward the motel desk. "Hi, Loretta."

"I don't know why I let you keep dragging me into this," was the first thing she said.

"Because you want answers as much as I do?"

Loretta laughed. "Neither of us believes that."

"Fair enough," he conceded. "I suppose you have news if you're calling?"

"You suppose correctly," Loretta said. "I did some digging on my own for Erika Willett, just to see what I could come up with."

"Let's hear it," he replied.

Loretta didn't take the bait. "How much do you know about this girl? Have you spoken to her?"

"Briefly," Ryan said. "We spoke a couple nights ago, when I ran into her by chance. We had a drink, got some surface level information out of each other. Like, think first date kind of questions." Loretta's disapproving grunt on the other end of the line was the only interruption, so he kept speaking, "She said she came from a military family. Parents are in San Diego, no siblings. I didn't get the sense that she opened up much to new people, so I took that conversation as a win."

"You're right about that much," she said. "She certainly didn't share much with you, and based on my research, she gave you half-truths at best."

Ryan frowned, uncomfortable with how much this upset him. Erika was used to running, used to hiding outside the law. It shouldn't surprise him that she had hidden things from him or misled him when they spoke for the first time.

He didn't like that he believed them to be more connected than they were. He'd have to remember not to make that mistake again.

"Tell me more."

"Her father, Grant, is retired Navy. That all checks out. He and her mother, Robyn, have lived in San Diego full time since his retirement about eight years ago."

Ryan stared down at the motel room desk which held the well-worn map with all his plotting and notes. The oldest red dot he tracked was from four and a half years earlier, an armed robbery of a gas station outside Oakland that resulted in the teenage cashier's death. There were no marks or notes from where her parents lived, but that could just mean he hadn't found them. "This all checks out with what she shared," he said to Loretta, somewhat vindicated that Erika had been partially honest with him.

"Well, here's where it gets good. Or, actually, here's where it gets very bad," she said.

He clicked the speaker phone option on his screen and sat down, taking out a notebook. "How bad?"

"Just...tragic bad. I don't know if it's going to explain anything for us, and this is all public information if you know where to look for it," Loretta explained.

Ryan scribbled the words *Erika: History*, at the top of a page and prepared to write whatever his friend said next.

"She used to have an older sister. Hailey was her name."

Setting the pen down, Ryan leaned back in his chair. The implications of what Loretta revealed made him rethink his plans to use Erika's background to get closer to her. It felt wrong to write down her pain as if it was another case for him to solve.

Was this what first sent her out on the road? Had she watched Hailey experience some grave injustice, leading to her nomadic secrecy in helping other victims?

"Five years ago, Hailey Willett was a twenty-year-old staying at her parents' home for the summer. Apparently, Grant and Robyn were out of town for the weekend, and Erika had some event with a friend. When Hailey had the house to herself on Friday, July 23, 2021, she ended her own life with a single gunshot wound to the head."

Ryan remained silent, looking down at the map that had no red dot over San Diego. This was not what he had been expecting.

"Erika was the one who found her when she got home that night," Loretta finished softly.

The climate control unit in the motel kicked on, adding a steady hum to the atmosphere in his room. It was loud enough that Ryan almost convinced himself he could end the conversation with that as an excuse.

"I have to confess something, Loretta."

"What's that, Ryan?"

"I don't know what to do now that I know all this," he said.

It occurred to him then that he was still behind Erika, still trailing her as she moved. Sure, he had caught up to her physically. He might understand that she was cunning and skilled, that she had a heart for those who needed justice. He recognized that she had ways of gathering evidence that existed outside the law. Ryan even knew that she was pretty and could be flirtatious when she wanted.

But he could chase her for the rest of his life and still not learn everything, still never comprehend what motivated her or caused her pain.

"I think part of your problem—and I say this with love since I'm guilty of it too—is that you haven't been treating her like a person."

Ryan's frown deepened. "What do you mean?"

"For months, when you were chasing her, she was an enigma. She was a ghost or an angel who had delivered you a miracle. You put her on a pedestal like she was this untouchable thing you had to capture to understand, that you needed to study. You wanted answers or closure, or something else she could give you."

He wanted to interrupt that he hadn't even known it was a woman he was chasing until a month earlier, but he let Loretta speak.

"And even when you found out who she is, or potentially is, it still became about what she could be for you. Her ability to solve crimes from the shadows is an obsession for you, and you still didn't stop to consider the fact that you were just one stop for her, that her own path has nothing to do with you.

"She's not a puzzle for you to solve, Ryan. Erika Willett is a person."

He waited to answer for a moment as he closed his notebook and pushed it aside. "Okay," he said softly. "How should I proceed?"

"I'm glad you asked," Loretta responded. "That depends entirely on you. When you hit the road all those months ago, what was your goal?"

That was an easy one. "To find the person who helped put Sloane's murderer in prison."

"And if that hasn't changed, then I think this is as far as you need to go," she explained. "We have enough circumstantial evidence that leads to Erika being our girl. If you asked me to put David's entire college fund on whether or not it was her who helped you with Sloane, I would do it in a heartbeat. You can rest easy in the future knowing that you found her, and maybe you could leave her a nice note saying thank you, then come back home to Cody and go back to work as a detective. How does that sound?"

Ryan didn't have to think about that one at all. "That sounds terrible."

"Then your goals have changed," Loretta reasoned. "And depending on what you want next, I will either advise you or tell you to come home."

"I'm not going back to Wyoming," he said. He had no plans to return right away. If he left Oak Island, moved on from Erika, he would still spend a few more weeks away. He wasn't capable of returning to a normal life after his months on the road and would need to decompress further.

He wasn't capable of looking Sloane's parents in the face, seeing their devastation.

"So, what do you want?"

He sighed, then folded the map back into its atlas and began packing his backpack. "There's still more I don't understand. There are questions I have that need answers."

Loretta sounded like she was chopping something in the kitchen, a sharp contrast from her usual typing noises. "She's not a lab rat, Ryan."

"No, obviously I know that," he said. His bag packed, he slipped it onto his shoulders and checked his pockets for his wallet and keys. As he left the motel and locked the door behind him, he kept speaking, "I want to talk to her. I think Erika is worth knowing, as a friend or something. Well, if she wants to know me, that is."

"I agree," she replied, the sounds of a sizzling skillet coming through the phone. The warm sounds of a dinner being cooked were at odds with Ryan's walk down the street. It was already dark on the island, and a light fog removed more of his vision than he cared to sacrifice, though the mist wasn't chilly enough for him to double back and get into his truck. He wanted the time alone on the sidewalk as he moved towards the houses farther from the coast.

"What are you going to do about it?"

"I don't know," he admitted. "It's not like I can come clean with everything."

"Why the hell not? You've shared your nutty story with many people who were far less sympathetic audiences. You've been laughed out of restaurants and bars for telling people what you were up to."

Ryan tried not to get frustrated with his friend's deliberate misunderstanding of his situation. "I can't just tell a woman in her early twenties that I've been following her all over the country for more than half the year, Loretta."

"If she's not the one, then it's a moot point. You'll leave town and move on, and she'll have a funny tale to tell her children someday," she replied. "If she is the one who helped us, then she'll know your character already, and I think she'll appreciate your honesty."

Ryan kicked a dead snake out of his way as he continued his prowl down residential streets. Cursing to himself silently, he tried to pretend he hadn't seen it. He could enjoy the beach during this time so late in the winter, but based on what he'd seen so far, he wanted nothing to do with the wildlife on Oak Island when the weather finally warmed up.

"Alright. I'll keep you updated on my plans," he lied before hanging up on Loretta.

Pocketing his phone, he stalked towards the coast, making his way through the mist to the house where Erika Willett was staying.

16

"WHEN DO YOU PLAN on visiting the Cahill hunting lodge?" Christina asked.

"I don't know yet," Erika admitted. They sat across from each other on the floor next to the coffee table. Since she was finished digging into camera footage for the night, she was flipping through a deck of cards playing solitaire while a rerun of *The Twilight Zone* played in the background. She'd lost the coin toss for the night and was stuck with Christina's preferred entertainment, but she didn't have to stare at it. Placing a six of hearts on top of its place in the four sorted stacks, she tried not to sound annoyed.

"I have to figure out a way to get inside, narrow down what I'm looking for. I'd have to make sure no one was there when I planned to go. Depending on how far it is from the main roads, I'll have to map out and memorize a hike so my car isn't seen there, and I can leave my phone someplace else."

Christina didn't look away from the screen as a rock came to life and ate the doctor studying it on her show. At least, Erika thought it was a rock. Perhaps it was an alien. For the time in which it was filmed, she found it to be rather graphic, but she didn't say so aloud.

"Could you send an anonymous tip? You could, like, get the place SWATed or something?"

Erika took a deep breath and reached for her patience. "Since I'm not in the business of attempting to murder people, no, I won't be SWATing anyone in the Cahill family or otherwise."

They sat silently for a few more minutes, each woman wrapped up in her own thoughts. Erika didn't usually stay in one place for so long. By this point, in most cases she'd have already found everything she needed, said goodbye to her new friend, and moved on. It was out of the norm for her to be interacting with someone like Christina for so many weeks.

She wasn't entirely sure it was a good thing, but she couldn't leave until she finished her job.

Before either of them could say anything else, the doorbell rang.

"Did you order something?" Christina asked.

If she wanted anything delivered, Erika would have sent it to her temporary PO Box in the town, and she never would have ordered food to the house when so many places were within walking distance.

"No," she said. "No one should be at the door." She felt her pulse quicken. There was no good reason for anyone to visit the house.

Christina ignored her and stuck her head in the window to see who was outside. "Ooh," she said. "It's that's guy who seems to be wherever we are. Is it Ryan, you said?"

She tried to calm her heartbeat enough to respond. "Is it really him?"

"Looks like it," her host responded. "I think you should invite him inside."

"Absolutely not," Erika responded, shooting up from her seat. "He'll go away if he sees no one is home."

"Newsflash, the lights are all on," Christina replied after a shiver. To punctuate her statement, Ryan Gibson rang the doorbell a second time. "And it doesn't look like he's leaving."

"Well, I'm not answering the door," Erika hissed.

"I don't think you have a choice," her friend hissed back.

"You're the one who wanted to keep everything quiet until we had proof!"

"You've been here for weeks, and we still have no proof. We have less than any proof. And I told you multiple times," Christina said, "that I think we can trust this guy. He seems like a good type, you know?"

"I already know he's the good type. I told you this. I studied him extensively when I was in Wyoming. It's just that he doesn't know that I know he's the good type, so what kind of type would I be if I let a stranger into your house?"

"But he's not a stranger?"

"He doesn't know that I know he's not a stranger!"

"He might! Because he's here!"

Erika watched as Christina looked out the window, scrutinizing the man waiting outside, unconcerned with being seen.

"Are you sure you want to bring someone else in on your case?" Erika asked. "This isn't the kind of thing we can walk back once we tell him everything."

The doorbell rang a third time while she waited for a reply.

"Well?" she asked Christina. "What if we tell him and he runs to Cahill?"

"And then what? I never get justice? So far, it doesn't seem like I'll get it anyway," Christina said, and Erika fought to hide her wince. "We could use the help, and maybe he has access to things we haven't thought of. I told you I trust him, so feel free to share what you can of my story. You can make your own decision after that," she continued. "I'll make myself scarce while you guys talk."

Erika watched Christina waltz back to her bedroom, whispering every curse she had at her disposal.

She peeked out the window one more time. Ryan kept his gaze on the front door, which was very gentlemanly of him since it was impossible he hadn't seen her staring at him already.

With shaky hands, she opened Christina's front door.

"HI."

That was it? That was all he had for her after eight months? Ryan wanted to slap himself. He should have crafted her a dissertation on how amazing she was, how smart he found her to be. He should have written a poem describing her mysterious nature and how much he respected and worshipped it.

He should have catalogued for her how many hours he spent thinking about her.

But no. All he said was "hi."

Erika looked up at him from her spot inside the foyer, dressed in only athletic shorts and a pullover. She appeared too amused to be scared, but too on edge to be expecting someone.

Ryan didn't know what to do with her. He could try to be cool, but he'd never been cool once in his life.

"If you wanted a second drink, you know where I work," she said.

Oh. Right. That was their last contact. A drink.

He smiled, even if it wasn't charming, and looked at Erika. "I do need a drink," he said, pulling the cheap bottle of merlot from his backpack's water bottle holder. "But I don't think I can wait for the coffee shop to open."

Instead of sending him away, she smiled. "Just in time then," she said.

Ryan passed the bottle of shitty red wine to Erika. "Can I come in?"

She didn't want him to go inside. He could tell, even through whatever lying skills she developed. He knew she wanted him to leave.

But an inkling he had, one he normally would have ignored, saw that she needed someone, and he was just enough of a bastard to push her on it.

"One drink. Then I'll leave. Promise."

She stepped back and opened the door farther, giving him space to pass her. "Fine. We can sit in the living room."

Ryan crossed the threshold then wiped the bottom of his shoes on a rug before moving into the common area. It was more feminine in décor than he was expecting with its stark white couch and fluffy pillows, a shaggy pink rug on the floor. He didn't think the space suited Erika, but then he remembered it wasn't her house.

A game of solitaire was spread out on the coffee table half completed while the television blared.

"You a big fan of *The Twilight Zone*?"

"No," she said quickly while turning the TV off. "It just played automatically after something else."

"Got it," he said. It seemed he was really spoiling this. If someone held a gun to his head and told him to engage in a normal conversation with her, he would be killed almost instantly. That's how hopeless he was behaving.

What he needed to do was take Loretta's advice and treat this conversation like the others that he had during his time on the road speaking with detectives.

Erika, if he was right, had been there, too, and might want someone to whom she could relate.

Ryan made and released a fist with his left hand repeatedly while he watched her pick up the playing cards and put them away.

"If you need something to keep you busy," she said without looking up at him, "then you can grab us two glasses from the kitchen."

"Sure," he said, shaking out his hand. Quickly, he moved through the space towards an open doorway since the longer hallway seemed to contain the bedrooms.

The kitchen was small but organized well, so his task wouldn't take him long. Only three rows of cabinets filled the space over the counter with its small gas burner, followed by a double sink. A large window took up most of the area over the sink. Without blinds or curtains, he was confronted with his own reflection in the glass, his hair sitting close to his head, weighted down from the mist outside. It was so dark in the night, and the kitchen so well lit, that it may as well have been a mirror.

Ryan tore his gaze away and opened the cupboard. With the glasses located, he made his way back into the living room.

Erika waited for him, sitting on the couch with her legs tucked beneath her. She looked so small, yet her face held confidence that made him nervous.

She didn't seem worried about seeing him, so had he been wrong this whole time?

He set the glasses in front of her, ignoring his worries, then twisted the cap off the wine, kicking himself for not buying her something nicer. It was the same one she ordered the other night, but that didn't mean anything.

"Here," he passed her the drink, then poured himself one twice as large.

"Thank you," she said. It was clear Erika had no intention of initiating their discussion. She obviously wanted him to start, so she could find out why he was there.

Ryan slid his backpack off and put it to the side, then sat on the ottoman in front of the small table.

He let them sip quietly before beginning.

"I'm going to tell you a story," he said quietly, reaching into his backpack for the map. He laid it on the table, facing it upside down for himself so she could see it. "And then I'd like you to tell me if you've heard it before."

Erika's eyes were glued to the map, moving quickly across it, taking in his notes.

"I'd only been a detective for two years when we found Sloane Mitchell's body next to the Shoshone River after a graduation party last summer," he choked out.

She tipped her head slightly, acknowledging that she heard him without tearing her scrutiny away from the map.

"It was, and still is, the worst thing I've ever seen."

17

ERIKA STARED DOWN at the map in front of her. She took in all the places he'd marked with red dots, each describing a case solved with an anonymous tip to an investigating officer.

Ryan was good. Really good, but she already knew that.

"We had nothing on the kid who did it." He was still speaking to her about Sloane. "Until incontrovertible evidence arrived and we were able to pull a confession from his friend."

His voice was smooth and steady as he continued the story, recounting to her what happened back in Cody, the actions afterward she hadn't stayed to see.

It was fascinating. She never really got to hear this part, what happened to the people she gave evidence to so they could prosecute a crime. She always left before they got the chance.

The way Ryan told it, what she'd done was a miracle, and exposure to that kind of phenomenon had transformed him into a religious observer of sorts. He spoke with reverence most reserved for cathedrals and fine art museums. His commitment to understanding who had helped him and why had undoubtedly taken on the form of an obsession, and Erika wondered if she should be worried.

She didn't feel worried. She felt flattered.

Ryan's story continued as he described how his town healed after getting justice for the violent murder of one of their own, then his own pilgrimage in search of the one who gave it to them.

"I searched everywhere I could think of," he said. "First, locally, for anyone who may have been involved. Former friends of the murderer, enemies of the mayor, other people who loved Sloane. But no one knew anything. I felt as if a ghost had passed through town untouched by a single person who could tell me about them.

"Then an article caught my eye about a small town in Idaho. A man murdered for his wallet outside a convenience store; the killer masked and untraceable. The article said there were no leads until an anonymous tip arrived for the investigating officers, giving them enough to arrest the man responsible."

Ryan took a break to swallow some wine then massaged his right palm. Erika took a sip as well before standing, so she could look down at the map and read all of it.

"The article didn't say much else, so I packed up my truck and drove there to ask them myself."

She pulled her attention upward so she could see Ryan in his seat. His wine was gone, the glass abandoned to the floor by his feet. His hands were on each knee, knuckles white, and Erika wondered briefly if he was hurting himself, but he seemed to need the tension for some reason.

"What did they say?" she asked, though she could probably guess with impressive accuracy.

"The detective there had a similar story to mine," he said as he looked up at her. "It varied in some areas, but I sensed that it was the work of the same person who helped me. His tale had that touch to it, you know? After that, I called my sergeant and requested an extended unpaid leave and followed every story I could dig up that resembled ours."

"Yeah. I get it," she replied, smiling sadly. She wasn't going to get out of this without giving him the truth, she realized.

It scared her, the end of her anonymity. Without it, she might lose her freedom.

But without her honesty, Ryan looked like he was about to lose his sanity, and she didn't feel right taking that from him.

"You're right," she said. "This is a story I've heard before."

He moved his head to face her instead of the ground in front of him, but he didn't interrupt her.

"You missed a few."

He blinked as if processing her statement took too much work. "What?"

She gestured down to the map. "You missed a few, but not many. This is actually very impressive."

Ryan gulped, then followed her hand. "Where? Which ones?"

"Toledo," she started, with her finger tracing along the worn paper of the map that had been folded and unfolded within an inch of its life. "A teenage girl who disappeared at the mall. It was some guy who worked at a kiosk who followed her outside. Then there was one in Wichita, a high school teacher hurt by one of his students. But other than that, you found them all."

He shot out of his seat then and paced the room, running a hand through his hair. She might have laughed at how messy it became, but she wasn't sure how to read his mood. It seemed like the best course of action was to let him walk it out for a minute and gather his bearings.

While he paced, she picked up their glasses to put them in the kitchen sink. She moved quickly, not wanting to leave him alone for any length of time.

When she turned around, she squeaked in shock, as Ryan had followed her into the kitchen.

His face was serious, and she panicked.

"You probably have a lot of questions—"

But she was interrupted when Ryan pulled her close and wrapped his arms around her, pressing her face to his chest. He held her still with one of his hands cradling the back of her head, not allowing for much movement. Eventually, she gave in and hugged him back.

"Thank you," he whispered into her hair. "I'll never be able to thank you enough for what you did."

∾

ERIKA DISCOVERED WITH SHOCKING immediacy how uncomfortable she was with gratitude and praise.

After the awkward disentangle from their kitchen embrace, she and Ryan sat next to each other on the couch with his legs crossed ankle to knee facing the coffee table and her sitting crisscrossed sideways pointed at him.

He seemed unable to comprehend being there with her.

"I just can't believe it," he repeated a third time.

"There's nothing to believe," she replied.

His attention moved back and forth between her and the map, as if trying to connect the two in his mind.

"No, it's just, you have to understand," he insisted. "I've been on the road chasing answers for almost eight months. Tracking you. A huge part of me didn't actually think I would find you. It still seems too good to be true."

"You think I made it up?" She teased him.

He laughed, catching on. "Of course not. I...uh," he sat and faced his body towards her. "Can I ask about your process? Or is that, like, privileged information?"

Erika didn't want to answer questions, but she wanted more time with Ryan. Turning him down meant risking his leaving, though he acted like he enjoyed her company as well.

She'd never had someone she could talk to about these things.

"How about you ask me whatever you're curious about and I'll decide if I want to answer."

"Right. That works," he replied then looked down at the map. "How do you find them? The cases, I mean."

"Well," she searched for an answer. "I think they sort of find me, if that makes sense."

Ryan gave her a sardonic glare. "So, file that under 'does not want to answer.' Got it," he said. "How do you find the evidence? Do you plant recorders for confessions?"

"Sort of," she said. "In the case of Sloane's killer, I followed him for days, watching his moves. I also watched his friends and picked the one who I thought would cave during a police investigation the fastest. Ricky was the obvious choice with his straightlaced attorney father, so it was his backpack where I planted it. For the other...things," she said, avoiding direct mention of the condom and brick, "Craig kept them."

Ryan scowled at the naming of Sloane's killer. "He kept them?"

"Yeah. In a safe in his bedroom," she said. "It was probably the best place for them since he knew your team would never get a warrant."

He scratched at his stubble and Erika found herself watching the movement with fresh interest. "How did you get the recorder back? And the other things?"

She winced. "Probably not something I should admit to someone who works inside the law."

"Shit, Erika." He sounded sharp, and she feared that her admission upset him. He was, if nothing else, a rule follower. She could picture him finding her methods inappropriate and deserving of reproach.

But that's apparently not why he was upset.

"That's got to be so dangerous," he said. "Are you staying safe?"

"Yeah." She picked at a stray thread on the sleeve of her pullover. "It's not guaranteed safe or anything, but I know what I'm doing."

Ryan exhaled, then shifted his weight back into the couch. "That's good, I think," he said.

They sat in silence for several minutes after that. If he was going to grill her for information, Erika wasn't going to offer it up for free.

Finally, he leaned forward, setting his elbows on his knees. He took in the map before pulling it closer and tracing her route between the red dots.

"I just..." he started then paused, moving his fingers back over certain cities. Randleman, Annapolis, Ketchum. "I just feel so in the dark."

The air was motionless between them, but Erika felt anything but settled. There were only so many plausible explanations she could give him.

"What do you mean?"

His top row of teeth pulled at his bottom lip and Erika watched as his confusion grew. "It's just...how do you *know*?"

She tried to keep herself still, betraying nothing. "How do I know what?"

How does anyone know anything? She wanted to ask sarcastically, but Erika knew that Ryan would reject that kind of flippancy.

"With some of these, it's obvious," he said. "Like back in Cody. We knew who killed Sloane, her sister knew, plenty of people were aware of what he did. We just couldn't prove it with legal means. It made sense that a vigilante third party might step in and rectify an injustice for us, even if I didn't understand how you did it. Thank you for that, again, though the thought of you anywhere near that scumbag makes me want to throw up."

"You're welcome," was all she replied.

"But with some of these," he pointed towards the other towns, "there was no suspect. The police and public didn't have anyone to accuse. There was just some faceless thief in Idaho, not even a locally known vagabond. Hell, with Tyler Jordan, they didn't even suspect murder; they just thought he drowned. No one would have known to look at the camera. How would you know to look at the security footage? How did you know about the drug deal in Annapolis? Who are you talking to that knows these things?"

He slowed down enough to take a breath. "And why are you here, now? What brought you to Oak Island?"

Erika sat quietly while he spoke.

"I don't think you'd believe me if I told you," she said softly.

"Please," he begged. "Everything I've heard from you checks out with what I know. I have no reason not to trust you."

Maybe I'm more worried about what will happen if you do *believe me.*

It seemed, in hindsight, inevitable that he would arrive at this question, and as she brainstormed ways to avoid giving him the truth, movement caught her eye from the hallway.

"I'm okay with you telling him about me," Christina said from the door. "I don't mind. I always said I thought we could trust him. I think you should tell him what happened to me."

The pounding in her chest almost shut out her ability to hear, but she knew what Christina was saying.

What would she do when someone knew the truth? Who would she become when she wasn't alone with this anymore?

Ryan was just staring at her, not responding at all to Christina. She knew that if she begged him not to ask, he would back off. He would give her space and respect her decision, but the not knowing would kill him eventually, and he would try to find answers somewhere else.

And she was tired of being alone.

"I know how to solve these crimes because I can speak to the dead."

PART II

JUSTICE FROM THE GRAVE

18

RYAN BLINKED, thinking he imagined Erika's response.

She wasn't looking at him, but she wasn't shrinking into herself either, which left him alone with the new information. Instead, she refolded her legs and started picking at her cuticles, like the task couldn't be delayed. The lack of eye contact offered the hint of privacy, one Ryan needed to collect his thoughts before saying anything else.

On its face, the statement she had just made was ridiculous, but he'd promised to try and believe her.

Without the noise of their conversation, Ryan understood just how quiet it was in the house. No mumbling voices from the television or dripping faucet allowed him to be distracted from her revelation. His imagination began creating whispers that said nothing until a car outside sped by, tires splashing in leftover rainwater that refocused his thoughts.

He wasn't a materialist or atheist, so completely denying the existence of supernatural elements in the world had never been his position. The idea of heaven was a comfort to him, one he carried close to his heart especially for cases like Sloane's.

Some people saw evil in the world and used that as evidence that a good God couldn't possibly exist and allow it to perpetuate. Ryan saw evil in the world as an aberration, a stain on something that was supposed to be good. He liked things like hope and love and thought that those immaterial powers were proof enough for him that there was something waiting for him on the other side of death.

He had simply never considered what his reaction would be when he was confronted with someone who claimed to know about it personally.

It might have sounded preposterous, but which was more absurd: a woman, working alone in her early twenties, solving all these crimes by herself, or the victims of the crimes helping her from beyond the veil?

He supposed it didn't matter yet.

"I've never heard anything like this before," he finally said.

Erika looked up from her fingers. "Well, I've never told anyone," she replied. "So, we're kind of in the same boat."

He nodded along, trying to piece together what he now knew. He felt like he'd studied for a grammar quiz only to be placed in front of an advanced calculus final.

She found evidence, helped people, got away with things no one should be able to get away with. She knew the truth of certain cases before investigating officers were even looking for it.

His mind was a jumbled mess he feared would never reorganize itself.

Suddenly, Ryan shot out of his seat and looked around the house. "Wait, you're staying here," he gestured around. "Does that mean Christina..."

"Yeah," she whispered. "Christina is gone."

The Christina Higgins missing person case was the one that Loretta had found for him, his reason for coming to the area. In his mad chase to find Erika, he would have investigated any unsolved murder or missing person, but his friend back home had insisted on the beach town as his next stop.

Thank God she had.

Ryan cursed under his breath before sitting back down. "That...that's terrible," he said. "I know it's been a few weeks, so the chances of finding her were slim, but I was still hoping."

"I get it," Erika said. "I would have felt the same way."

He shelved his internal debate about whether he thought living people could talk to the dead so he could communicate with Erika in the present.

It was a skill Ryan developed during many years of investigating. Gathering evidence from witnesses was much easier when they thought you believed them.

"So, how does this all work?" It seemed as good of a question to start with as any.

"Well, I actually don't know how *it* works," she said.

"No, I meant your process, I guess. Once you meet someone who needs your help," he replied, trying to clarify his question. "How does this usually work?"

"Oh," Erika said. She crossed her arms and chewed the inside of her cheek, like she wasn't used to telling someone about this. He would have guessed it might even be her first time telling someone, and he worked to suppress his pride that it was him. "Typically, the victim finds me when I stop in a place that feels right. I stop for any number of reasons, really. Maybe I see a town's name that speaks to me, or I feel a weight settle in my diaphragm after a particular exit on the highway. There was one time I just happened to be out of gas and when I pulled over, I saw a sign for a police tip line for a recent murder.

"Once they realize I can see them, hear them, they start talking. I get to know them, find out what happened when they were alive. From what I understand, it takes a lot of energy to stay here after death, if that makes sense."

"Energy. Right," Ryan repeated back. "How does that manifest?"

She sat up, possibly invigorated by his willingness to try and understand. "Mostly, I only see people who died young. The oldest I ever saw was a man in his late thirties, I think. And they all have a strong, personal motivation to stay," she explained.

"Like justice or vengeance," he continued.

"Yeah. I guess I should feel thankful. If I could see everyone who's ever died, that would get crowded," she joked, but neither of them laughed.

Ryan scratched his jaw and tried to root the conversation in something he could comprehend, something that would ground him as he learned more about her. "It seems straightforward. With how many places you've been, you don't stay in one place more than two weeks," he said. "Yet you've been in Oak Island for almost a full month. What's different this time?"

Erika sighed and rubbed her eyes. "Multiple things," she confessed.

"The first and most glaring is that Christina doesn't remember her death. I've been searching all over the island for her body or anything missing that belonged to her."

"Is that unusual?"

"None of this is 'usual,'" she scoffed. "But this is my first experience with a victim who has no recollection of their death. It means I have to solve it from scratch, which I'm not accustomed to."

"Right," he said. Secretly, he wanted Christina to still be alive, for Erika to be mistaken. She was still a missing person, after all. But he kept that to himself.

"So, you have no idea what happened to her?" he asked, fishing for reasons to hope.

"Not necessarily," Erika admitted.

Ryan frowned. "What does that mean?"

"Christina doesn't remember dying, but she does remember what happened before," she explained. "And this is the second complication."

He looked at her from his spot on the couch and waited.

Erika pulled her knees to her chest and hugged them. "Two nights before she was reported missing by her manager at the bank, Christina was violently raped by Carter Cahill under the pier. After he finished, he stole her bracelet as a trophy, and she remembers nothing else."

Ryan felt his neck heat as he turned to look at his hands.

His stomach turned at the thought of what happened, and he tamped down his imagination. It would help no one for him to picture it.

"Shit," he said. "The chief of police, Carter Cahill."

"Yes. So, among a litany of other things getting in my way, that's why it's more complicated this time," she explained.

Ryan wanted to crawl out of his skin and hide in a ditch somewhere so Erika couldn't see him. "This is extremely complicated," he agreed. "You know that I've been meeting with him?"

"Yeah. I figured that out."

He didn't want to think of Carter as being capable of something this vile, but only in the sense that he didn't want the act to have occurred at all. Chief Cahill wasn't his close confidant, and he hadn't known Ryan for very long before putting a hole in his father's house with his fist.

Perhaps he was more than capable of other kinds of violence.

This was all so new to him. Ryan wasn't yet used to the civilian side of investigating, and he sure as hell wasn't used to the supernatural aspect.

"Is she, um," he choked out, "is she here now?"

Erika looked over his shoulder to the hallway, legitimately checking. "No. She's leaving us alone," she replied. "Maybe we should save strategy for another time. It's almost midnight."

"Why?" Ryan sat up straighter. "What happens at midnight?"

Erika looked confused for a moment before erupting in a fit of giggles. "Nothing, sorry. You looked so scared," she said through her laughter. "What normally happens at midnight is that I get tired, so all plans we make need to wait for tomorrow."

"We're making plans now," he stated more than asked.

"Yes. I assume you want to help?" He nodded and she continued, "Then I can fully update you on everything I have later on."

"You seem like the type that likes to work alone."

Erika shrugged. "You already know all my darkest secrets," she said. "It would be silly for me to turn down extra help. Well, if you want to that is?"

"Yeah. Right. That sounds good." He stood up from his seat to find his backpack then reached for the map, failing to hide his excitement.

He was going to get to watch her work, to help her. He couldn't believe it.

"You don't have to leave," she interrupted.

"Oh," he said, though he didn't move.

"We can keep talking," Erika said. "Just not about, well, let's call it 'work.'"

"Right," he huffed a small laugh. "My old sergeant called it 'shop talk,' and he had to ban me from it multiple times. He says I have a tendency to fixate."

She eyed the map then smiled at him conspiratorially. "You don't say?"

"Fine. I suppose it's obvious," he said, widening his smile.

It was nice, he decided, to share humor with someone who knew what he'd been through. Loretta was helpful, but she wasn't with him in person, and she didn't seem to grasp the depths of his search. Sitting with Erika felt like the relief of crossing the finish line of a track meet, accompanied by the sharp pain of lactic acid released into his legs while he took his first full breath. It was its own sort of companionship, though he was excited to update his friend back home.

Erika interrupted his thoughts. "I was so afraid of being found out for so long," she said. "I couldn't picture what would happen if someone found out what I do, what I am. The idea of it consumed me."

Ryan kept his hands clasped as he listened.

"Now that it's not just me," she continued, "I'm almost relieved."

"How so?"

"I'm not sure," Erika smiled at him from her side of the couch. "But I'm glad it's you."

Ryan had a hard time maintaining eye contact as he replied, "Me, too."

19

CHIEF CAHILL WATCHED as Officer Pratt took oversized bites into his breakfast burrito every time he brought it to his face.

The stuffed mouth did not come with the added benefit of Tanner keeping it shut.

"It was the Grey twins," he garbled out. "Spray painted the side of the laundromat. The manager, Martin, said he thinks it was retaliation. He mentioned that he had to fire them because they were dicking around more often than not. So, check that one off the list."

Carter drummed his fingers, waiting for more. "And?"

Tanner stopped chewing for a minute. "And what?"

"And what did you do about it?"

"Oh," he replied. "I sent the kids home and told them not to do it again."

There were times when the chief enjoyed working with Tanner. He was a decent fellow, he showed up for work on time, and he didn't dig too deeply into places he wasn't invited. Locals and tourists alike didn't mind talking to him or find him threatening.

But on mornings like that one, Carter wanted to put his chair through a window dealing with the man's weaponized incompetence.

"That's it?"

"Sure," Pratt shrugged. "They're fifteen, what are we supposed to do about it? You always say you don't like arresting local teenagers. It just leads to them being afraid of us, and they won't want to come to us when something really goes wrong."

Carter cracked his knuckles before answering. Tanner was technically right on the advice he'd given the man, but he had deliberately missed the point. "You should follow up by calling their parents. Make sure they're aware of what their boys did. Then you call the school, and ask them to issue a Saturday suspension, make them clean bathrooms or something."

"Ah. Good idea," Tanner replied. "I'll add it to my list this morning."

He wouldn't, and it would be another thing on Carter's plate.

"How are your rounds with Detective Gibson?"

The officer appeared to give the question legitimate thought before answering. "He seems like a good guy, though he can be on the quiet side. We haven't run into any incidents where I could get a read on how he operates in the field yet."

Because you avoid work.

"Sure," Carter replied. "Do you think he'd fit here with us?"

Tanner settled back in his seat. "You recruiting?"

The chief shrugged. "Never hurts to try when you see potential."

"I gotcha," he said. "Well, he seems fine to me, but I'm just one guy."

Carter nodded. "I might have him work with Officer Barker next," he said, and turned towards his computer, effectively dismissing the other man.

"Oh, Chief," Pratt said after wiping his hands on his pants, not getting the hint. "I know you're heading up that Higgins case," he began. "But I keep fielding calls from her parents. Do we have any leads so I can update them?"

"Nothing new," he said. Christina was a transplant, not from Oak Island, and she grew up in some Georgia town where her parents still lived.

Not that he wasn't relieved that they weren't bothering him, but he found it odd that her parents only called for updates once a day when their daughter was missing. He expected them to be in town, banging on the station's doors daily, but they didn't seem all that concerned about her.

"It's weird that they aren't here," Tanner echoed the chief's thoughts. "If it was one of my kids, I'd be leading the search myself."

"If they aren't worried," Carter replied, "then maybe she has a history of this sort of thing. Running away and whatnot." It sounded so plausible, he almost believed it himself.

The other man made a face. "Little old for running away. Twenty-eight-year-olds with full time jobs and a mortgage don't just split town."

"Sometimes they do," he said. "I can pull some of her financial records from the bank, see if there's anything there. There are plenty of reasons for someone to split town."

If Tanner Pratt had been a skilled investigator, he might have asked why that wasn't already done.

But he wasn't one, so he didn't ask.

"Nice. Well, let me know if you find anything so I can tell her parents."

20

WHEN RYAN BECAME AWARE of his surroundings, all he felt was pain, and someone tapping him for his attention.

He shot up and grabbed the hand touching him before they realized he was awake.

"Ouch," Erika whispered. "What the hell?"

"Oh," Ryan said. "Sorry."

Locating the source of his pain, he rubbed his neck, which was stiff from using the arm of Christina's couch as a pillow. In fact, most of his body was stiff.

"That couldn't have been comfortable." She winced over him. "I'm sorry. I just assumed you probably didn't want to sleep in Christina's room."

You got that right.

"Wait, is Christina here right now?"

Erika shook her head. "No, she'll give us privacy while you're here. Unless you want her to join? I could speak for her, if you like?"

Cold sweat formed on his lower back. "No, that's okay."

Erika checked her phone for the time before sliding it into her back pocket. "It's almost six, so I've got to get to work anyway. Do you want to meet this evening?"

"Sure," he said, massaging the soreness in his right hand. "Here?"

"Yeah." She smiled down at him. "Where else?"

Ryan sat up fully, with his body returning to normal after a horrendous night on the couch. He didn't have an alternative to her place besides his motel or a public space, so he didn't offer one. "I don't have a lot to contribute yet."

"That's okay," she said. "I have less than I'd like to, but I had an idea. You're working with the chief, right?"

"Not directly, but I do see him every time I go to the station. I don't think he takes a lot of days off."

"If you have a moment alone with him, maybe you could ask him about Christina's case, see how he reacts or if he shares any official progress with you. I'd take anything new at this point," she admitted.

Ryan nodded along with her reasoning. He understood the frustration of an investigation facing a stand-still, or worse, growing cold before anything could be done.

"I'd love to help," he said, standing up to pack his things. He hoped that he came across as casual in his acceptance. Because the truth was, he was prepared to beg on his hands and knees to watch Erika work on a case like this.

Ryan might finally feel the closure he was seeking after Sloane's murder.

AFTER AN ACCIDENTAL EXPOSURE to a horror film when he was a teenager, Ryan became convinced that encountering a ghost would be the most terrifying experience he could imagine. He was utterly unprepared for the low simmering fear of knowing they exist but being powerless to see them or identify them.

Was one sharing the public bathroom with him?

Following behind him as he crossed the street?

Sitting behind him in the patrol car?

Fortunately for him, Ryan's latest companion, Officer Barker, didn't require much socializing while he worked. If Ryan had been less wrapped up in his own head due to the revelations from the night before, he might have found the silence unnerving. As it was, it gave him time to think.

He didn't worry about the implications of an afterlife. That would be a waste of his time, and frankly, Ryan wasn't sure what to do with it besides only saying nice things about people who had passed on, which he did anyway. When it came to ghosts, and who they could talk to, that existential question would have to wait.

Ryan isolated the new information he could actually work with, starting with Carter Cahill.

He had apparently completely misjudged the man. It wasn't like he'd thought Carter was a saint, but Erika's revelations left him doubting his ability to read people.

Ryan was now forced to operate as if the man was a monster and gather evidence about him for Erika, somehow without anyone around him catching on to his motives.

"Lunch?" Paul Barker asked. It was the first word he'd spoken in the last hour.

Ryan looked up and saw they were parked outside a small restaurant near the beach. While Tanner took multiple quick stops during his work-day, Paul appeared to enjoy a single sit-down meal for himself.

"I could eat," Ryan said, just as his stomach growled.

The men were told to seat themselves and Paul chose a booth, taking the seat that faced the door.

Ryan pretended to be okay with his back towards the entrance and sat across from him.

After a few bites of his meal, Officer Barker was apparently ready to chat. "What do you think of Oak Island?"

"It's nice," Ryan replied, as he picked at a fry. "The area. The people. I like it here."

Paul nodded and took another swig of his Coke. "That's good. This isn't any official offer or anything, but I'm sure you can tell the Chief is gunning to have you here. It's not every day we get a fully trained detective interested in this area, ready to work."

"Right," he said, gulping down his next bite of food. "What's it like working for him?"

"He's fair," Paul said. "Really strict with us, but for good reason. He wants everything done by the book, but he's also open to some leniency when it comes to locals who made a mistake. It helps build community cohesion. The people trust us to keep them safe, so they don't balk often when a tough decision gets made."

"Seems like a good man to answer to in our line of work."

"Exactly," Officer Barker affirmed. "The one before him was good too, but older. When he retired and Chief Cahill was instated, it was like we all got this boost of energy at the station."

"So, you don't have any issues," Ryan continued, "working under someone that young?"

"Not at all. I could see how it would get messy, but Chief does a great job of keeping it professional without being stuffy. He might get the occasional post shift drink with one of us, but only one, and he never speaks about his personal life."

Ryan raised an eyebrow. "He has that kind of privacy here?"

"Definitely not." Paul almost smirked but kept his face neutral. "Everyone knows his family, it's just that he won't talk about it. It keeps that healthy line of command barrier in place."

"He reminds me of someone I used to work for," Ryan conceded before finishing his meal.

21

AT RYAN'S INSISTENCE, Erika hosted him that evening on Christina's porch, rather than in the living room.

She understood his aversion and decided not to break his protective mental fence by telling him that Christina was more than capable of eavesdropping on them outside as well.

"I'm glad you take your coffee black, too," she said, leaning back in her Adirondack chair while they both sipped away. "I can make you something fancier when I'm at work, but this kitchen isn't very well-stocked."

Ryan sputtered over his sip, and it almost made her chuckle. He was probably wondering if the coffee belonged to Christina before she died.

Coffee was coffee. He could ignore the chain of ownership.

"It's perfect." He smiled over the mug. "Sorry I don't have much to report back."

She tried to appear reassuring and gave his knee a comforting squeeze. "It's more than I had an hour ago. Knowing how the people who work around him feel can be useful. It lets us know what we're up against when it comes to proving what he did."

Which was beginning to feel insurmountable. The people of Oak Island loved and respected Carter Cahill. Erika was starting to worry that nothing short of a high-definition video of Christina's rape and murder was going to get the conviction she needed for the other woman to move on.

"What do you have so far?" Ryan finally asked. He began their conversation with what he'd learned that day, likely as a show of good faith. She could tell he was eager to hear what she knew.

"Less than I'd hoped for at this point," she confessed. "Christina's lost memories are a problem for me. Usually, I know how someone died because they told me, or they could bring me to the place where it happened. A lot of times they can point out the lost evidence for me, like a glove or other piece of incriminating clothing. Even if they didn't want to talk about it in detail, I could extrapolate the events if I knew who was responsible."

Ryan picked up his mug and sipped his coffee, while Erika set her mug down and recrossed her legs. "Have you dealt with anything like this before? This kind of blindness to the situation."

"Not exactly, but every case is different," she replied. The chill of the evening was starting to get to her. "The Tyler Jordan case was particularly hard."

"I remember Corn," Ryan replied. "I can't imagine what that was like. Sloane is the youngest death I've ever had to deal with as a detective, including accidents. A child's murder would be unthinkable."

"It was worse than you're probably imagining," she said. "He was so young, he didn't understand what had happened to him. Like, he didn't even realize he was dead. He had this vague understanding that he wasn't supposed to play in the hot tub, and I think he associated his newfound separation from other people as a punishment."

Erika watched Ryan's grip on his mug tighten but continued her story.

"Two separate times, I saw Juliet around town while he was with me and he would run up to her, trying to get her attention. He didn't know why she was ignoring him.

"Eventually, he told her he was sorry, that he would never break a rule ever again if she would 'pull him back up.' That's when I knew to check for footage."

"Jesus Christ," Ryan whispered.

"Yeah, until I had that tip off, I thought Tyler just wanted to stay because he had the energy and didn't know how to pass on quite yet. I thought my job was just to keep him company in the meantime," she said. "Not everything I do involves fancy evidence gathering. Occasionally, someone just needs help processing their death."

"Got it," he replied, and she watched him battle with his next question. "I need to ask, even though I'm pretty sure I don't actually want the answer. But I think I need it."

Erika nodded. "You need to know about Sloane."

"Yeah," he croaked out. "I need to know."

"Are you sure?"

"Yes," he said. "Part of me hopes that if it's terrible, that if she suffered more after she died, that you might lie to me. It would kill me if I found out things somehow got worse for her. But it's worse not knowing." Ryan paused, then turned in his chair to face Erika. "I need to hear the truth."

There's the Detective Gibson I found in Cody, Erika thought to herself. In many ways, he was the same sitting in front of her as he existed in her memory. His fake slouch, trying to appear casual but his movements too firm to be relaxed, the insatiable need to solve the case.

But he was more reserved there in Oak Island, and she hoped she wasn't the cause of his newfound hesitancy.

"Sloane Mitchell approached me when I first got to Cody. There's never any question, by the way. I always know what they are immediately. Does that make sense?"

"It does."

She offered him a sad half-smile. "She must have been a very loving and adaptable girl when she was alive," she said, and Ryan tipped his head in agreement. "When I met her, she told me what happened to her. It was terrible, but she didn't have any bitterness or revenge in her heart. She didn't fight what she realized couldn't be changed. Some of them linger because they won't accept that they're gone, you know?

"Anyway, she knew she needed to stay and see Craig put away for what he'd done, not because she would benefit, but because it was necessary. She worried that he would do it again if he got away with hurting her."

"She was right," Ryan said. "After Ricky spoke to us and Craig was arrested, we found pictures in his closet indicating that he was following around another high school girl, sending her notes the way he had to Sloane."

"Oh," Erika gulped. "I didn't hear about that."

"Yeah, you, uh, probably saved her life," he said. "Thank you."

"Of course," she said. "I never get to see anything that happens after I leave."

Ryan didn't respond to her statement, probably knowing that his experience after receiving help from Erika was extraordinary and not what she was wondering about.

"How is her family doing? All things considered, I guess."

"Not great, I'd think," Ryan said with a humorless laugh.

"You'd think?"

"Yeah," he sipped again. "Our families don't talk anymore." He cleared his throat before she could respond and he continued, "So, Christina?"

"Right. Well, as I said, I don't have much. There's footage of her and Carter walking towards the pier the night he attacked her, but there's nothing in the video to indicate what happened next. They just seemed flirty together, really. We know what he did next, according to Christina, but nothing indicating how she died."

Ryan frowned at her statement. "So, we don't even know for sure that Carter was the one who killed her?"

Erika gave him an exasperated look. "Don't tell me you're defending him."

"No, shit, not at all. Just, I have to look at this from my perspective. I come from law enforcement, obviously, so I need to see things how they could be proved in court. We have circumstance and motive, but nothing concrete."

"I'm going to need you to take off your detective glasses for a moment and remember that it's not like Christina can testify. None of this is admissible evidence."

"Fair point," he admitted. "Then explain to me what happens next."

"We need to find her body," she said simply.

"It's been four weeks," he said, sounding pragmatic if not belittling. "He could have dumped it in the ocean, the forest, anywhere really."

"Ugh, don't remind me," she said. "What I'm hoping for at this point is really anything that connects him to her. She says he took her bracelet, so finding that in his possession could get a third party involved. If we get enough to implicate him, we can at least remove him as the investigating officer in her case and maybe get some search dogs for the national forest next to his hunting lodge."

"He has a hunting lodge?"

"Apparently, his family does, yeah," she replied. "Another place for him to hide things."

Erika didn't mention that, eventually, she would search around the lodge herself due to Christina's encouragement. It would likely be a far safer exhibition than digging through Carter's primary residence, probing for clues about Christina's body.

Ryan appeared to file this information away while he clasped his hands together. "What do you need from me?"

"Anything you can find," she said. "I wouldn't discount much at this point. If you can see how much the official missing person investigation has turned up, or if Carter is hiding something, we can work with that."

Ryan stood, clinging to his backpack, the action making Erika smile. He had seemingly not separated from that bag for almost eight months, refusing to be parted from his precious maps and notes for any length of time. She found it sort of cute that he retained that habit even after he'd uncovered her identity.

"I have one more question about what happened back in Cody," he began.

"Just one?"

"Yeah, and then I'd like to not talk about it again," Ryan said, slinging his pack over his shoulder.

"Whatever you want to know."

"I wasn't the lead investigator on Sloane's case," he said. "It was my supervisor. Why was I the one you gave the evidence to?"

Erika nodded, expecting to get this question eventually. "Well, I watched you for a while."

"I'd expect nothing less," he said with a half-smile.

"But the deciding factor was Sloane."

Ryan appeared to hold his breath, waiting for more.

"She said I could trust you, that you would do the right thing," Erika continued. "And she said you might need it."

"I might need it," he repeated. "Did she tell you what that meant?"

"No," she said.

Erika waited for him to answer her unspoken question, but she didn't let herself be surprised or disappointed when he didn't say anything. Ryan just stared at his hands as they rested on the patio ledge.

"Same time tomorrow?" She interrupted his thoughts.

"Yeah," he replied, then looking over her head through the house's windows. "Do you think we could meet at my place this time? It's room six at the Seaside Motel."

Erika's smile fell slightly, but she didn't push him on the location change. "Of course. See you then."

He squeezed her shoulder reassuringly as he went past, and she watched him walk down the steps on the home until she could no longer see him.

22

"WHY ARE YOU MISSING Sunday dinner? You know this upsets your mother," Robert Cahill's voice filtered through the speaker phone sitting on Carter's desk.

This was just what he needed. A lecture from his father.

"I'm not missing for sure, but one of my officers has his own family event this weekend. He asked for the time off a while ago, and I doubt I'll have the manpower to replace him that day," he said reasonably. He did his best to sound contrite, saddened and disappointed by the news. Oh, the horror of missing Sunday dinner. Carter wasn't entirely sure he pulled it off.

Missing Sunday dinner with Robert, in reality, was better than overtime pay.

"You're being ridiculous," the man said. "When are you going to stop playing cops and robbers and come home to your family? It's not too late to develop a real career and start a family. You owe it to your mother and I."

That was the rub. With the exception of Carter becoming a police officer, he and his father had mostly the same goals for him. He, too, wanted to have his own family, his own career success. But that wasn't enough for Robert, and sometimes the younger Cahill wondered if he would have been better off cutting ties, becoming a complete disappointment instead of a partial one.

"I'll get married when I meet the right person," he tried to compromise.

"Ashley, your history with women is abysmal," his father replied. "You have horrible taste. Most of the women you date are trash, and while I don't begrudge a young man his youthful indiscretions, you are no longer young, and it's time to start being serious about who you choose to spend your time with."

Carter couldn't hold back his reply. "And your idea of serious is a nineteen-year-old freshman studying for a communications degree?"

"She comes from an excellent family!"

"Great," he cut in, then, risking further wrath, said, "There's someone in my office, I've got to go."

Then he hung up on Robert.

It felt good to disrespect the man so openly, even if Carter knew he would pay for it later. But before he let himself think about the future, he clasped his hands in front of his face and rested his eyes.

For a couple seconds, nothing existed, and he didn't have to slam someone's face into his desk.

"Whoa, sorry to interrupt," a voice came from the door.

Maybe Carter would get to beat the shit out of someone after all.

Instead of any easy target, he looked up and saw Detective Gibson. Carter checked his watch and realized the man was right on time for being back after his day shadowing officers.

"I didn't take you for a praying man," Ryan joked.

Chief Cahill chuckled. "I'm not," he said. Not anymore. "How has your week been with Pratt and Barker?"

"Good. Fine, it's good," he said. Carter knew Tanner well, so obviously Ryan was lying, but too polite to accuse the other officer of being the lazy blowhard that he was.

"Well, that's good," Carter replied, "because today you're graduating."

"I'm what?"

"You're with me for the rest of the day. I realized I haven't given you a full tour of the station yet." He stood and grabbed his keys. "Let's roll. I need to get out of this office for a while." He walked down the hall, knowing Ryan would follow him obediently.

RYAN GETTING TO SPEAK directly with Chief Cahill was a lucky break, though spending any extended amount of time alone with the man made him nervous.

Even before he learned about everything with Christina, he could tell Carter had a tendency towards gratuitous violence and a temper that appeared to exist without a healthy outlet. He seemed to have a short fuse, yet he'd seen no indication that the men and women who reported to him held anything but respect for the chief. He would have thought that if Carter didn't have some kind of self-control, it should have presented itself at work sooner.

"This shouldn't take too long," Carter said as they walked down the hall, past the places Ryan had already seen. "I know you've had a full day already, but we're a small station." They walked together with Ryan attempting to stay in step with the chief. "We have one interrogation room," Carter said while pointing to an open door revealing a room with the lights dimmed, sitting unused. "It's multipurpose. We use it for interrogations, sure, but also interviews, high profile discussions, or anytime someone needs privacy for a conversation."

"What's a high-profile discussion around here?"

Carter chuckled then shrugged. "Usually, it's just me and the mayor talking over the quarterly budget. Oak Island doesn't get a lot of celebrity visitors if that's what you were asking. I wish something more exciting happened in there that I could tell you about."

"That's alright," Ryan said. "Not everything exciting is good."

They continued their path down the hall, skipping over the bathrooms —a larger, locker room style for men, and a single, family style restroom for women—before stopping in front of a locked door.

Carter pulled a wallet out of his pocket, swiped it over the sensor, and pressed open the door. "This is the evidence locker."

Ryan followed him inside, trying not to appear too eager.

Aside from the sturdy shelving, and clearly temperature-controlled air conditioning, nothing remarkable stood out about the room. It might appear to the untrained eye that it was underutilized with many shelves remaining empty or holding only a few labeled items, but Ryan saw many similarities to his own back in Cody.

Low crime usually meant low evidence inventory.

"We hold onto everything for about six months after a case is resolved, either by plea deal or a finalized trial. After that, we send drugs to be taken care of in a lab setting and personal items get returned to the family. That sort of thing."

Ryan nodded along with Carter's explanation, reading all the labels he could see without moving the packages around. "Do you have any evidence on the Higgins case?"

It wasn't a totally out of the blue question to ask. Christina was what brought Ryan to Chief Cahill's door in the first place.

"There isn't any," Carter admitted. "We don't deal with them often, but apparently that's not uncommon for a missing person case."

"So, there are still no leads?" Ryan asked.

"Not really. When we did the initial search through her home and workplace, we didn't find any evidence of her packing up to go somewhere, nor did we find anything she'd regularly carry with her, like her phone, wallet, and car keys."

"And her phone's location? Surely, you've tracked that," he replied, unsure if he kept the accusation out of his tone.

If he was offended by the question, Carter didn't show it. "Her phone was on the beach near the pier the Friday night before she was reported missing. Then it either died or was turned off," he said. "For all the leads we have, she could have just walked directly into the ocean."

Convenient.

"Her family seems confident that she'll come back at some point," Carter continued.

"What makes you say that?"

"They sent her cousin to stay at Christina's place," he said. "The girl seems to be waiting for her there. She promised to call me if Christina returns to town."

Ryan nodded along as if the update didn't concern him. If Erika had been interacting with the chief and lying to him about her reasons for being there, that would have been good information to have.

She was creating loose ends in this case that seemed out of character for her.

"Hey," Carter said, as if recalling something. "You have any luck finding that guy?"

It took a beat for Ryan to know what he was talking about. "Oh," he said. "Not really. It was always a long shot, you know?"

"Sure," the chief replied while he offered Ryan a fraternal slap on the back. "But if you find your anonymous case solver, let him know we could use all the help we can get on this one."

"I'll do that," Ryan smiled while he stepped farther into the room and away from Carter's touch. When he turned, he saw a new shelf in the back, covered in unpackaged items.

Items might have been a generous description. "Junk" was probably a better word for it.

"What's this?"

"Unofficial lost and found," Carter said. "The guard station at the beach has their own, as do most private establishments, but occasionally items get found and people bring them to us in case someone comes looking."

Ryan's eyes raced across the items. He tried his best to catalogue everything there without appearing too eager.

He skipped over the mismatched sandals, the wallets, and the bathing suits. When he saw something shiny, he slowed, taking in the section containing jewelry.

Ryan saw a few watches, several earrings without a partner, and some necklaces or bracelets.

Arriving at the latter, he committed to memory exactly what they looked like.

Cherry charms. Rose gold. Chunky branded clasp.

"Did you lose something?" Carter joked at Ryan's fixation.

"No, sorry," he replied. "Let's finish the tour."

23

"OH, THAT WOULD HAVE BEEN such a huge break for us," Erika lamented from her spot in Ryan's motel room.

She was sitting crisscross at the foot of the bed facing him with her computer in her lap, while he leaned against the headboard with his legs extended. Erika had arrived as scheduled at Ryan's motel room and hadn't mentioned that Christina's house would obviously be more comfortable.

Ryan was clearly dealing with the implications of what he now knew about her, and while she wanted to resent his fears, she also couldn't blame him for having them.

Revealing her skills to another person was a novel experience for Erika, so she was going into their newfound partnership as blind as he was.

"I was so sure I had something there," Ryan said, alluding to the lost and found jewelry.

"Me too," Erika said. "But Christina said it was a platinum tennis bracelet that used to belong to her grandmother. Nothing gold or covered in charms."

"You have to admit, it would be the perfect place for Carter to hide things like that if he has multiple victims," he continued. "If anyone recognized anything from his stash, he has all the plausible deniability in the world."

"I wouldn't discount that theory completely. He still might be doing that, but perhaps Christina's jewelry was too valuable. It would have been catalogued or stored somewhere else and then connected back to her."

"True," Ryan agreed. "But that still puts us back at square one. We don't have any evidence that could bring reasonable charges against Carter."

Erika folded her laptop and set it on the floor beside the bed. She'd found no new footage from the night in question, and since sharing the investigation with Ryan, she hadn't broken into any Cahill Group houses to look for anything that belonged to Christina.

He might be used to working inside the law, but Ryan's moral compass was likely slowing Erika down.

"There are other places I could look," she said. "I think Carter's primary residence or his family's hunting lodge could have something hidden."

Ryan paused his flipping through his notebook and looked up at her. His expression was carefully blank, but he couldn't hide the concern in the way his brow scrunched up. The obvious care there made her feel guilty, and she resisted the urge to lean over and massage the creases over his nose.

"That seems needlessly reckless."

"It's not reckless, it's calculated," she argued.

"We need to be careful about this, Erika."

She bit her lip to hold herself back from saying something hurtful, from trying to cut him off completely from the investigation. "I just feel like we're running out of time."

He rubbed his eyes, probably already weary of the argument. "Let me try something," he said. "I work with him all the time. Well, I work with his officers, but I always run into Chief Cahill at the station before we get started. We're friendly, and I think he's trying to recruit me to his force, so maybe I can fish for an invite to go hunting with him. That way, I can scour the property without breaking any laws."

Erika lifted an eyebrow but didn't argue. "Are you sure you can convincingly swing an invite without totally clowning it up? Duplicity isn't one of your strong suits, which is admirable, by the way. But I can't have you revealing our intentions."

Despite the obvious chastisement in her statement, he blushed at her compliment. "At least let me give it a shot."

Erika unfolded her legs to get comfortable, letting her left foot touch one of Ryan's through her sock. "Okay," she said, relaxing her posture. "I'm curious to see what you can get for me on this side of the law."

He grinned at her comment. "You'd be shocked to see how most people in this country live. Not committing any crimes on purpose, just going about their normal days not breaking into other people's homes. Completely unreasonable."

"Oh, the horror," she gasped, then chuckled and settled into her new position.

Ryan quieted and watched her as she moved. When his face grew more serious, almost sad and he didn't say anything else, she got nervous.

"What is it?"

"Can I ask you a personal question?"

Erika felt something sink in her gut. "Maybe."

"I'm curious," he said softly, "if you got to say goodbye to your sister."

She tensed, unable to cover her response. "I see you've done your research."

"Never mind—"

"The answer is no," she said. "I told you, it takes a lot of energy, and they must have an intense desire to stay. Hailey didn't even want to be here the first time."

He put his head in his hands. "I'm sorry."

"You don't have to do this," she replied, uncomfortable with his regret.

"Yes. I do. Give me a second," he stopped her. After clearing his throat, he gripped his upper thighs and took a huge breath. "I can't imagine how this looks to you," he began. "I know that I'm just some stranger you've never met that followed you all over the place for way too long. It probably feels creepy as hell, the fact that I know all these things about you.

"But I'm asking you to understand that it comes from a place of admiration. I was just a man, in his hometown, with no big city cases to solve and very much okay with that. I didn't want recognition; I wanted the people to be safe. Until Sloane's death, I had that, then Craig took it away, just like he took her away from us, from her family. And for a few terrifying weeks, I thought he was going to get away with it.

"Then this thing happened, this miracle of a solved case, and I had to know. I dropped everything to learn the why, the how, the *who*. And yes, I learned way too much about you in the process, and I apologize if that feels invasive. It probably is. If you want me to back off or to keep our partnership exclusively about Christina, then I can do that. We don't have to share anymore if you don't want to."

Erika responded to his monologue with a brief moment of out of character hesitation. Sure, Ryan had invaded her privacy to a certain extent, but she wasn't exactly the poster child for respecting boundaries.

Instead of chastising him or accepting his apology, she sat up and crawled in his direction.

"You're wrong about one thing."

He still couldn't look at her. "What's that?"

When he didn't turn towards her like she wanted, she moved closer, eventually straddling his lap and tipping his face so he could look up at her.

Ryan's hands remained fists at his sides while she spoke.

"You're not a stranger to me," she said simply. "I learned about you, too, to make sure I could trust you."

He looked directly at her then, their faces at an even height.

"What did you learn?"

"I learned that you're smart," she continued. "I found out that you have one of the highest solved case rates in the state of Wyoming. I know that you're honest, almost to the point of naivety, but that you refuse to compromise on your ethics. You're a rule follower, which means you probably won't go far in life."

Ryan cracked a small smile at that.

"You care deeply about your community, what's true and noble, and you want to save everyone you meet," she said. When he opened his mouth, presumably to argue with several of her points, she stopped him by squeezing his jaw open slightly.

"And I know that you grind your teeth in your sleep."

"I don't—wait, what?"

"I wasn't in your house or anything, silly," she reasoned.

"That's not a silly question," he argued. "This whole conversation started because of your breaking and entering addiction."

Erika ignored the jab. "My second night in Cody, I sat four stools away from you at a bar," she explained. "I was watching you pore over your notes from Sloane's case. You must have been so stressed, not taking care of yourself. Eventually, you fell sleep on your notebook facing me."

He finally unclenched his fists and interrupted her. "I'm surprised I didn't notice you," he said.

"I was wearing a hat," she said.

"I feel like I still should have noticed you."

"Anyway, while you slept, your jaw moved so aggressively, I almost threw an ice cube at you to wake you before you cracked a tooth."

"I wish you would have," he said, as he moved his hands from the bed and settled them on her waist.

Erika kept talking like she didn't notice. "No, it wasn't time yet. I couldn't have you thinking of me when the package of evidence arrived."

She'd settled into his lap, leaving no space between them, and he tightened his grip incrementally.

"I think," he swallowed, the noise audible to her ears, "that it would be nice not to be alone tonight."

Erika leaned closer, shoving down any thought about Christina by herself in the stilted house.

"Me too," she whispered against his mouth.

RYAN BLINKED AWAKE, feeling something foreign, a sensation he hadn't felt in over a year.

The other side of the bed was warm, though based on its emptiness, recently vacated. He sat up slowly and saw Erika tying her shoes at the motel room's desk.

"Having regrets?"

Her head snapped up. "What? No," she assured him. "No regrets. I actually wouldn't mind a repeat performance. I like the chest hair, by the way." She winked and returned to her shoes.

Ryan resisted the urge to pull the sheet up and cover himself like a scandalized maiden, though he did have some concerns that had nothing to do with Erika seeing him.

"I have kind of a silly question," he said.

"What is it?"

"Was there, um," he began as he struggled with the phrasing he wanted to use. Erika simply waited for him with an expectant look on her face. "Were any of them, you know, watching us?"

She frowned, then stood up from the chair and began buckling her jeans. "Watching us?"

"Yeah, any of your...do I call them friends? Ghosts? Did anyone see us last night?"

Erika snickered, then realized he was serious. "Ryan, I'm hardly an exhibitionist for the dead," she insisted. When she was done dressing, she walked over to him and sat on the edge of the bed and gave his hand a comforting squeeze. "It was just us. I promise."

"Good." He squeezed her hand back, ignoring the dull pain in his own. "Are you working today?"

"Not at the shop, but I'll be doing as much as I can for Christina," she explained.

"I'll be at the station today," he said. "Please promise me something?"

"What is it?"

"Give me a chance to get into Carter's home by invitation," Ryan implored. "I don't want anything illegal to sabotage our efforts at a conviction, and it's just flat out safer to do it this way."

"Fine," she relented. "Same time tonight?" Erika asked over her shoulder as she walked to the door.

"Same time tonight," he agreed.

24

ERIKA UNLOCKED THE DEADBOLT on Christina's house and stepped inside, kicking her shoes off and hanging her coat on the hook.

The sunlight was coming in at an odd angle through the living room window, and she realized she'd never been inside the house at that time of day. There was nothing unusual about it, but the shift in her vision unsettled her.

"You look well rested," Christina's voice interrupted her.

Erika froze, then looked over to where the other woman stood, arms crossed as she leaned against the door frame.

"I fell asleep while we were working," she lied. "We were going over all the leads we have for your case."

"Anything interesting?" Christina asked.

Finally moving her feet again, Erika walked back towards the living room. "Another potential location of your bracelet has been eliminated," she said. "It's not in the police station's evidence locker or lost and found."

"I guess that's not nothing," Christina confirmed, though her tone implied the opposite. She uncrossed her arms and joined Erika in the living room.

"It's not nothing, but it's not much," Erika said.

"Really? Are you sure he's helping us?"

Erika resented that last pronoun. There would be no "us" when it came to Ryan. There would be Ryan and Erika, and Erika and Christina, but no friendly trio, and she didn't know how to communicate that gently.

"Yeah." Erika tucked her feet underneath her on the couch while Christina sat down beside her. "He thinks he can get invited to the hunting lodge to try and find something there."

It was a huge weight off her shoulders, even if she didn't admit it out loud. Erika never got used to the anxiety of searching somewhere she didn't belong. It wasn't like riding a bike or learning to drive when practice allowed for growing confidence.

There was no abolishing the apprehension of breaking and entering.

"Compelling," Christina said, "but ultimately I don't know if that will work."

"Why not?"

"Well, if Carter knows he has a guest coming, won't he get rid of anything incriminating?"

"Maybe he's got a big enough ego to slip up, thinking Ryan is his friend," she replied, though she hadn't convinced herself. Christina had a point there.

"Whatever. We can't do anything about it until later, anyway," she said. "Why don't we go to the beach today? We can walk down the pier, feel some sunlight. Or, well, you can feel the sunlight."

Christina's face held humor about her situation, but for Erika, the mood swings were jarring. The woman seemed uncomfortable speaking about that night with Chief Cahill yet appeared totally fine going back to the place where it happened.

She was unfamiliar with sexual trauma herself, but she could try and relate it back to losing Hailey. For example, she never went into her sister's room ever again, but she did find that target practice at the range with her pistol made her feel morbidly close to her sister.

Everyone heals differently, but it's never linear.

"Sure," she said with a smile. "I'll get changed."

~

ON EITHER A STROKE OF AMAZING luck or some kind of freak coincidence, Ryan wasn't assigned to ride along with any of the regular Oak Island police officers.

His usual hosts, Tanner or Paul, both had the day off, and Chief Cahill had apparently caught up on all his managerial housekeeping.

"This is kind of a special occasion for me," Carter had said as they walked together towards his squad car. "I don't often get to be out with the people for a regular day anymore. It always feels good to reconnect with the community."

"Makes sense," Ryan offered back while he buckled his seatbelt and buried any misgivings he had about being in the same vehicle as the other man.

They'd been driving around Oak Island for only a couple hours, and already Ryan could see how someone like Chief Cahill would get promoted over someone older, like Officer Pratt.

Where Tanner was jovial and somewhat crass, Carter was serious and unapproachably proficient. Where Tanner avoided work, opting for social calls, Carter sought out duty like a greyhound and communicated with locals in a kind but distant manner.

Ryan and Carter had already stopped by a former graffiti site to ensure its continued cleanliness, cleared out a known spot for homeless drug use near the beach, and answered a reported theft call from a clothing boutique that had turned out to have been a misplaced box that was still in storage.

It was early, and Ryan was already more tired than he'd been since arriving on the Island. "Busy day," he commented.

Carter shrugged without looking at his passenger and flicked on his blinker to turn left. "This would have been pretty typical for me back in the day," he said. Then, without requiring follow-up from Ryan, continued, "I think my field days are pretty different from Officer Pratt's."

"I never would have guessed," Ryan laughed.

"Right." Carter let out a rare smile. "I know how it looks, keeping someone like Tanner around, but it's hard to staff a small-town police department. Plus, the locals like and trust him. If something disastrous happens, either an accident or a weather event or anything else, then I'm able to handle logistics without being interrupted while he comforts and interviews witnesses. The dynamic comes in handy more than you'd think."

"It sounds like you run an effective force," Ryan complimented somewhat begrudgingly. He was having a hard time mentally coming to terms with who Carter was. He felt as if he was staring at the man without glasses on, seeing two overlapping police chiefs that didn't quite combine seamlessly.

Carter, the selfless, hard-working one who took care of his town, overshadowed by Carter, the man who violently assaulted women.

"I bet you could use a vacation," Ryan hedged.

"Fuck, don't we all," Carter said.

When the man didn't continue, he tried again. "I hope to be around a while, but I'm not sure if I fit."

"Hey, like I said, the Oak Island emergency responders are always taking applications. Seriously, we'd kill to have you on the force," Carter said, not seeing Ryan's wince at his use of the word 'kill.' "And I think you fit just fine," the chief continued. "What makes you think you don't?"

"Oh, it's not the people," he insisted. "It's really the climate I'm worried about. I grew up with a lot of snow in Wyoming, so I'm not sure how relaxing I'd find the beach. And I'd really miss the hunting we have out there."

"Ah, well there you go," Carter said while parking in front of a boxing gym. "That's easy. I don't go near the beach for fun, especially during tourist season. That's not my scene either."

"Oh, really?"

"Hell no. I was just born here. And you can't tell from all this," he pointed outside to the houses on stilts next to the water, "but we also aren't far from some of the best hunting on the East Coast. My dad has a lot of properties and one of them is a lodge on the edge of a national forest. We use it for hunting, and we even have several deep freeze units in the basement if you want to keep the meat you catch."

"No shit? That's awesome," Ryan said, hoping he sounded appropriately enthused but still cool about it. "I'd kill for an opportunity to check that out sometime."

"Well, it's almost brown bear season. I've got a busy schedule coming up, but I can take you out there in three weeks if you're still here."

It felt way too easy, getting an invitation this quickly, but Ryan wasn't about to complain about it. "I'd love that, man. Thanks," he said.

Carter's invite also made Ryan think there was nothing to be uncovered at the lodge, but he could brainstorm on that with Erika later.

Secretly, he'd be relieved if they never found anything incriminating, and Christina had simply run away from her attack, finding solace and comfort in a new place. She could have split town and found a new life for herself, hiding out in a big city.

Stop hoping for the impossible, he lectured himself internally.

He looked through the windshield at the gym where they were parked, its sign advertised personal training in a variety of fighting sports. "What's happening here?" Ryan didn't think it was the kind of place that would call the police if someone inside had thrown a punch, and he couldn't imagine anything worth stealing was inside.

"What's happening," Carter replied as he opened his driver's side door, "is that I want to hit something. Come on in."

RYAN'S FIRST THOUGHT when he regained awareness was, *Hell smells like a sweaty sock.*

Because that is where he had to be. There was no way he was still alive and experiencing the blinding pain present in his head and face.

"Is he okay?"

"Hope so," responded a familiar voice. "Looks like he's waking up. Can you grab him a wet towel or something? And definitely some ice."

Ryan tried to open his mouth but groaned with the effort. Everything felt like shit.

"Hey, man." Carter was kneeling next to him, waving a hand in front of his face. "Good, good, you're awake. You were only out for a couple seconds."

Based on the way his head felt, it was a good thing he hadn't been out longer, but Ryan already missed the sweet oblivion of unconsciousness.

"What happened?"

Carter smiled, as if none of it was a big deal. "You can't drop the pads like that, man."

Vision clearing rapidly, Ryan glared at Chief Cahill. "You hit me."

When they'd walked into the gym together, Ryan had anticipated a space filled with heavy bags hanging from the ceiling and a weight room with a boxing ring in the middle. He'd never participated in fighting sports aside from the basic training required to become a police officer. When he saw that the gym was just an open space covered in foam mats, he realized he was wholly unprepared.

"Hey, it was an accident," he replied, unconcerned. "But, lucky for us, the gym's medic is here, and he can check you for a concussion."

After walking in, Carter had handed him a jump rope and insisted they warm up. That preceded Ryan's hands being shoved into boxing pads before Carter started taking swings at him.

It all happened rather quickly.

When Ryan tried to sit up, Carter pressed lightly to his shoulder. "No rush," he insisted. "Might want to stay down for a minute so you don't get too dizzy."

He had no desire to lie down any longer on the disgusting gym mat, but he also wasn't in a position to argue with the Chief. It was obvious their skillsets were mismatched, at best.

Instead, Ryan stayed on the ground, vision focused above him on the post-industrial style exposed ceiling. He tried to count the steel beams to keep awake, or follow the air ducts with his eyes, but both tasks inflamed his growing headache.

Excellent. This was the last thing he needed.

"Do you feel better?" Ryan asked.

Carter frowned. "What do you mean? I'm fine."

"You said when we got here that you wanted to hit something," he explained. "Did hitting me make you feel better?"

"That's not exactly what I was going for, dude." Carter laughed as a man in a white polo walked over to them. The man placed an ice pack on Ryan's head and reached for a small pen light to begin the concussion protocol.

"But, yeah, actually," Carter continued. "I do feel better now."

25

ERIKA STOOD IN FRONT of the bathroom mirror putting mascara on. It was out of character for her to bother with make-up, but she'd seen the tube and began swiping without too much reflection into why she had a newfound desire to look pretty.

On a normal day, it was better for her to go unnoticed. Erika knew she was somewhat attractive, but she could easily play it down without going overboard. Keeping make-up free, wearing modest, unlabeled clothes that fit, and keeping her hair in a ponytail were all ways she could become relatively invisible. She almost didn't recognize the woman in the mirror with her hair down wearing bright colors.

Christina leaned against the door frame next to her. "What's all this for?" she said as she pointed to the tube in Erika's hands.

"I don't know," she replied, which was technically true. She refused to admit she had any reason to change her routines. Erika was simply getting ready for a business meeting, and it was important to be professional about those things.

"How could you not know? I've never seen you wear a stitch of make-up, and now you're digging around in my old stuff," Christina accused.

Erika dropped the cosmetics and tried to hide her blush, which only made it worse.

"Sorry," she said quickly, then began washing her hands to give herself something to do. "I don't know what's gotten into me."

As she dried her hands, she looked back into the mirror and met Christina's eyes in the glass. They were filled with accusations, and Erika was tempted to call the woman out on it, to remind her that her assistance was free and she didn't have to be in Oak Island at all.

Yet, guilt consumed her. She really should be more focused on wrapping up Christina's case and allowing the poor woman to move on.

"It's fine," Christina said. "It's not like I can use it anymore."

Erika didn't release her breath until she could no longer see Christina in the reflection.

Would all the ghosts she'd helped in the past have become increasingly hostile if their cases had taken her this long to solve? She didn't think so, but she couldn't discount that either. Christina just needed to have more patience.

Erika was about to speak up and apologize or explain herself further but was interrupted by the doorbell.

"Oh, look," Christina called out from the hallway. "It's your new best friend," she said, then disappeared into her room.

With no small amount of relief that confronting Christina would have to wait, Erika rushed to the front door but gasped when she opened it to see Ryan.

"Oh my god. What the hell happened to your face?"

Ryan sported the beginnings of a black eye, the swelling of which was giving his left eye an unnatural squint. "Chief Cahill happened," he said.

Erika's concern turned to confusion. "He hit you? Why?"

"It was at a boxing gym, but yeah, he hit me."

How the man had managed an appointment to his position from the mayor remained a mystery to Erika. She was inclined to believe Robert Cahill had pulled some strings to get his son the role as chief of police, but from everything she'd heard since coming to town, the two men hardly had a close, functional relationship.

Either the mayor was an idiot, or corrupt, or Carter had been an impressive cop at some point, earning the role. She was inclined to think the worst of the man and didn't want to admit he might have had any positive traits.

She opened the door farther. "Come inside and sit down," she insisted. "Let's ice it and you can rest."

"No more ice or rest. I've had plenty of that today," he said, remaining outside. Even with his injury, he stood with strong posture, the contrast enhancing his strength rather than diminishing it. "Right now, I need food, and I'd like to eat it with you."

She smiled and met him outside, grabbing her jacket and closing the door behind her. "Lead the way."

Their steps down the wooden staircase were in sync, and Ryan held his hands in his pockets while he moved. Not knowing what to do with them, Erika shoved her own in her pockets as well.

When they reached the street, she spoke. "Why did Carter hit you in a boxing gym?"

"Honestly? I don't think he meant to," Ryan said. "He started off just tapping the pads, moving his upper body. He talked through the first few swings, showing me what I should do when it was my turn. Then he picked up speed, and once he got going, it was like he didn't know how to stop."

Erika suppressed the shiver that ran through her body. Christina had described his actions similarly, a man swept away by his baser instincts, and the comparison was as informative as it was unsettling.

"I don't think I want to talk about me," Ryan continued easily. "I want to hear about you."

"I'm not that interesting," she said.

He burst out laughing when she said that, and she smiled at him. "False humility won't get you very far with me," he said, looking down at her.

"Fine, but you'll have to ask me something specific," she responded. "I can't just sit around talking about myself."

"If you did, I'd still listen to it," Ryan said with a frankness that kept the statement from sounding too affectionate. "When did you realize you were different? Or, maybe, when was the first time you spoke to someone who wasn't with us anymore?"

Erika glanced in his direction before clarifying. "You want the origin story."

"Yeah," he said. "I'd like to know more about how you got here."

She'd been lucky, if one could call it that. Her first experience with the dead could have been one of the gruesome murders Erika now dealt with as an adult, but she remembered the first ghost with the tiniest hint of fondness.

"When I was in the fourth grade," she began, "my best friend Nora's dad died. There was no murder or foul play involved, not even a tragic car accident. I think he had some kind of heart condition, and he passed away in his sleep. It was peaceful, but unexpected for his family.

"Nora was obviously devastated, really retreated into herself. I tried to stay close to her, but she didn't want anything to do with her old friends. Most of them seemed fine to abandon her. I don't blame them. They were just kids, too, and grief is hard even on people who understand it, but I didn't want to be that kind of friend, even if it was tempting."

"That would have been hard," he agreed. "Supporting someone with that kind of loss when you were so young."

"I suppose," Erika said noncommittally. "She hadn't been to school through all her father's services, so I asked my mom if I could help her when she went to visit their home. One afternoon, my mom and I went to see them and dropped off some homemade meals. You know, post funeral neighborly stuff."

"Of course," Ryan agreed.

"Well, when we were there, I saw him. I was so confused, wondering why we were all pretending to be sad when he was right there, or at least some version of him was. I already understood he wasn't the same, but I didn't get it yet. Eventually, I asked Nora if she was saying her dad died so she could get attention."

Ryan cringed but didn't interrupt her.

Erika chuckled a bit at the dark memory. "She started beating the shit out of me right there in the living room. Our moms had to pull us apart and mine made me apologize for making such a cruel joke."

"When did you fully comprehend what he was? What you could see?"

"I was sitting on the chair in a corner, on time out, while my mom wrapped up the visit with Nora's mom. Since I was alone, her dad sat next to me on the ground. He said that he was sorry if he scared me, or if I was confused.

"He told me that he didn't know why I was the only one who could see him, but that he knew what happened to him. He explained that he needed to stay a while and make sure his family was going to be safe, and he would appreciate it if I kept his secret for him."

"That must have been terrifying," Ryan said.

"I think it should have been, but it wasn't. I was more so relieved that my friend hadn't lost her father completely, even if she thought she had."

Streetlights did their best to illuminate their walk through the mist, though their efforts were in vain. It stayed mostly dark, and the evening's relative chilliness forced her to pull her jacket closed.

They approached the pub, and Ryan pulled the door open for her. "Were you able to stay friends with Nora?"

"Kind of," she replied. The memory of her childhood friend saddened her. She had tried to fix it, but it never went back to the easy playfulness they had before, and a few months later Erika's dad was restationed to another naval base.

"I'm sorry to hear that," Ryan said as he walked with his hand on her lower back. He guided her to a tall bar table with four stools and sat on the one next to her.

"You are going to have to tell me more about your eye." She changed the subject. "I need to know what I'm up against if I have to take care of you."

"I'll save those details for later tonight," he laughed. "I'm probably going to ask you to wake me up every three hours."

"Presumptuous of you to think I'd stay with you." She leaned her elbows on the table. "But now I'm worried. How concussed are you?"

"Hopefully, none. But the medic who was there said I should be careful." Ryan leaned back in his chair but rested his hand on the back of her own. She could feel his fingers drum lightly against the wood supporting her back as he looked around the room.

"Well, if you get me a doctor's note, maybe I can be convinced to poke you awake every hour or so," she said.

She silently admitted to herself that that sounded better than sharing the house with Christina and her growing agitation.

Ryan smiled at her joke before looking around the pub. "If you see a doctor, let me know so I can flag him down."

They quieted when a waitress dropped off waters and menus. Ryan thanked her before putting one menu in front of him and passing Erika her own.

She watched his gaze consume the menu while his left hand rhythmically clenched and unclenched into a fist, and for once, she could relate to his anxiety.

The pub was well attended but not overcrowded, with a mix of some faces that were beginning to register as familiar to Erika, which was deeply unsettling. There was always the possibility that these people were going to start recognizing her as well, so she should have been more aware of who else was present.

Just as she was about to ask Ryan if they could pick a different spot, they were interrupted.

"Gibson!"

Ryan pulled his gaze from the menu, then his expression hardened. "Chief," he called out, as Carter made his way to their table.

Erika stiffened but didn't slouch or give in to the temptation to make herself smaller. She wasn't doing anything wrong, and she felt bolstered by Ryan's presence.

Carter Cahill walked up to their table and took a seat uninvited, sitting his tumbler of brown liquor on the top. "Erika, right? Christina's cousin?"

"That's me," she replied with more confidence than she felt. She had to remind herself that since her lie about being related to Christina, it wasn't weird or automatically scary that Carter remembered her. He probably saw it as his duty.

"How do you guys know each other?" Carter asked, pointing between them. His expression seemed neutral but came across as unnatural, as if he were feigning relaxation and fun instead of experiencing it. She could tell, easily enough, that it wasn't his first drink.

"I met her at the coffee shop," Ryan said. "Found out we were both new to the area, so we decided to grab a bite together. It sure beats eating delivery alone in my motel," he chuckled, but it turned into a cough.

"Sure," Carter said as he tipped his glass up for a drink.

Ryan leaned back in his seat and crossed his arms. "Did anything come up at the station after I left?"

"No, once you were out—sorry about that, again, by the way—I went back to the office and finished up some administrative stuff. I'm grateful for my role, don't get me wrong, but it comes with a shit ton of boring work I'd pass off to someone else if I could. You sign up to be a police officer to keep people safe, you know? Anyway, it's hard to fulfill that calling from behind a desk."

He was chattier when drinking, but no less serious, Erika noticed. Based on everything she knew about him, that wasn't terribly surprising, though her curiosity tempted her to dangerous places.

Carter might spill more secrets when drinking, but she should not be foolish enough to ever be alone with him.

Ryan and Carter conversed idly about schedules for the week. "If you want," Carter offered, "I can run you through some of our spring break protocol. I don't know how long you'll be here, but if you're still around we could use the help."

"I'll consider it," Ryan replied.

"Just know, if you want to work during tourist seasons, you can be a beach volunteer, or I can compensate you as a member of the force. What we're doing now probably won't fly then. It'd be too confusing for my men."

Ryan nodded. "I understand."

"You're staying for spring break?" Erika asked.

"That depends on what you're doing," he said to her lightly, not offering anything secret to Carter, but the statement held a deeper meaning.

Ryan apparently didn't believe they would solve this case by then.

The chief began explaining tourist season safety tips to Ryan while Erika felt someone else approach the table.

The skin on her arms pebbled when she realized who it was.

"This looks cozy," Christina said, taking the final seat at their table. It took all of Erica's strength to not turn her head and look at her, to engage with the newest dinner guest, but she really didn't want Ryan to know Christina was there.

What was she doing there?

"Hell, it's certainly big enough," Carter responded to something Ryan said before looking at Erika. "Did Ryan tell you the news?"

"That you're a total scumbag? Yeah, we already knew that," Christina said unhelpfully. Erika couldn't figure out why she was there. Her presence could only harm any progress they might have made in gathering evidence against Carter.

"Depends on the news," Erika said without letting her gaze move to the side. "I heard about the gym accident."

"No, not that." Carter laughed but had the decency to look apologetic. "I invited Ryan to stay with me at my family's lodge in three weeks. If weather allows, we could go hunting in the national park."

"Really." She perked up, then looked at Ryan, who had the wherewithal to look sheepish for not having updated her.

"Three weeks is too far away," Christina said.

"I asked if you could join," Ryan said, still oblivious to the occupied fourth chair. "As a welcome to the community sort of thing."

"If I'd known you were interested in hunting," Carter continued, "then I would have told him to invite you. Along with the big game available, we have an outdoor hot tub, and the hiking is second to none. Heck, maybe I'll find a girl my dad hates, and we can make it a party."

"Is that why you did it, Carter? Was I not good enough for Daddy?"

Christina was making it hard for Erika to focus. "Sure. If I'm still in town, I could tag along."

Ryan frowned at her statement, but he couldn't voice his confusion in front of Carter. He saw this lodge trip as her opportunity to investigate; in his mind, that meant she'd still be around.

She just might have to move faster than she anticipated.

"This trip is going to be awesome," Carter said, ignoring Ryan's concerned look. "It'll give us an excuse to get away from all the early spring breakers, too." He punctuated his excitement by finishing what was left in his glass.

"Don't even lie, you piece of shit," Christina said. "You love when all the college girls flood into town and get drunk around you."

Erika shoved her stool behind her and stood up, shaking Ryan's hand off her shoulder. "I just realized I'm not feeling well," she said to everyone at the table. "I'm going to bed."

Troubled, Ryan stood with her. "I'll walk you home."

"You really don't have to," she said.

"Y'all are boring," Carter added. He slapped Ryan's shoulder before stepping away. "I'll be at the bar if you want to come back after you see her home."

Ryan said something noncommittal, but Erika was already rushing for the door with Christina hot on her heels.

"You can't do that to me," she said.

"I'm not doing anything to you," Christina replied. "I'm dead, remember?"

"You know what I mean," Erika whispered back as they stood just outside the door, waiting for Ryan. "That was too risky."

"Well, don't you think it's risky to become vacation buddies with the man who probably killed me?"

Erika didn't respond because Ryan burst through the pub's entrance looking for her. "Hey, I'm so sorry," he said, and pulled her into a hug.

It was a warm and earnest hug, but she couldn't enjoy it or relax into him with Christina's glare still pointed directly at them.

"Why are you sorry?"

"I didn't realize how upset you were, sitting there with Cahill. You were probably worried he'd ask you Higgins family questions you couldn't answer," he explained. "I should have noticed and gotten you out of there sooner."

Yes, that's why he would think she was upset. Erika must have successfully kept Christina's presence to herself.

"That's not your responsibility," she said.

Ryan looked like he wanted to argue but seemed to change his mind. "Let's get you home."

He put an arm around her shoulder, and she allowed him to hold her while they walked, but she didn't tell him that Christina followed right behind them, her presence like a hot iron against Erika's back.

26

RYAN FELT LIKE AN ASS.

He should have known to get rid of Carter sooner or order their food to go. Something. While he was aware of what Chief Cahill was, what he'd done, Erika was far more intimately acquainted with the consequences of his actions. It was no wonder she wanted to get out of there.

"Are you alright?" he asked, knowing he wouldn't get the truth.

"Yeah. Fine," she replied.

She was being understandably short with him, and she seemed more on edge than usual, but at least she didn't shrug him off.

They walked back to Christina's house in silence the rest of the way.

Ryan wanted to break it, to get some clarification from Erika. He could feel her pulling away and it made him want to panic, his inclination to cling to her stronger. They were too many blocks from the coast for him to hear the ocean, but he swore he could feel its crashing, feel it pushing him away when he didn't want to move.

The stairwell leading to the house's front door appeared before he was ready.

"When Carter invited you to his hunting lodge three weeks from now, you said you'd think about it if you're still in town. What did you mean?"

Erika climbed two steps before turning to face him. "Exactly what I said. I wasn't speaking in riddles, Ryan."

The tension in his gut thickened. "Why wouldn't you be here?"

"Because, hopefully, by then we'll have enough evidence to throw Carter in jail. After that, I'll move on to the next one."

"But that was the whole point of my getting the invite," he argued. "We could search it together, legally." He glared at her, a realization settling on him. "Or you never planned on doing it that way. You were always going to go behind my back and search it yourself."

Erika rolled her eyes then flapped her arms at her sides. "Well, yeah. How did you expect it to go? He'd invite you over and Christina's bracelet would be proudly displayed on the mantle? Maybe he'd show you the headstone he carved for her burial site in the backyard?"

Ryan flushed slightly at the picture she painted of him. "Fine," he said. "Then why exclude me? I still would have wanted to help."

"I'm not used to having help."

"But now you have it, so it doesn't make sense for you to throw it away," he replied.

"I don't understand," Erika frowned.

"I could help you," Ryan said. "I have experience, resources, all the skills and resources you could ask for at your disposal. We could work as a team, solve these things faster, then maybe you would finally get a break."

"I don't really do breaks," she deadpanned.

"You could," he insisted.

"This is what I do," Erika said. She seemed to be trying to soften her voice, but she was still on edge, refusing to lean on the handrail that ran up the stairs. "Alone. I don't want a team, but I'm not opposed to us staying in touch after this or anything. We can still be friends."

Ryan ignored most of what she just said, deeming it absurd to relegate what they had to a long-distance friendship. Did she think he was stupid?

She was lying. If she wanted him in her life at all, she would have mentioned it. "How long?"

"How long what?"

"How long do you plan to live like this? Spending your life on people who don't have theirs anymore?"

It was the wrong thing to say. He could see that as soon as the words left his mouth.

Erika crossed her arms as she looked down at him, not bothering to hide her irritation any longer. "Is that what this is?"

Ryan didn't reply right away since she wasn't really looking for an answer.

"You think that I'm trapped here, doing this," she continued. "You think I'm cursed or that I can't get off this path I've chosen, that I'm stuck somehow. Poor Erika tormented by dead people crying out for justice. She must be lonely and need a hero. Hell, that's a best-case scenario. Maybe you think I'm lying or insane.

"And then that's where you come in. Ryan Gibson, on his white horse, ready to save me from my own haunted existence. You'll ride up and sweep me away from my despair and anguish, and I'll look up at you and tell you that I never knew passion or freedom until you showed up. The world was a bleak and misty place, but you brought me sunshine and hugs and a happily ever after."

Ryan glared at her, keeping his hands in his pockets.

"And then," she finally appeared to be wrapping up, "then we'll be even, right? Because that's what this is really all about. You think you owe me for helping with Sloane's murder case, and you don't like being the one who gets saved. That's not the role you assigned yourself in life."

He didn't say anything, letting her turn and retreat up the stairs. He wanted her to have a little bit of distance after thinking she got the last word.

"Maybe you got a few things right," he said.

She stopped without turning back towards him.

"But so did I. You're alive, Erika. Maybe it's time you start acting like it."

Ryan stomped into the night, resisting the urge to sit outside on the stairs all night making sure nothing could hurt her.

"THIS IS BAD," Christina said, an unmistakable anger in her voice.

How astute, Erika thought to herself. She'd just alienated her only living ally, throwing away the one person who saw her, and she was no closer to helping Christina than when she arrived on Oak Island.

Since she started this multi-year road trip alone, she had never once left a case unsolved. Erika was dedicated to a fault. She stayed in towns and cities looking for justice at her own expense, often putting herself in danger. She'd faced everything in her path head-on, whether it was breaking into the lairs of hardened criminals or a week without food when work was scarce. Erika always fulfilled her commitments.

But she was tempted this time to abandon her mission. She never had this much trouble finding the evidence she needed, never worked this blindly for proof of someone's sins. She'd never faced animosity from a ghost like she had with Christina, whose growing hostility was beginning to scare her.

So, Erika wanted to leave. Leave Christina's case for whoever stumbled across her body, Carter's justice to someone who wanted credit for it.

Leave Ryan and go to some place he couldn't find her.

She almost laughed at that final thought. It was the least plausible of the three fantasies. Erika knew in her gut that Ryan would always find her. There'd be no escaping him, and she wasn't sure she wanted to.

"I know it's bad," she said in agreement.

"Three weeks is too far away," Christina hissed. "If there is anything left there, it will be long gone. He'll have it gutted top to bottom before he brings Ryan anywhere near it."

If he hasn't already done that.

"I know," Erika replied.

"You need to get there first," Christina insisted.

"I know."

"We can't let him get away with what he did," she implored further.

"I know," Erika bit out, harsher this time.

Her tone seemed to sufficiently chastise Christina, who remained quiet as she followed Erika into the bathroom. She leaned back against the bathroom wall, where she watched her wash her face in the mirror. The suds covering her closed eyes were the only reprieve she got from the woman whose house she was borrowing.

Erika prepared for bed as if Christina wasn't lurking behind her.

Once she was done brushing her teeth, she went to the living room, instead of her bedroom, with the other woman following closely behind.

She gathered her usual hunting items—flashlight, pick set, gloves—along with a book of maps she'd acquired from a local gas station which she began diligently unfolding on the coffee table. She removed her laptop from its case as well as an analogue compass.

Christina watched as Erika worked, waiting for her to speak.

Erika didn't want to talk to anyone, but with her roommate, that often wasn't an option.

"When are you going to go?" Christina asked softly from her spot in the doorway.

"Tomorrow," was all Erika replied, as she tried to put together a plan that wouldn't get her killed, or worse, caught.

27

RYAN SQUEEZED THE GRIP strengthener with his left hand while his right alternated by clicking his pen. His chair at the temporary desk Chief Cahill assigned him rocked back and forth with his movements, squeaking tightly whenever he hit a certain joint on the left side.

He felt antsy but with no direction. It was like watching old track footage of himself, seeing where he failed but knowing he wasn't ever going to compete again, never going to get another chance to redeem himself.

It was only one in the afternoon, but he felt like he'd lived ten years since leaving Erika on the stairs.

Early in the morning before his shift, he stopped by Christina Higgins's house and rang the doorbell. When no one answered, he banged his fist on the door repeatedly until he was sure Erika was actually gone or just very dedicated to ignoring him.

Then he went to the coffee shop, but she wasn't there either. It was just Fiona, the shop's very frustrated owner, saying Erika called out for the day.

Her car was no longer in the port next to Christina's, and he feared the worst. Ryan's confrontation the night before had scared her away, and he worried that he'd never get to explain to her what he meant. He wasn't trying to change her, but he wanted to ask her to make room for him somehow.

He hated that she wasn't there so he could apologize for hurting her.

"Dude. Knock it off." Tanner's voice came across their shared desk. When Ryan stared at the man blankly, Officer Pratt pointed to the pen. "Seriously, that's annoying."

Ryan set the pen down and moved the grip strengthener to his right hand, watching as Tanner slurped audibly from his mug. Then, like clockwork, the man burped fifteen seconds later.

Ryan closed his eyes for patience and remembered Sergeant Vincent.

"There are a lot of rich, powerful people saying our jobs are obsolete," he said once while they were supplying crowd control for a local protest. "People who say we do more harm than good, that crime is a social ill and it needs to be massaged out of a populace with gentle means. They think with the right schools and programs we might become too evolved for crime. They'll say our salaries, meager as they are, could be better used on prevention.

"And, unfortunately, those people will have examples they can use. There are plenty of bad cops out there. Corruption is endemic and there will be no shortage of officers who will inadvertently become the faces of a movement that wants us abolished."

In that moment, they both had watched as Kurt Lewis leaned against a stop light pole, playing with a piece of hair on a woman he spoke with, having abandoned his station.

"Under no circumstances are you to let yourself become one of those faces, Son."

Tanner Pratt was probably not what Sergeant Vincent had in mind when he gave that lecture, but Ryan had a hard time coming up with something that would be more wasteful than Officer Pratt's salary.

"Where are we going today?"

Tanner shrugged, finishing his coffee. "Cahill hasn't given me anything yet."

Ryan stopped moving in his chair to look across the desk. "You mean there's no schedule?"

"No, there's a schedule. I'm on patrol today, but the chief hasn't told me where to go yet."

"You get told where to drive for every patrol," Ryan stated.

"Well, obviously. How else am I going to know where to go?"

"How long have you been on the force here?"

Tanner, having the self-awareness of a deaf bat, said proudly with a grin, "Almost twenty years. The front desk ladies are planning an anniversary party for me."

Ryan was saved from responding when Chief Cahill walked into the communal office area.

"Good morning, team," he said to no one in particular as he moved through the space. He was greeted back with various versions of the same sentiment before he approached the shared desks of Tanner and Ryan.

"Pratt, I need you covering the beaches today. Out of towners are arriving earlier than we expected," he said.

Ryan was impressed. If Carter held any annoyance at the man's ineptitude, he didn't show it.

What he couldn't hide, though, was his obvious exhaustion. Ryan wondered when the man made it home from the pub the night before.

"Gibson, you're welcome to go to the beaches with Pratt, or you can come with me. I'm covering for Officer Childs today."

"I'll go with you," Ryan said, standing to join Carter.

On his way outside, Ryan wondered if his preference for sharing a vehicle with an accused murderer over Officer Pratt said more about himself or about Tanner.

Midway through that thought, he decided he didn't care.

As they crossed into the hallway, Carter's phone buzzed but when he looked at the screen, he grunted and put it back.

"I swear my dad is losing it," he shared.

Having met Robert, but not knowing whether he was invited to speak poorly about him, Ryan only responded with, "Oh, yeah?"

"Yeah," Carter said. "He's really intense about his properties, obviously, but I feel like it has gotten worse the past month. He'll call me in the middle of the night and make me check on a house if a silent sensor trips. As if I don't have better things to do."

Ryan listened quietly but felt the urge to squeeze something with his fingers.

"Apparently the police were called on our hunting lodge a couple hours ago. I know a few of the local cops there, so I made sure they were the ones who checked on the house rather than a bunch of strangers. They're perfectly capable of putting a lid on things without resorting to a property search, but my dad has been ringing me constantly ever since," he explained.

"How annoying," Ryan choked out.

Erika, what have you done?

"Right? As if I could do anything else about it. It's not my jurisdiction or my property. I'd just be stepping on toes out there."

Carter pushed open the station's door but stopped, causing Ryan to have to sidestep to avoid running into him.

Outside on the steps stood several police officers Ryan didn't recognize, as well as an irate Robert Cahill.

"When I call," Robert spoke with an eerie calm, "you answer the goddamn phone, Ashley."

～

TO ANYONE WHO SAW HER, Erika appeared to be a confident hiker, walking the trails alone with her map and compass. She mostly kept to herself, smiling at the occasional couple walking past. It was easy to be anonymous during her walk with the exception of a small family that passed her early on. Nobody said anything, but the family patriarch gave her a look as if he wanted to say something about her being alone on the trails, a look that bordered on an invitation to join them, but Erika avoided the confrontation by walking faster with her head down.

The Croatan National Forest had many visitor parking lots that connected to hiking and hunting areas throughout its land. One of the trails started a few miles away from the Cahill lodge.

She had a larger pack than she typically carried for what she'd affectionately termed "house hunting" since she didn't know how long she would be outside. In addition to her standard supplies, she had the map, compass, as well as food and water. Not wanting to actually need those last few items, she covered ground quickly.

Forty minutes into her hike, she stopped and checked her place on the map. The trail continued, but one mile east of her current position was the Cahill property.

She looked to her left and right, ensuring her solitude, before entering the denser forest.

It was trickier to navigate the untouched woodland, a path not worn down by outdoor enthusiasts, but Erika wasn't going to disappoint Robert Frost by chickening out this far into her plan.

I chose the road less traveled by, and that has made all the difference.

The consistent and unrelenting crunch of forest debris beneath her feet was the only companion she had as she huffed between trees. No other animals joined her, no birds or squirrels tittering in the fog. The dead sounds of her steps against fallen foliage made her feel like the only living creature around.

Perhaps Erika should have been frightened by that prospect, but instead it relaxed her. She almost wished she could take her time, photograph her progress and enjoy the area. It would be nice to sit and eat her snack while breathing in the clean air.

She swatted the desire away like a gnat and trudged on. She reasoned that she could do that later, once she'd helped Christina.

Why are you spending your life on people who don't have theirs anymore?

Erika ignored Ryan's voice echoing in her mind and moved forward.

It was still early when she saw the house. The sun was low in the sky, diminished further by low hanging clouds in the trees. The chill was persistent, yet Erika's skin was coated with sweat from her exertion.

Besides the traditional wooden siding, she wasn't sure what qualified it as a lodge. It appeared to her to be a large single-family home, designed to make one feel as though they were Paul Bunyan when they stayed there. It was nice, if not a bit obvious in its intentions.

She skirted the property, walking adjacent until she could see its front. The driveway was gravel, holding no cars, but the garage was closed so she wouldn't be fully confident of her isolation until she went inside.

Erika pulled a neck gator over the bottom of her face. She didn't have time to avoid cameras, but she wasn't going to let her face be photographed that easily.

A few more crunching steps toward the tree line, and she stopped, resting her hand on an oak and looking over the land.

Once the gravel road entered the property, it split into two, creating a circle in front of the house. In her uninformed opinion, homes meant for hunters should be obscure, should create the illusion of having participated with nature since its inception. The whole point of hunting was to sneak up on the animals. What good was it if your entire property was this developed?

Erika shook her head and walked into the open. If there was a camera, it could see her without any obstructions, so she ran towards the door.

She pulled gloves out of her pack and knelt before the lock.

It appeared to be a simple deadbolt, and seeing no signs of an alarm system, she got to work.

Except for her own tampering with the lock, and the occasional creak when she shifted her weight, Erika worked in silence.

She took longer than she wanted, about four minutes. It was minimal, but if she had silent trip alarms to worry about, she needed to search quickly, all but disregarding subtlety.

She stepped over the threshold and looked to both sides, seeking any kind of security system she missed, and finding none. Frowning, she closed the front door and walked into the living area.

As far as she could tell, she was alone in the house. Erika used that as an excuse to throw open drawers and cabinets without caring about the noise she made.

Nothing in the living room but games, old magazines, and blankets. There was a stark absence of family photos, which wouldn't have been odd except the lodge wasn't a rental or for sale.

The kitchen revealed a similar theme with the cupboards filled with innocuous cookware and utensils. A walk-in pantry explained nothing about the occupants of the house except that they might not be there for a while since everything was nonperishable. She searched under the sink and found nothing but generic cleaning supplies.

Leaving the kitchen through its second entrance, she opened the garage and found it thankfully devoid of any vehicles. On one side, there was a wall of various firearms that she was almost positive weren't stored legally.

The other side displayed mountain bikes in a similar fashion, but they looked far less used than the guns. Erika saw nothing of importance and closed the door.

The first door at the beginning of the hall after the garage was open, revealing a small first floor bedroom. Erika moved inside quickly, observing everything she could.

A small closet held a few men's jackets, only stocked for visits and not full-time living. The dresser was similarly empty with all six drawers vacant. There was no bathroom attached, so Erika dropped to the floor, looking under the bed.

Nothing.

Two bedside tables remained. She jumped to her feet and yanked open the drawer on the one to the left side of the bed. A frame, facing down, slid backwards from the force, and Erika picked it up gingerly, avoiding some of the stray shards of glass that crunched beneath it as she lifted.

The photo, obscured marginally by the shattered glass, was of Carter Cahill and a woman Erika had never seen before.

"This must be your room," she said to the frame. She didn't waste any time wondering about the woman's identity while she replaced the picture and stood up, moving to the other bedside table.

She pulled open the drawer and stared at its contents.

It was more populated than most of the other storage spaces in the bedroom, but Erika ignored the mouth guard case and stray pens rolling around, her eyes fixated on a platinum tennis bracelet.

Carefully, she used two fingers to pick it up and inspect the clasp for an engraving.

The *MGH* for Christina's grandmother's initials was all the proof she needed that this was what she'd been looking for.

It would be difficult, probably impossible, to pull prints from the piece of jewelry, but she would try anyway. She needed a firm tie from Carter to Christina on the night she was murdered for anyone to search his property.

Before shutting the drawer, Erika saw a silk pouch shaped like a small envelope tucked into the corner of the drawer. It reminded her of the way her mom stored jewelry, in little drawstring bags, rather than a large jewelry box. She slipped her fingers under the flap and peered inside.

The silk pouch held what looked to be an engagement ring with a yellow gold band and three small diamonds inset across its surface.

"Oh my God," she whispered. "Is there really more than one woman?"

As if it burned her, Erika shoved the silk envelope back into the drawer and slammed it shut. Whoever it belonged to, it wasn't Christina, and she needed to keep moving.

The bracelet was circumstantial, and she wasn't going to waste her trip by not canvasing as much of the house as possible.

Standing in the bedroom doorway, Erika stayed motionless, listening for anything out of place.

She didn't detect any tires outside, no sirens or speeding vehicles. Checking her watch, she saw that her comb through the first half of the lower level had taken only fifteen minutes.

If there was a silent trip alarm, she had, at most, that much time left to search.

Down the hall she looked through a closet and a half bathroom, both filled with harmless content, and she started to get anxious.

Erika almost skipped the last door, wanting to go upstairs before anyone arrived. But she pulled it open as she walked.

It was stairs to a basement, a floor in homes she hadn't seen since getting to the island, but she'd forgotten that this lodge was more inland.

She pulled her neck gaiter over her head and wrapped it around both handles, using it to keep the door from latching closed. There was no need to risk getting locked down there.

Erika held a hand against the cream drywall as she stepped downward, her heartbeat in time with each foot hitting a stair while she descended.

Thump. Thump. Thump.

At the base, she was greeted with a dark, windowless space that only offered shadows because of the light from behind her. She watched her hand glide beyond the start of the darkness before it hit a switch, which she flicked.

The fluorescents were jarring with the rest of the house only lit by faint sunlight through the clouds.

Erika blinked before taking in the environment.

The large, rectangular room appeared to serve one purpose: storage.

Not just any storage. This wasn't a basement one dumped undesirable items into over their shoulder without a second thought. The space held ten enormous deep freeze units, five on each side, meant for freezing game.

For all her judgements about the utility of the Cahill Lodge for actual hunting, Erika really hoped Robert and Carter were conservationist savants. If anything besides animal meat was stored down there, she really didn't want to see it.

"Stop being a coward," she whispered as she walked up to the first deep freeze.

After a deep breath, she steeled herself against what she might find and pulled open the lid.

"What?"

The freezer was filled with food, thank God, but it wasn't from hunting. The whole thing was filled to the brim with frozen pizzas, chicken tenders, burritos, and even a couple handles of vodka.

Erika huffed out a laugh. To each their own, but that seemed like a huge waste of such an expensive unit.

Less apprehensive, she moved to the next one and threw it open without pause, then screamed.

"Shit, eww," she said before closing the lid.

Several deep breaths later, she tried looking inside again at the face staring up at her.

It had, indeed, been a head looking up, but it wasn't human. Erika thought it might be an elk, but it was hard to tell for sure when it was separated from its body.

"Dear God," she said to the animal. "Shouldn't you be, like, at least cling wrapped or something?"

The head was sitting, fur and all, on top of the rest of the meat in the freezer. Not that she would ever eat anything served to her by Robert Cahill after what she'd seen, but at least the rest of the cuts appeared to be wrapped appropriately.

She wasn't sure what decisions led to the elk head lying on top, but she decided it wasn't her business and moved on.

The freezers continued on in much the same way as the second one, minus any animal faces staring at her, and after the fourth she could sense a pattern in the contents. It seemed that they might be organized by animal type, which made sense to Erika. She could tell some units held smaller game, like birds and fish, while others held giant unidentifiable chunks of meat from much bigger animals.

She'd lost hope of finding anything when she got to the last freezer. She was running out of time, and she needed to leave.

In front of the last freezer, she lifted the lid.

For a second, she didn't believe it.

"Oh, no," she choked out and turned away leaving the lid open while she tried to hold onto the contents of her stomach.

IF ASKED, ERIKA would say that she was comfortable with death. Not her own, or anyone she loved, but she understood that it was a reality of the natural world and was unavoidable. She didn't shy away from grief or wondering what happened on the other side.

She spoke with the dead more than the living. If anyone was comfortable with it, Erika Willet was.

In the Cahill lodge, she crawled up the stairs, not bothering to stand upright, using her hands on the steps, as she made her way to the door held unlatched by her neck cover. She pulled it off and finally stood, her legs shaking as she went. She left all the lights on in the basement, then propped the door open with an umbrella holder.

The thing was, and this discrepancy hadn't occurred to her before, that while Erika was an expert in death as an idea, and dead people as ghosts, she hadn't laid eyes on a dead body since she walked in on her sister Hailey five years earlier.

Finding the frozen body of Christina Higgins, especially after talking with her for many weeks, had been a sight she wasn't prepared for.

Erika walked into the kitchen and paused in front of a landline phone. In the distance, she could hear them: the law enforcement response to her tripping a silent alarm in the house.

After ten seconds, she noted the slight increase in sound, indicating the vehicles moved closer.

On the off chance that they weren't coming to the Cahill Lodge, she couldn't risk Christina's body going undiscovered by someone outside the family. Erika picked up the landline phone. She didn't expect it to work but was relieved to hear a dial tone and typed in a few numbers.

Once it rang, she left it on the counter and ran towards the back of the house, a faint voice from the phone following her as she sprinted.

"9-1-1, what's your emergency?"

Erika ran, past the bedroom, beyond the basement, and into a mudroom at the back of the house. She threw open the door, not bothering to close it behind her, and sprinted across the back yard and straight for the woods.

28

CARTER CAHILL SAT, hands cuffed, in a chair at the table in the Oak Island police interrogation room. The town had never needed more than one, and as chief, he'd had no complaints about the smaller amenities, but now he was regretting not asking the mayor for a budget raise. Another interrogation room sounded nice.

There wasn't anything wrong with the room. It's just that he was sharing it with his father.

"What the fuck did you do, Ashley?"

Carter didn't roll his eyes or even lift them up from where they were aimed at his hands on the table.

"I'm not the only one cuffed, Dad," he reasoned. "So, what did you do?"

There was no response. He wasn't expecting one. He just wanted the lawyer to get there as soon as possible so he could leave.

Time moved slowly in the interrogation room on purpose. The space was deliberately void of any entertainment value, no colors or fun distractions for the eyes. Only room temperature water would be served, removing any distractions for their tastebuds. Any passing officer would encourage more water consumption, hoping that an urge for the restroom would trick them into talking. Carter was familiar with the tactic, had used it himself, but Robert wasn't used to being ignored.

"What's taking everyone so long? This is preposterous."

They had been told by the attending officers that they had total privacy in the room, that nobody would hear what they said until official interviews began, but Carter knew that trick as well. Someone might still be listening, gathering information, it just wouldn't be admissible. They'd have to get that evidence out of them another way.

"I'm going to sue everyone in this department," Robert blathered on.

Carter almost smiled. That threat probably included his own son.

The wait continued in silence.

Eventually, a man with a briefcase was ushered through the door.

"You've got to be kidding me," Carter said.

"You shut your mouth and be grateful I'm sharing my lawyer with you," Robert bit back.

"How generous! I get to be represented by your shitty real-estate lawyer. I can't wait to spend life in prison knowing that my equity is safe."

"Everyone shut up," Max Everitt, the lawyer, said with authority Carter had never witnessed from the man. He turned to Carter. "Real-estate law is more of a hobby of mine. I specialize in criminal law."

Carter raised an eyebrow at Robert who only shrugged in response.

"Now," Max continued, "I can get both of you out of here today, but I need you both to shut the fuck up. No one says anything without my permission. Clear?"

Father and son nodded in unison.

Max walked over to the two-way mirror and knocked three times, then sat down and opened his notepad.

Officer Barker stepped inside and closed the door. Carter wasn't surprised to see him doing the interview. Officer Pratt technically had seniority but no one, including Tanner himself, would have wanted him to handle this situation.

Paul Barker didn't waste any time. "You've all been told why you're here?"

It was a stupid question, but one that needed to be asked. Everyone mumbled their agreement.

"Christina Higgins, missing for four weeks, was found dead in the basement of a lodge outside Croatan National Forest this morning. Both of your names are on the deed according to public records."

Carter glared at Robert, who just shrugged. The younger Cahill hadn't known his name was on the deed.

"Obviously, you're both being detained for questioning," Paul continued.

"Mr. Barker," Max interjected. "Any evidence against my clients is completely circumstantial. Until you have a warrant for their arrest, I don't believe you can legally detain either Mr. Cahill. I request that they be allowed to leave."

Carter had to fight every instinct in his body not to drop his head in his hands.

Paul was too professional to show any reaction. "First of all, sir, I can detain them for twenty-four hours without a warrant, so you're wrong. Second, I can call the judge and have a warrant for both their arrests in about ten minutes. The fact that we haven't requested them was done entirely out of respect for Chief Cahill."

Max settled into his seat, unbothered. He apparently hadn't thought he would win that one. "Proceed with the questions then," he declared with an air of unearned generosity.

"Thank you," Paul replied, with no sarcasm in his voice. Carter was privately proud of his officer's demeanor, though he would have appreciated a wink or something to let him know someone was on his side. As it was, he felt entirely alone. "Now, did either of you have any kind of relationship with Ms. Higgins prior to her disappearance?"

"No," Robert said immediately.

Max looked at Carter. He didn't indicate how he would answer before he spoke.

"Yes," he said.

Paul didn't react to the news. "In what capacity did you know her?"

"Mr. Barker, my client is not obligated to give details about his personal life, and I resent—"

"We were physically intimate but not romantic," Carter said to Paul, pretending the other two weren't in the room with him.

"Ashley, shut your fucking—"

"Let's all settle down." Officer Barker's voice allowed for no negotiation on his demand. "This is all preliminary, and I assure you, Mr. Everitt, that relations with Ms. Higgins are hardly incriminating. I do have one follow up for Chief Cahill, if I may?"

"You may not," Max declared.

"Ask whatever you want." Carter overruled the lawyer.

"When Christina Higgins was declared a missing person, you never contributed to the investigation by sharing your relationship with her," Paul said. "Why was that?"

Robert grumbled while Max looked at Carter with an expression that begged him not to speak.

"I didn't say anything because it would be the second missing woman from town associated with me socially," Carter admitted.

"Oh, for fuck's sake," Robert spit out. "Not this again."

"What do you mean by 'second'?" Paul asked, ignoring Robert. "Higgins is the first declared missing person we've had in two years."

"My girlfriend, Lindsey Payne. A few months ago, she disappeared, leaving only a note telling me she was ending our relationship. I haven't been able to find traces of her anywhere since she left town."

Max interjected. "This is getting off subject. Can we be more efficient with the questions, please?"

Paul ignored Max. "If you were worried, why didn't you file a report?"

Carter glared across the table at Robert. "He told me not to."

"Because you got dumped, Ashley," Robert yelled. "Yeah, it's embarrassing but you need to move on. How would it reflect on this family if you used the resources under your command to chase after some white trash that left you?"

"She wasn't white trash," Carter growled.

"Of course she was!"

"What does that even mean?" Carter replied. "We live in a beach community! This isn't Augusta National or whatever you're always fucking role playing at!"

"Everyone shut up," Max interrupted, for the first time helpfully. "We are here about Christina Higgins, no one else."

"Thank you, Mr. Everitt," Paul said. He was, somehow, still unruffled by the entire conversation.

Carter made a mental note to request a raise for Officer Barker if he ever got out of this mess.

"Now," Paul continued, "Chief Cahill, you said you had a casual relationship with Christina before she disappeared. When was the last time you saw her?"

"Don't answer that," Robert and Max said at the same time.

"Can both of you stop interrupting me?"

"Carter," Max implored, "Please don't answer any more questions. Officer Barker, can I have a moment alone with—"

"Get out."

All three sets of eyes turned towards Carter.

"Both of you. Get the fuck out," he repeated.

"Ashley, what the hell do you think you're doing?"

"I want Robert and Max gone, then I'll talk," he directed his request to Paul. "I waive my right to an attorney."

~

"WHAT THE HELL IS HE DOING?" Tanner asked Ryan, confirming Robert Cahill's sentiment.

Ryan stood next to him in the observation room behind the two-way mirror. The entire exchange was as entertaining as it was confusing.

This was not what he expected. When the neighboring county's police arrived with Robert Cahill in tow announcing they had found Christina Higgins's body, Ryan was stunned but elated. Erika had actually done it. She'd found Christina and the woman would receive justice and move on.

And Ryan would hopefully have the opportunity to apologize to Erika. If she forgave him, maybe he could go with her, wherever she went next.

"I don't know," Ryan said to Tanner. "I didn't expect him to act this way."

"What way is that?"

Innocent.

"Usually, people being interrogated aren't as forth coming as he is," Ryan replied.

Tanner didn't seem surprised by what he saw. "Maybe guilty people aren't," he said, unknowingly echoing Ryan's opinion.

"Her body was found on his property," he countered.

They watched as Robert yelled at his son but was eventually ushered out of the room along with Max, probably to a holding cell. Once they were gone, Ryan and Tanner quieted, waiting for the two men left to speak.

"Tell me about your relationship with Christina," Officer Barker said, opting to start at the beginning instead of when she disappeared.

"I met her at a pub, maybe two or three months ago," Carter explained. "I didn't know her before, but she said she'd seen an article written about me last year in the paper. She said it was her civic duty to buy a local hero a drink."

Officer Barker took limited notes but listened without interrupting.

"We had a drink together and she was really flirty. Overwhelmingly so. It's not hard for me to recognize when a woman is interested in me, but she was painfully obvious about it, which at the time was more flattering than weird. I was still getting over Lindsey, so it was nice to get attention like that."

Ryan could only see Paul's back, so he couldn't guess his expression when he responded. "We should probably come back to Lindsey after this. It sounds like you think there might be foul play there."

Carter agreed but looked ill at the thought. "Yeah, we can do that."

"Back to Christina," Officer Barker prompted.

"Right. After the drink, she put her hand on my thigh and asked me to go home with her."

"Did you?"

"I tried to turn her down at first," Carter said. "I told her that I'd just gotten out of a relationship and didn't want anything serious. She acted like she didn't care, said she was fine with casual, too. Women say that all the time, you know. They're usually lying. I was still going to turn her down, but she insisted it was fine. Eventually, I said, 'fuck it' and went home with her."

"Did your casual arrangement extend past that first night?" Officer Barker asked.

"Yeah," Carter said, appearing to grow uncomfortable. "She would text me once a week or so, asking to come over and I'd usually agree to it. It was fine for a couple times."

Tanner interjected, "I'll bet it was."

Ryan ignored him.

"What changed that made it 'not fine' later?" Paul asked.

"What always happens when a girl says she wants something casual," Carter explained. "She started asking to sleep over, leaving her stuff at my place so she had to come back for it, cleaning up after me and trying to appear domestic. It was like she was trying to use a back door method and trick me into a relationship with her I didn't want."

Paul's shoulders moved subtly as he wrote. "What did you do about it?"

"I ended the arrangement."

"When was this?"

Carter scratched his chin and looked around, appearing to grasp the information from his memory. "Maybe two weeks or so before she disappeared?"

Officer Barker continued with his questions. "Is that the last time you saw her?"

"No," Carter admitted quietly.

"When was that?"

Chief Cahill looked like he was going to be sick. "Probably pretty close to when she went missing. I can describe what she wore, if you want. Maybe it matches what she was found in."

"Why would he offer that information?" Ryan asked himself out loud.

"He's probably trying to help," Tanner offered. It was a fair assumption for the officer to make since he respected and trusted the chief and didn't have the information Ryan had gotten from Erika. Pratt didn't know what Carter had done to Christina.

What are you trying to do, Carter?

"That would be great," Paul responded to the suggestion. "I can get that from you later. Tell me what happened the last time you saw Christina."

Carter visibly swallowed and closed his eyes briefly before he spoke.

"I was at the pub where she first approached me, getting a drink after work. I was there alone, so when she walked up to me again, I didn't have a way of sending her off without being rude. When she sat down next to me, I just let it happen without fighting it.

"She was casual and friendly. For a while she didn't even bring up the subject of us together, just wanted to hear about my job and the prep for spring storm season, my thoughts on the increase in tourism. At one point, Christina even mentioned that she was looking to move closer to her parents, back home for a new job opportunity."

Tanner and Ryan watched as Paul scribbled some more notes. "At any point in the night, were either of you intoxicated?"

Carter spoke slowly, "I only saw her consume one drink, but I can't speak for what she had earlier. I think I had four or five during the time we spoke. She kept flagging the bartender, making sure my glass was full."

"How long were you at the bar?"

"Maybe an hour and a half?"

Officer Barker wrote something else down. "Did you and Christina leave the bar together?"

"Yeah," Carter admitted. "We did."

Behind the glass, Ryan spoke to Tanner, "I don't understand."

"What's not to understand?"

"Even if he didn't do it," Ryan thought out loud, "he should have a lawyer filtering through this. Even a first-year public defender wouldn't let him say any of this to the police."

Tanner cracked his knuckles and kept staring through the two-way mirror. "Chief Cahill usually knows what he's doing."

Carter continued to speak to Paul in the interrogation room, "Towards the end of our time at the pub, she started getting closer again, like that first night. I had a buzz, but I wasn't drunk or anything, so I just reiterated what I told her before. I knew we were looking for different things and I didn't want to hurt her.

"She insisted it was just one more time. Christina said she was moving back to Georgia, getting closer to her parents and that I wouldn't have to worry about her again after that night."

Officer Barker interjected with what could be considered to be his first unprofessional question of the afternoon. "And you believed her?"

"Maybe I just wanted to," Carter responded. "Unless I'm working or I spend time around my family, I go home alone most days. Usually it's easy to ignore, but she was just standing there and willing to give me one more night. Not to be crass, but did you ever meet Christina?"

From his perspective, Ryan couldn't tell if Paul affirmed or denied the question.

"Well, she was very beautiful. Alarmingly so. Any saint would have a hard time turning down that offer."

"He's not wrong," Tanner said from beside Ryan. "That girl was smoking hot."

Ryan couldn't hide his disgust when he turned to look at the man next to him. "Dude."

"What? I said *was*."

Paul continued his questions, oblivious to the conversation behind him. "To which of your residences did you both meet for this rendezvous?"

"Neither," Carter said, frowning. "She said she wanted to try something new. We left the pub and walked together, though I didn't know where we were going until we got to the pier. She wanted us to have sex on the beach."

Oh my God, Ryan thought. *Is he dumb enough to tell the truth?*

"Did you?" Paul asked.

"Yeah, but it was weird. Like, really off," Carter said.

"Sex on the beach usually is," Tanner said.

"Can you shut up?" Ryan bit out at Officer Pratt. He couldn't miss any of the interrogation.

"Could you explain what was off about it?" Officer Barker asked.

"Sex with Christina up to that point had always been normal. Obviously very enjoyable, I think for both of us, but she never had any upsetting or memorable requests for me."

"Like kinks or fetishes," Paul continued the thought.

"Exactly," Carter replied. "She might have been enthusiastic or playful but nothing that would have stood out to me. But when I tried to, you know, get things started with her on the beach that night, she shoved me away then slapped me. I backed up and asked her if she changed her mind, but she said no."

Officer Barker scribbled something down in his notepad. "Did she explain her reaction?"

Carter interlaced his hands in front of him on the table and took a deep breath. "She said, 'I don't want you nice. I want you to fuck me like you hate me.'"

Ryan ignored Tanner whispering *nice* under his breath and watched through the window.

"Were you amenable to her demands?" Paul asked Carter what might have been the most euphemistic question Ryan had ever heard.

"It was easy to fall into it," he replied. "I don't want to describe in too much detail my past intimate relationships or what happened that night unless I have to, but I was surprised at my own reaction to her and the situation in general. She would tear her nails into my neck or bite me, and it was hard not to respond similarly. I was definitely rougher than usual, but I didn't cross any lines."

Officer Barker shifted in his seat. "What would crossing lines look like in those circumstances?"

Carter's knuckles were white where he still had them clasped. "I didn't hit her back or anything, and I'm pretty sure I didn't leave any marks. I got verbally aggressive, which I'm not proud of, but that's it."

Paul apparently had enough information about the lurid details of the encounter, so he moved on. "Did you and Christina leave the beach together?"

"No," Carter said quietly.

"No?"

"After, uh, we finished, she completely flipped on me. She started screaming and sobbing, telling me that she would hate me for the rest of her life. At one point, she yelled, 'how could you do this to me,' as if she had been the one on the fence about the whole thing instead of me." Carter cleared his throat before finishing his thought. "At that point, I'd sobered up and I just felt tired and dirty. So, I left."

"You left her under the pier," Paul repeated back.

"Yeah," Carter whispered, clearly ashamed. "I left her there." He shifted in his seat, giving himself time to think. "When she didn't show up for work Monday and her coworker reported her missing, I kind of hoped she just went back to Georgia like she said she would. Then her parents started calling and I knew."

Officer Barker crossed his arms and leaned back in his chair. "Knew what?"

"That I fucked up."

29

IT TOOK ERIKA ALMOST a full half hour to catch her breath in the woods after fleeing the Cahill Lodge.

She'd moved quickly through the trees retracing her steps in the woods until she broke the tree line and found herself alone on the hiking trail. There, she stood, panting until she could calm herself down. She'd been fortunate that the area was so unpopulated while she recovered from her escape.

Once she had enough breath in her lungs, she hiked back to her car.

Erika had no desire to return to Christina's empty house right away, so she spent the afternoon driving with no destination in mind. Part of her wished she had the foresight to pack all her belongings so she could split from the town completely, but she would have had no way of knowing that she'd find something so definitive at the Cahill Lodge, much less evidence that wouldn't require her to send any packages to the police.

So, she drove for hours without stopping except for a short break on the side of the road to cry after she left Croatan National Forest.

It wasn't out of character for Erika to have a strong emotional response before she left behind a person she'd been helping. She was a logical person, but she wasn't a stone, and she'd spent more time with Christina than was typical for her.

She cried for the woman, and her bizarre attachment to horrible scary movies. She cried for the town, which was about to go through the traumatic process of losing trust in one of their leaders. She cried for Ryan, whom she feared would never be able to return to his normal life after her.

She cried for herself, a little bit, but would never admit that out loud.

"I hope you found peace, Christina," she whispered as she parked in front of a diner an hour south of Oak Island. Erika wasn't running away from everything waiting for her there exactly, but she wasn't in a rush to return yet either. Any remaining responsibilities could be put off until the morning.

And she really, really didn't want to return to Christina's empty house. That somehow seemed creepier than sharing it with her ghost.

She walked into a mostly empty restaurant, managed only by a man behind the counter flicking through television stations on a mounted screen.

"Sit wherever you like," he called over his shoulder without turning around.

Erika pulled a stool away from the counter and sat down. "How late are you open?"

"You can sit there all night if you want to," he replied, before grabbing a laminated list of food options and putting it in front of her. "Full menu is available, but it's just me tonight and I'm not as good at the breakfast side of things. Burgers are where my real talents are."

"Good thing it's dinner time," she replied easily. It was a little after nine in the evening, and Erika still wasn't ready to make her way back to the island. "I'll just start with a coffee."

The man poured her a mug from a standard drip machine, and she noted his name tag when he dropped it in front of her. "Thanks, Brian."

"Just holler if you need more," he said, then leaned against the counter to watch the station he chose.

It was a local news station, giving updates on interstate highway construction plans scheduled for the warmer months. "Damn," Brian mumbled. "That's gonna cut off my access to travelers."

"Sorry to hear that," Erika replied almost automatically.

The news anchor moved some papers to the side before speaking.

"When we return, we have a statement from the Oak Island police force about the impending investigation into the death of Christina Higgins."

Erika tensed slightly but tried to relax. It was inevitable that the news would latch onto a story as devastating as Christina's, but she hadn't expected it to be the same day. Oak Island police needed to tighten up their leaks.

"Terrible business about that girl," Brian said.

She sipped her coffee before responding. "Has there been a lot of coverage about it so far?"

"Not really. Just that she was missing and they located and identified a body. I'm hoping it was an accident, and she didn't suffer or nothing, but they did mention she was found on someone's private property."

"That's suspicious," Erika offered noncommittally. She could almost feel the bracelet burning her skin through the bag. It was unlikely that she'd need it as evidence now, so she would leave it at Christina's house before she left.

Brian shrugged, his eyes still on the screen. "Could be. I got some friends in Oak Island, so I'll probably ask around if anyone knew her."

"Why? It's not like it would help anything."

"Because it's interesting," he admitted. "It's not good, and I don't like it, the morbid fascination, but when beautiful women die young, everyone pays attention."

The anchor returned, repeating the intentionally vague statement given to her by the police. "At this time, persons of interest are being held for questioning, but no charges are yet being considered." She finished her short speech with an entreaty to keep Christina and her family in the audience's thoughts and prayers.

"I wonder who they are," Brian said. "The 'persons of interest.'"

"Probably some pretty bad people," Erika said.

RYAN STOOD IN THE HALLWAY between the open offices and the interrogation room, sipping on coffee he couldn't taste. There wasn't any reason for him to be standing except for the fact that he worried if he sat down, he would fall asleep.

"I thought we got a rush on the autopsy," Tanner complained.

"We did," Ryan replied. "But the coroner couldn't get started right away."

"Why not?"

"They had to wait for her to defrost," he said.

Tanner gagged, which was annoying, but he also left Ryan alone after that.

Carter and Robert were being detained in separate cells, though the elder Cahill's lawyer was working overtime to get an order from the local judge to release them or charge them with something. Even without the order, unless Christina's body came back with enough evidence to dispute Carter's story, they'd have to let him go in a couple hours anyway.

Waiting on the justice system to work properly could be exhausting, and this scenario was reminding Ryan far too much of Sloane's death.

"Gibson," Officer Barker called out, then gestured for Ryan to follow him. He followed him down the hall and into Chief Cahill's office with Paul closing the door behind him.

"I've got the coroner on the line," he explained, then put the phone on speaker and sat in one of the guest chairs in front of the desk.

It appeared that even with everything he'd just learned about his chief, Paul refused to disrespect the man by sitting at his desk like he owned it. Both Paul and Ryan sat in the visitor chairs, facing the front of the desk.

"Dr. Ellis," Paul enunciated clearly in the direction of the phone. "I have Detective Gibson here. We're ready for the results."

"Thanks, Barker," a woman's voice came through the line. "We'll start with what you care about most. Cause of death was likely hypothermia."

Ryan closed his eyes while Paul quietly cursed beside him. "You're telling us she was alive when she was put in the freezer?"

"Yes, for several hours at least," Dr. Ellis replied.

"Were there any signs of a struggle?"

"None," the doctor replied, "which at first, I found odd. People buried alive always eventually try to claw their way out once panic starts to set in and oxygen gets low. In this case, we should have seen the psychological effects of late-stage hypothermia with the cold becoming so unbearable it starts to feel hot and the person experiencing it sheds their clothing. In Christina's case, she didn't move around much once she was inside the freezer."

"Why was this different?" Ryan asked.

"That's where we move to her stomach contents and blood work. Christina had some light alcohol consumption in the twenty-four hours before her death, but not enough to impair her."

"That checks out with Chief Cahill's story," Paul interjected. "The clothing she was found in matches the outfit he described her wearing that night."

"A couple drinks wouldn't have been enough for her to just pass out in the freezer, though," Ryan pointed out.

"No, but an over-the-counter sedative would," Dr. Ellis replied. "The girl had at least an entire bottle of NyQuil in her stomach. Maybe more. Not enough to overdose, but enough to make her sleep through the effects of the hypothermia."

"She drank the whole bottle?" Paul asked.

"Or someone forced her to drink it," Ryan countered.

Dr. Ellis paused at the other end of the line before answering, "I suppose either are possible."

"If she took it herself," Ryan continued, "we'd have found the bottle somewhere on the premises."

Paul nodded, not to agree with him, more to ingest the information. "What else did you find?"

"She had intercourse before she died, and we found semen, but we won't have a DNA match until we get a sample from the chief."

Ryan swallowed back the bile rising in his throat. "Any evidence of sexual violence?"

"We found skin and blood under the nails. Again, waiting on DNA, but the blood type is a match for both the Cahill men," she explained. "Premortem bruising would be hard to identify after how long it's been but there's no scratch marks on her, nor are there any broken bones or sprains. I did find a splinter in her left buttock, likely from the pier."

"Nothing about that contradicts Chief Cahill's story," Paul insisted.

"Are you saying that Christina drugged and froze herself to death?" Ryan asked incredulously.

"No, I'm saying it's going to a be a tough sell getting a warrant for Carter Cahill's arrest with what we have," Paul explained. "We can't ask her what happened, and nothing on her body contradicts his version of events. Both Robert and Carter have said that they haven't been to the lodge in three months, though we can't know that for sure since there's no alarm system, just a silent trip that gets set off by animals occasionally. And while Carter lives alone so we don't have a verified alibi for the early hours in the morning when she would have been placed in the lodge, the chief worked double shifts for the rest of the weekend. We all had eyes on him for the forty-eight hours after he did this."

"If I may?" Dr. Ellis's voice came through the phone.

"Go ahead," Paul said.

"I like to leave the speculation and investigating portions of this process to you guys," she said. "But it seems like an uncharacteristic lack of foresight from the chief to leave the young woman in a climate where all the evidence against him could be preserved, especially when the natural environment offers much better hiding places for a body. The person responsible could have buried her in the forest or dumped her in the ocean."

Paul steepled his fingers together pensively. "That's a fair point."

"So, who could have put her there?" Ryan asked.

"We still have Robert in holding," Paul said. "He's giving us an exhaustive list of anyone who could have had access to the lodge—cleaning staff, family, visitors. They'll obviously all have to be questioned."

Ryan sat back in his chair, rubbing his hands across his face in disbelief. It was like Cody all over again: a trusted official no one wanted to blame, and a wild goose chase interviewing people he knew didn't do it.

"We don't have enough evidence to hold Carter," he said aloud.

30

IT WAS RAINING by the time Erika made it back to Oak Island. She planned her return strategically, in the early hours of the morning, when she would be the least likely to run into anyone. At one point, she considered parking a mile away from Christina's house, keeping her return more anonymous, but the rain and her own fatigue won out.

She needed to sleep, pack, and then decide where to go next.

Leaving Ryan behind could be sticky, as there was the possibility of him tracking her again. She couldn't discount the man's investigative skills and tenacity.

But she wasn't worried about him revealing her secrets. In that way, she could trust him.

She pulled the car into the port next to Christina's unused sedan and grabbed her pack from earlier. The house on stilts was unchanged since she left it the morning before, but she didn't eagerly run for the door, wondering who would win the rights to movie night between the two of them. There was no need to rush back to an empty house.

Slamming the driver's door behind her she'd made her way to the steps when she stopped and stared at the person sitting there.

"Christina?"

"Hey, girl." The woman sat on the steps with her arms wrapped around herself in a familiar stance.

"You're still here," Erika replied, sitting down next to her. They were protected from the rain where they sat, staring out on the unbusy residential street where Christina's house stood.

"Yeah," she replied. "At least it's not quite so cold anymore."

Erika didn't respond right away. The people she worked with usually left or moved on to wherever they went next after a case was solved. If they stayed for some reason, they stopped speaking to her.

The fact that Christina stayed meant that something was wrong.

"I found your bracelet," she said. As if that would help. The other woman said nothing, no sarcastic comment or gratitude.

"There's more, isn't there?" Erika asked Christina.

The woman nodded. "I think so," she said.

They watched the rain for a few more minutes until Christina stood up with Erika right behind her.

"The tide should be pulling back out soon," Christina said. "There's something I want to show you."

Without a second thought, Erika followed her friend into the wet, inky darkness of what remained of the night.

RYAN WATCHED ROBERT and Carter Cahill walk into the precinct parking lot. The elder Cahill arguing loudly with his lawyer, headed towards a car under an umbrella, while Carter stepped onto the sidewalk with his hands in his pockets, ignoring both his vehicle and the rain.

From his spot behind the window, Ryan's visuals were limited, but his anxiety was high. He pumped the grip strengthener repeatedly, passing it back and forth in his hands. He wished it would alleviate his tiredness as well.

He felt Officer Barker before he heard the man speak.

"You got good instincts," the man said. Ryan only acknowledged his compliment with a nod, not moving his eyes from the window. Carter was well out of his line of sight by that point, but he couldn't stop looking for him.

Paul continued, "We'll find whoever did this. It's a tragedy our community won't allow to go unsolved. The people will be out for blood."

"What if we can't prove he did it?"

"You seem pretty confident that it was Chief Cahill," the officer observed.

Ryan shrugged. "I don't see who else it could be."

It wasn't like he could explain what he knew to anyone but Erika. Visions of the dead experienced by people Ryan had just met were hardly admissible evidence.

"We need something more concrete than your gut feeling, Gibson," Paul reminded him, with no judgement in his voice.

The man's statement almost made him smile. "You remind me of my old sergeant," he said.

Vincent held the same serious yet approachable nature that Paul did. They also shared a no-nonsense commitment to hard evidence.

"You want fingerprints, DNA, video, any physical evidence if you can get it. You never want to rely on a single person's recounting of a crime. Witness testimony is extremely unreliable," Vincent had lectured him once. "People forget things, misremember events due to stress, and in a lot of cases, they're flat out lying. Never base your case on the words of one person."

Ryan stopped pumping the grip strengthener and held his breath at the memory.

Officer Barker, observant as he was, noticed the change. "What is it? Did you think of something?"

"Yes," he replied. "But I don't know what it means yet," he said, handing the fidget tool to the officer. "I've got to go."

Ryan ran out into the rain and raced to his car, igniting the engine before his door was fully closed. As he sped in the direction of the house where Erika was staying, he prayed she would still be there.

Am I too late?

31

"WHERE ARE WE GOING?" Erika asked Christina.

"The caverns," she replied. "Like I said, the tide should be pulling back out in the next hour or so."

"What's in the caverns?"

"You'll see," was all Christina said back.

They walked past the pier along the coast, taking the paved road toward the large rock formations at the end of the island. The rain was relentless, though Erika was grateful it wasn't accompanied by any thunder, even if she could use the visibility lightning offered.

It was still dark, but the overcast sky was moving from black to grey with the impending sunrise. Her phone was still in the car, but her watch said it was just past five in the morning.

She watched Christina step off the sidewalk and onto the tops of the caverns. From their perspective, it was a somewhat flat walk towards the ledge, but Erika knew the rocks dropped off eventually, creating a wall towering over the north end of the beach, the entirety of which was only visible during low tide. There were only a few hours in the middle of the day when it would be possible to walk alongside the boulders.

"It doesn't seem safe to be out here," she said to Christina.

"Just watch your step. We're going just a little bit farther," she called over her shoulder. With seemingly no other choice, Erika followed Christina onto the stone formations.

The ocean, which up until that point had been competing with the sound of the rain, was much louder as the waves buffeted against the rocks where they stood. Erika watched each step, making sure she had enough texture underfoot to keep her from slipping.

"Come out this way," Christina insisted.

Erika followed dutifully but continued her slow pace.

"You missed the beaches during peak season," Christina explained from her position at the edge of the boulders. "It really is beautiful here, but not in a corporate, manufactured way. The beach is for everyone, as are the bars and restaurants. This town was good to me, until it wasn't."

"I'm sorry," Erika said, finally catching up to Christina.

They stood together, watching the navy-blue waves take turns beating into the side of the natural wall where they stood. It was like something from a pirate movie, right before the Kraken comes out of the water to capsize the ship, dragging the crew into the abyss.

Erika hoped they found what Christina was looking for soon.

"You know, I had it all planned out," she said, ignoring Erika. "We were going to get married at the Baptist church here in town. We could have had a reception with everyone we knew. I even had ideas for us to take photos out here on top of the caverns."

Looking to her left, Erika saw the other woman with her eyes closed, face tilted towards the rain, smiling.

"What are you talking about?"

"I'm talking about Carter Cahill," Christina said, harsher than she'd been speaking before. "When Lindsey left, it was my turn."

The waves continued their relentless attack on the rock formation while Christina raised her voice above the noise.

"Once she was gone, he was supposed to want me. He was supposed to pick me."

Erika was even with Christina then, though she took a step to the side to distance herself.

What have I enabled?

Christina continued, "When he said he didn't want a relationship, I was devastated. I wanted to rip my own heart out of my chest and force feed it to him."

Erika backed away another step from the woman. "What are you talking about? He attacked you."

"I needed him to hurt like I hurt. To suffer like I suffered when he rejected me," she said, eyes wild as she slapped her hand against her chest for emphasis. "Do you know what it's like to love someone who is still pining for another woman?"

"Oh my God," Erika whispered.

"He sure as shit didn't help me. I spent years praying for Carter Cahill to love me."

"Was any of it true?" she asked.

Maybe Christina had lied about some parts but hadn't completely falsified the story. Maybe there was still an opportunity for justice if Carter had committed some crime.

"The truth doesn't matter if I win," Christina reasoned with a small, sinister smile.

"How is this winning? If you recall, you're fucking dead," Erika hissed out.

This woman was insane. Erika couldn't believe she'd been blind to it for so long.

"Easy," Christina said. "Originally, I didn't know what waited for me after death. I just didn't want to be here if I couldn't have him. It wasn't worth it to keep going, so I thought that as long as I was leaving, I could take some of his happiness with me. They would find my body at his lodge and assume he killed me after we had sex, or more likely, they'd believe he raped me.

"Imagine my surprise when I woke up, still here. Then you showed up, my sweet little bleeding-heart ghost whisperer, believing everything I told you," Christina explained. "It was perfect. I could finally have everything I wanted. Carter will go to jail for my murder, and I'll be there, waiting with him, in whatever form this is," she gestured toward herself. "I'll take him whatever way I can get him."

"You're insane," Erika whispered.

"It doesn't matter. No one will know the truth except me."

"Revealing the truth is what I do," Erika replied with more bravery than she felt.

"Not for long," Christina said.

Before Erika could respond, Christina rushed her, jumping through the air to just an inch away from her face before whispering, "*Boo.*"

As a reflex of being surprised, Erika stepped backwards, only to learn that the surface of the boulder had ended, and nothing but the ocean was behind her.

CARTER HADN'T RUN THIS FAST since high school football.

His feet pounded into the pavement with a steady repetition, slamming into the growing ground water from the rain. It splashed against his ankles, slowing him only marginally. Each touch to the ground was timed with his breathing as he rushed towards his goal.

Hit. Hit. Hit. Hit. Hit.

The movements returned to him as second nature, though he didn't allow his mind to wander while he moved. His only thought was to move faster.

After leaving the station, he walked with no goal, not ready to go home, but unwilling to face the men he usually outranked after being questioned by Officer Barker. It was humiliating to be apprehended in front of his force like that. How could they respect him going forward, knowing he'd impeded an investigation? He withheld information about a relationship with someone who'd been declared a missing person, and that might prove unforgivable.

They would be well within their rights to ask the mayor for a new chief. He sure as hell didn't respect himself after his behavior the past months. Maybe he wasn't suited to lead until he got his shit together.

At the very least, he was likely to face some kind of suspension, which he would happily agree to. At worst, he could be accused of murder, which he'd like to avoid if possible.

Those were the musings that plagued him as he walked but no longer distracted him as he ran.

Because walking with no direction had led him towards the coast, passing the pier he never wanted to see again and leading to the caverns where he saw a person, probably a woman based on her size, standing there alone. He walked a bit faster, trying to gather any information he could about her emotional state.

Nobody who cared about their own wellbeing would be on a cliff like that.

Carter thought maybe he was seeing things in the night, that the woman was some kind of waking dream due to his lack of sleep, but as the cloudy sky changed from black to grey with the impending sunrise, he knew there was a person at the top of the rocks.

Was she an idiot? The boulders that lined the sea were dangerous in good weather and much worse on a morning like that one. She would have almost no traction under her feet. He thought about calling out to her, warning her away from the ledge, but there was no way she would be able to hear him through the rain, especially that close to the sea. He adjusted his listlessness and made his way to the caverns, walking at his same pace until he saw her fall over the edge.

Then he stopped thinking and ran as fast as he could.

Hit. Hit. Hit. Hit. Hit.

Carter quickly erased the distance between himself and the caverns, only slowing slightly when he arrived so he wouldn't slip.

"Hey!" he called out as loudly as he could with his heavy breathing, but he didn't stop for a response, nor did he expect one.

He didn't hesitate or think of calling for back-up for himself. Instead, Carter raced to the edge and dove over the boulders, straight into the sea so he could find the woman.

32

"GET UP."

The delicate voice was out of place, though Erika wasn't sure what that place was. She thought maybe her mother might be waking her up after a long car ride, one that had dragged on into the night past her bedtime. But she wanted to push her away and keep sleeping. Her head hurt, and Erika was less likely to feel it if she kept her eyes closed.

The voice returned, harsher, and was feminine but definitely not her mother.

"Get up," she insisted. "You're running out of time."

Time for what?

Erika's eyes flew open, and she realized that she was running out of time to stay conscious if she didn't get air soon.

But which way was up?

The current slammed her body into a hard, jagged surface as she scrambled to find where the water turned into air so she could finally inhale again.

Clawing at anything she could find, she felt dryness above her, so she pushed against what must have been a lateral wall towards the pocket of air. It was pitch black, so she had no way of knowing how much space she would have above water until she got there.

Erika broke the surface of the water and gasped, desperately pulling air into her lungs. Still blinded, she knew she couldn't stay there long. A sharp pain on her left temple indicated she'd hit her head at some point on her fall, but that could wait. She must have been under the caverns, in the caves that stayed full until the tide went back out in the morning.

But where was the exit? What direction did she enter from?

A fresh wave must have buffeted against the opening because the small pocket of air Erika had been relying on disappeared and she was shoved farther into the cavern.

The exit must be behind me.

"A little farther," the voice came through the water as if spoken aloud.

Still sightless, Erika kicked herself away from the wall and let the water push her until she needed oxygen again. Another pocket of air arrived just in time, and she broke through the surface and gulped at it greedily when her hand made contact with a sudden dip in the wall to her side.

The water moved with strength she couldn't overpower, but she noted that its force was recurring. With just a hint of predictability, Erika could sense when a wave crashed into the cave and when the tide pulled back out for another ambush.

Hoping for a place to breathe, she stuck her hand into the crevice and grabbed the corner, pulling herself closer. The water broke and she rose above it, gasping while she moved her hands around blindly.

Something artificial broke Erika's perusal, a plasticky material that felt like a tarp, and she quickly moved it out of the way and kept digging.

Behind the plastic was what felt like fabric then something gummy and...

Erika yelped, and if she'd had more room in her lungs, would have shrieked.

Bones.

When she tried to rip her hand away, it snagged on a small chain, and it was all Erika could do to keep focused on her task and not break down into a whimpering mess, letting the sea consume her.

"Hold the chain," the voice commanded. "Take it with you."

Erika twisted it around her wrist and yanked it with her, right as a hand grabbed her shoulder and pulled her back through the tunnel.

BENEATH THE SURFACE, Carter had no visibility, the salt and darkness partnering to blind him further. It was impossible to tell in what direction he was moving when he was fully encased under the water, so he waited for a push then a pull, finding which way was up by instinct.

As his head broke through the sea, a wave slapped into him, the force of which slammed his body against the rocks. He grasped desperately at the boulders but failed to get a solid grip and was soon pulled back into the ocean as the waves retreated, regrouping for another surge.

Carter swam through the waves yelling for the woman whenever he kept his head above water in between attempts to see under the waves for where she went. The morning sky would have been brighter by then except for the continued onslaught of rain, the density of the clouds showing no signs of surrendering their ownership of the sky.

The woman had likely slipped into one of the caves, but it would be almost impossible to find her without the return of low tide.

When he faced away from the ocean, a wave crashed into his back, throwing him into the rock formation. His shoulder took most of the force, but he was able to stop his head from slamming into the boulder.

He couldn't save anyone if a concussion put him at the bottom of the sea.

As the tide withdrew to collect for another wave, he saw a gap in the rocks that looked big enough for him to fit.

Carter took a deep breath and pulled himself into the opening.

Any visibility he had outside vanished as he kept his head close to the top before another wave pushed him under again.

Using the tide to guide him into the cave, he kicked along with the current pushing him.

Grabbing a protrusion to his left, he pulled his head above the water line and called out.

"Hello? Anyone in here," he yelled into the space, though he didn't think his voice carried far. There was too much water, too many waves crashing, and not enough open space for an echo to reach another person's ears.

Tightening his grip, he held himself steady against the tide pulling back out so he wouldn't lose progress.

"Hey!" he yelled again, louder, to no one's ears but his own.

Almost ready to turn around, Carter thought he heard a faint sound of distress, an echo of a person's voice calling to whoever could hear.

"I'm coming in," he called out, then pushed himself into the darkness.

When his hand collided with a warm, clothed arm, he grasped it as firmly and as gently as possible before trying to leverage his other arm to fight through the water. A wave pushed against them, trying to force them farther into the darkness, but he held steady.

He didn't have enough space or vision to check on the woman, but based on her thrashing, she was conscious.

Soon, the tide pulled out again for another wave which he used to his advantage.

Even a man as strong as Carter couldn't out match the force of the ocean, so he knew they needed to break out of the cave before it pushed them back in, eliminating any progress he made.

The woman he carried wasn't exactly dead weight, but he could tell based on her size she wasn't going to be any help swimming.

Carter's vision returned just in time for him to see another wave approaching.

"Hold your breath!" he yelled and yanked them both under, just in time for him to grab the corner of the cave's entrance. His left forearm burned with the strain of keeping them from being shoved backward, while his right twisted unnaturally trying to hold onto his passenger, and his lungs screamed at him for relief.

It was a huge wave, fighting him every second of its existence, but at least that meant an equally strong recession of water would help them both back out into the open.

Just in time, the water pulled away from the caverns and Carter brought them both above the surface.

He turned to see Christina's cousin, Erika, if he remembered correctly, trying to keep her head above the water line.

"Grab onto my neck," he instructed loudly while pulling her arms around him to show her. When he was confident that she wouldn't fall off him and be lost to the sea, he began to move.

Carter had never been a big swimmer. He liked land sports, like football and hunting, but he also really liked being alive, and he wanted the people around him to stay alive as well, so he pushed through the waves with Erika on his back with commitment, if not technical skill.

The caverns only lined the sea for about two hundred yards, but it was the longest two hundred yards Carter had ever experienced. The current was constantly pushing him into the sides of the rocks or dragging him out into the ocean. He couldn't be sure, but he felt as though the undertow was fighting sideways against him as well.

Erika's grip was firm around his neck, though she seemed to be aware of how tight she held him so he could move. It would have sucked if he had to fight the elements as well as his partner's strangling grip on his swim to shore.

When his feet finally touched sand, he stumbled but held strong. None of the sand was dry, and it was still raining, but he carried Erika several yards away from the sea before setting her down.

Carter was no EMT, but all police officers have some emergency medical training, so he began the well-formed habit of checking her for injuries. He noted a welt on the side of her head, but no broken bones.

She coughed and sputtered, taking greedy gasps of breath as she lay on the sand, but he was relieved to not have to revive her. Carter was about to ask her what the hell she thought she was doing standing over the cliffs, but he froze when he saw what she held in her hand.

"Where did you find this?"

33

RYAN SPED THROUGH STOP SIGNS and empty residential streets with an alarming carelessness that he never exhibited behind the wheel of a car.

"Where are you, Erika?"

Her car was in the spot under Christina's house, though no one had answered when he banged on the door, eventually breaking inside to search for her himself.

She'd returned to Oak Island. He knew that much, at least.

But as he tore through neighborhoods as if they were racetracks, that thought was not even remotely comforting to him.

Because, in the dark recess of his mind, he thought that maybe they had gotten it wrong and now she was in trouble.

He should have asked more questions. He had no details, no fine print about her relationship with the dead. Could she be hurt by a ghost physically? Was she trapped here until Christina let her go?

Ryan hated this feeling, the one where all he could do was wait for the devastating news of finding out he was too late.

He remembered the emotional gut punch from eight months ago, as he sped to a crime scene with a yet unidentified murder victim as a text message from Sloane's mother all but confirmed his worst fears.

Sloane never came home last night.

The windshield wipers struggled to slap water away from the glass fast enough for Ryan to see where he was going. He hoped that anyone who would normally be walking to the beach was staying inside, otherwise, he was likely going to run them over.

He sped by the coffee shop and pub, even the seafood restaurant where they got their first drink, but all of them were closed. He drove down every street she mentioned walking during her nights breaking into houses and she was nowhere to be found.

An incoming phone call interrupted his focus, but he answered despite his annoyance.

"What?"

"Get to the beach," Officer Barker's voice came through the handsfree Bluetooth. "Possible injuries from a fall and a potential casualty."

"Who is it?"

"I don't know about the body," Paul explained. "But Pratt called it in when he saw Chief Cahill dragging a woman out of the water."

Ryan hung up and cursed, then swung his truck around for an illegal U-turn in the middle of whatever street he was on.

Please be alive, Erika.

ERIKA WANTED TO INTERRUPT Carter's attempts to resuscitate her by telling him that she was, in fact, awake and he was starting to hurt her, until she realized he wasn't administering any CPR.

He was gripping her upper arms and shaking her.

"Where did you find this?" he demanded, yelling at her over the sound of the rain. "This doesn't belong to you!"

She tried and failed to wriggle out of his grasp, wanting to ask what he was talking about. He released only one arm long enough to rip something from her hand and dangle it in front of her face.

"This," he yelled. "Where did you find this?"

The chain she pulled out of the cave swung from his hand before her eyes. It was a necklace that held a small cross decorated with pink gemstones. It had clearly been worn by its time in the water but appeared to have been on the expensive side before its destruction.

Apparently, Carter recognized it, making her next sentence almost too heartbreaking to utter out loud.

"In the cavern," she gasped out when she caught her breath long enough to speak. "There's a body."

Carter ceased his shaking as Erika watched confusion slowly take over his expression. He released her arms and settled back on his heels, disbelief warring for a spot on his face but eventually losing to devastation.

"Oh, God," he uttered, as he fell backwards and gripped the chain harder, sobs wracking his body. "Lindsey. It's Lindsey."

As Carter wailed, the sounds coming from a man as large as him foreign to Erika, the rain continued to spill onto the sand. It seemed cruel for the clouds to remain discharging on them that way, while he was clearly hurting.

Erika would have comforted him, maybe to hold his shoulder or ask him who Lindsey was to him, except for the scene unfolding about twenty yards behind him.

It occurred to her that in all her years communicating with the dead, she had never seen two deceased people together before.

She watched, unable to intervene, as a blonde woman she recognized from the broken frame at the lodge dragged Christina away from Carter by the ankle, while the former screamed for freedom.

"Let me go!" Christina's fingers pulled through the sand but left no trace of her presence. Neither woman made indentations in the beach at all, each movement disappearing from Erika's vision as soon as it was executed with no indication that they had been there.

The blonde woman didn't respond, only moving Christina farther from the man's heaving body. When she finished moving, the blonde dropped onto Christina, straddling the other woman, and began strangling her.

Though Christina's fingers left no mark on the beach, her nails clawed at the other woman, tearing through skin and leaving the occasional mark on her face and neck as she gasped for air.

Erika couldn't rip her eyes away. Could somebody die twice? She'd never been present when a ghost moved on or left her, and she watched with a terrified fascination as Christina didn't exactly choke through the strangulation. She fought as if she remembered the act of losing her breath, but she appeared to be fading away instead of expiring.

"No," the blonde said, answering Christina's demand to be released, her voice matching the one Erika heard in the caverns.

Despite the brutality of her actions, the blonde did not seem to be relishing in her behavior, more so resigned to the necessity of it. Her face was stern but serene, and she held Christina still until the woman obsessed with Carter disappeared completely.

When, finally, the blonde sat alone on the sand, she whispered to Christina once more, "he doesn't belong to you."

A siren blared in the distance, ripping Erika away from her trance. She had to move quickly or else become trapped in a bureaucratic law machine when she had work to do.

She stepped around Carter, who ignored her, lost in his lamentations, and walked over to where the blonde still knelt in the sand.

"You must be Lindsey," she said quietly so Carter couldn't hear.

The woman didn't say anything, just stared at Carter with a heartbreaking expression.

"I can help you," Erika tried again.

Lindsey stood, never pulling her gaze from the sobbing man. "He was going to propose," she said, ignoring Erika's words. "I found the ring in his room at the hunting lodge but never told him. He would have been disappointed if I ruined the surprise."

Her voice held a profound sadness that almost made Erika break down in tears alongside Carter, but the sound of emergency vehicles closing in gave her urgency.

"Tell me who killed you, and I'll find them," she choked out.

Lindsey finally tore her gaze away from Carter and looked at Erika.

"Not everyone was happy for us."

34

RYAN SKIDDED TO A STOP right behind the emergency vehicles at the beach, ripping open the door as he looked through the people moving towards the water.

He saw officers start the process of taping off the area as a crime scene, but no paramedics rushed to the shore.

He didn't see Erika.

"Pratt," he called out to Tanner, who was standing near the vehicles. Ryan jogged to his side, wishing it was another person, but desperate enough for information to talk to him.

"What's going on?"

Officer Pratt wiped rain from his forehead and pointed at the people moving on the beach. "Cahill jumped off the cliff, diving after someone," he explained.

When it appeared that it was all the information Tanner had, Ryan walked through the beach shrubbery lining the rocks. There was no direct path to the beach from where he parked, but he moved quickly and saw Carter sitting in the sand alone, soaking wet.

"Cahill," he called. The man didn't respond, so Ryan jogged closer across sand compacted by rain, ducking under the crime scene tape. No one stopped his progress, and the chief still hadn't acknowledged him, so he stood in front of the man's line of sight. Carter's reddened eyes and dead stare didn't offer him any hope.

"What happened here?"

He sat still, forearms resting across his knees and what looked like a necklace hanging from one of his hands. Though he made no indication that he'd heard Ryan, Carter responded, "Erika fell off the cliffs," he explained. "So, I went in and got her."

Ryan forced himself not to overreact to the news. If something was wrong with Erika, there would be paramedics racing to help, but the first responders exhibited no such urgency. Looking around, he couldn't see any sign of her on the beach at all.

"Where is she now?"

Carter shook his head, eyes still plastered on the ocean. "I didn't see her leave. She was gone before all my men showed up."

Paul jogged over to them from where a group of other officers were finishing the perimeter. "Ryan, I'm glad you're here."

"Why the perimeter?" he asked.

"Chief says there's a body in the cavern," he said. "But we need to wait another few hours before the tide is out far enough and we can retrieve it for identification."

"It's Lindsey," Carter interrupted. "I know it is."

Paul looked down at his boss with no small amount of confusion and pain in his face. "This doesn't look good, Chief."

Carter laughed humorlessly. "Who cares how its looks? Nothing matters anymore."

BY THE TIME RYAN was in his car headed back to his motel, he thought that he'd never be dry again and that there was no amount of sleep that would return him to any kind of functional state.

It took three men, Ryan included, to hold Carter down while the forensics team went into the cavern to retrieve the body. He behaved as though possessed, as if he could reach the remains first, he might find her alive and discover that the past several months were just a horrible nightmare.

Eventually, one of the paramedics sedated him, but not before Carter got another clean swing at Ryan's face.

Texts and missed calls from Loretta, his brother Travis, and even Colleen filled his phone, but he had no intention of calling anyone back. His old concerns about his brother's wedding seemed laughably superficial compared to what he'd seen since arriving on the island, and any communication with them at this point would only function to alienate him from his family more.

A text to Loretta letting her know he was alive would have to suffice.

His skin had been pruned throughout the day. He could feel it pebble beneath his clothes as the AC blew out of his truck's vents, and he hated it. Ryan hated that he couldn't escape it, the water still running down his neck from his hair, the rain continuously pelting against his windshield. All he wanted was to be dry and to sleep for several days.

Once parked, he slammed his door and meandered towards his motel room. What was the hurry? It's not like he could get more drenched, and the rain finally felt like it was slowing down.

When he got to the steps in front of his room, he didn't pause when he saw Erika sitting on them. He walked past her, expecting her to follow if she had something to say. As he worked the key into the lock, he couldn't hear her moving behind him, but he could feel her, so he held it open for her to walk through with him when he was ready.

His motel room didn't offer many options for sitting, so when Erika sat on the edge of the bed, Ryan chose the desk chair to give himself some distance.

They sat in a soundless stalemate until Ryan relented. "Are you going to tell me what happened?"

Erika was just as soaked as he was, shivering on the side of the bed. He'd seen many versions of her since she entered anonymously into his life months before. He saw the formidable investigator, the mysterious shadow, the brilliant puzzle solver. More recently, he got to experience the warmth of her affection and her humorous friendship. Ryan could spend lifetimes getting to know all of Erika's idiosyncrasies.

But if he never had to see her look so pitiable and defeated as she did at that moment ever again, he would be grateful.

"I think so. At least, I'll tell you some of it."

It was a vague answer, but he understood. "I was trying to find you all morning," he said.

She lifted her head to look back at him. "You were?"

"I knew something was wrong," he explained. "After Cahill told us his version of events, I knew I had to find you."

Erika nodded and placed her gaze firmly back on the floor. "I should have been more discerning."

Ryan leaned forward, placing his forearms on his thighs. "How much did Christina lie about?"

"Most of it. Probably all of it, in a way."

She held herself responsible for not figuring it out sooner, and Ryan could tell it was eating away at her. "Has that ever happened before?"

She rolled her eyes. "Have I ever been lied to before?"

"No," he replied firmly. "In all your time spent helping people find justice for themselves and helping people like me put truly evil men and women in jail, have you ever been misled and manipulated like this?"

Chewing her lip, she considered the question. "I guess not."

"Then you can't blame yourself," he said. "You were trying to do the right thing."

She didn't respond right away, and the only noise that filled the space was a steady dripping of water from Ryan's sleeve to where it thumped into the industrial carpet.

"I was trying to ruin an innocent man's life," she whispered.

Ryan wanted to comfort her. She clearly needed it, but he had more questions. "Is he?"

"Is he what?"

"Is Carter Cahill innocent?"

Erika nodded. "That's sort of a funny question," she said. "Innocent might be the wrong word, but all the things they're about to accuse him of? He didn't do them."

He found it interesting how she worded it. It was as if she knew what was coming even though she hadn't been there with Ryan and Paul as the team excavated the body from the caverns once the tide pulled out. There hadn't been much left of the woman, but everyone was confident they'd have an ID shortly.

"We found a body," was what he said out loud. "Carter thinks its Lindsey Payne, his ex."

"He's right," she replied as she stood from the bed and approached the window, pulling one of the blinds down to see out of it.

A brief wave of panic rolled over him as he considered what her paranoia might imply. "Is Christina still—"

"No," she interrupted. "She's gone."

Her response did not invite any follow-up inquiries, though he was dying to know what happened there. Instead, Ryan reverted back to some of his more urgent concerns. "The investigating officers want to pin all of this on Carter," he said. "Lindsey, Christina, all of it. Right now, they're holding him for impeding the Higgins investigation by withholding evidence."

Erika's answer was quick, expected, and entirely unsatisfactory. "I'll handle it."

Ryan clenched his fists but held back his immediate response. "Are you going to let me help you?"

"No," she said, moving from the window back to between Ryan and the bed. "Not the way you want to."

Relaxing his hands he resisted the urge to stand up and crowd her space in confrontation. "That's not fair."

She laughed. "Fair? That's what you're complaining about?"

"I've been here for this investigation, I've helped you. We're a team here. You can't shut me out like this."

"Oh, are we a team? Funny," she said, as she turned away from the window and crossed her arms. "Because as someone who's on my team, you've been rather dishonest with me."

A pain flared in Ryan's right hand under her perusal. "I don't know what you're talking about."

"At first, I was kind of flattered," Erika continued, shifting her weight as water still dripped from her clothes to the floor. "You followed me all over the country, obsessing over the person who helped you close Sloane's case. I'm not unaware of the impact of what I do. It didn't surprise me that I'd developed at least one dedicated fan over the years."

"Sloane was important to me," Ryan reasoned.

"Certainly," Erika agreed. "Your families are close. What I did meant a lot to you, so when I saw you for the first time at that pub, I was scared of being discovered but not surprised. The longer I do this, the more shocked I am that I continue to move around undiscovered.

"And when you confronted me with all your evidence, I liked it. All the people I've helped laid out in front of me like a shrine to my work. Your devotion fed my ego in a way that made me not ask any questions."

She stepped closer to him then, though Ryan remained frozen in his seat, one hand grasping each chair's arm.

"When you stayed, and started asking about Christina? I didn't question that either. You also love solving cases, and what better way for you to get closure on Sloane's murder than to solve someone else's. It made sense, and frankly, I actually liked having you around. Apparently, my solitude made me vulnerable."

Erika closed the gap between them and put her hands on top of his, leaning her face towards him in a way that made it impossible for Ryan to look anywhere else.

"But then you started alluding to the future. Us, working together, traveling around the country and solving these cases. That was the red flag for me. Because, Ryan, in your soul, you're a detective and a man of the law. Me? I'm a nomad and a criminal with good intentions. We don't fit."

They glared at each other for a few beats.

"I made some calls yesterday when I was on the road," she finally admitted. "I'm disappointed in myself that I didn't catch some of your story while I was in town. It explains so much. But your suspension? Well, you're lucky that the Oak Island PD didn't also make those calls to verify your story before basically begging you to work there."

The sounds of their clothes leaking onto the carpet in soft, rhythmic thumps provided the only noise in the room, with both of their breathing halted as they waited for him to respond. To deny it, to excuse himself.

Ryan leaned forward, almost completely closing the distance between them before speaking.

"Get out."

Ryan watched as she stood up, opened the door, and slammed it behind her.

How dare you.

It shocked him, the resentment that he felt towards Erika as he battled with whether or not to run after her. He wasn't prepared to feel anything but righteous anger, but he was sad, too. In fact, Ryan was sad enough to say the wrong thing, beg her to come back so he could explain himself. Instead, he gritted his teeth and took off for the small motel bathroom instead of following her. He couldn't speak to her right then, or he'd say something too honest.

Those thoughts slammed into him as he turned the shower on as hot as it would go and waited for it to heat. With his fists on the counter, he glared at his reflection until he couldn't stand the sight of his own face anymore. His eyes were sunken, empty, and he needed a shave, but it was the hatred in his eyes that scared him the most.

He took a shower, a longer one than usual. The chill from the storm was still lingering, clinging to his bones even after his time with Erika. Ryan stood under the spray, soaping and shampooing until the water stopped being hot, while he convinced himself it was worth it to do the right thing even if it meant she didn't choose him.

"It's better this way," he said into the steam. "Just rip the Band-Aid off."

If only he could make himself believe it.

RYAN SAT ON THE SIDE of the bed, staring at the wall. He wished he could lay down and sleep, knew he would need the rest for what was to come later. Carter would need an ally, and he might be the only option.

It was a humiliating clarity he finally possessed, understanding that between the two of them, Carter was likely the better man.

Ryan picked up his phone and made a call he'd been avoiding since he went on the road.

"Well, son," Sergeant Vincent's voice came through the speaker. "I wondered when I could expect this call."

"I figured after all these months, it might be time to stop avoiding you," Ryan said into the phone.

"Far past time, in my opinion," Vincent replied. "How are your travels?"

"Not what I expected."

"Those sorts of trips rarely are. I spoke with Loretta," he hedged.

Ryan nodded, even though no one could see him. "I see."

"We agree that it's time for you to come home," Vincent said. "You made a mistake."

"I made more than one mistake," he whispered back.

As a police officer, Ryan never slept with his phone on silent. It was a habit he'd probably never break, so when his phone had woken him up that late spring night, he'd answered without pause.

"Yes?"

"Ryan," Sloane's voice came through. "I need a favor."

Checking the clock, Ryan winced at the time. He was supposed to wake up for his shift at the station in less than four hours. "What is it?"

"You know Mike's graduation party?"

"The one your parents said you couldn't go to?"

Sloane's silence at the other end was the only confirmation he needed.

"You might be the only teenager on the planet who calls a cop for help after they've been partying," he muttered.

"Please," she begged. "I just need a ride home and I don't want to ask my parents. Everyone's drinking too much, and I don't want to be here anymore."

"What's the address?"

Sloane rattled it off, and Ryan made some mental calculations. "Look," he said. "That's less than a twenty-minute walk from your house. Grab a friend, and you should get there just fine. It's not even cold out." And before hanging up, he finished with a comforting sentiment: "Nothing bad ever happens around here. I would know."

Ryan had never regretted anything more than his decisions that night.

Sergeant Vincent interrupted his memories. "No one blames you for Sloane's death," he said. "She should have called her parents or sister for a ride, and she didn't. That's not your fault. As for the mistake that got you in trouble, well, no one around here blames you much for that either."

Ryan had never directly disobeyed an order from Vincent. It wasn't in his nature to break rules, but everything about Sloane's death had destroyed his ability to reason, his control over his baser instincts.

"Absolutely not," Vincent had said once they had the suspects in custody, placing a hand on Ryan's shoulder. "You are way too close to this. You're too emotional. There's no way I'm letting you in there for the questioning. Hell, I should have taken you off this case entirely."

They had both been standing behind the mirror of the interrogation room, watching as Ricky sat there sulking. They had arrested both him and Craig after Erika's evidence package arrived and were waiting for Ricky's father to arrive as his legal representative.

"Please let me do this," Ryan had begged. "I want to hear why he didn't come to us. I need to hear it from him."

"No. You will wait for his dad and keep your ass on this side of the window. Do I make myself clear?"

Ryan clenched his teeth before gritting out a reluctant agreement.

But then Vincent had made the mistake of leaving Ryan alone while he interrogated Craig, and Ryan had entered the room holding Ricky.

The kid looked up at him, then turned away.

"I'm not saying shit 'til my dad gets here."

It would be cliché for Ryan to claim he had blacked out in that moment, that he was blinded by rage, but it also wasn't untrue. He just knew that before someone caught him and he was dragged away by his arms, that he'd been alone with Ricky long enough for the nineteen-year-old to have a broken nose, and Ryan to have fractured one of his fingers.

He wiggled those fingers to work out the persistent soreness before saying anything to his old sergeant.

"I guess I regret that mistake far less than the others," Ryan admitted.

"You won't get any argument from me there," Vincent said. "Your suspension ended months ago, and the other officers are ready to have you back. Hell, even his dad didn't bother pressing charges."

As a part of his agreement to testify against Craig, Ricky's dad had signed his son up for community service but demanded a two-month suspension for Ryan's attack.

"There needs to be restitution here," the lawyer had argued fairly.

Ryan's punishment was a two-month suspension. Without any professional obligations to distract him from the guilt he was drowning in, he set off to find the one thing he could think of that might offer redemption.

The person who helped him solve Sloane's murder.

When the suspension ended, he was too deep into his investigation to return home.

"I think you're right," Ryan said to Vincent.

"I usually am," he replied. "When can we expect you back?"

Ryan thought of Carter, and the two dead women the town of Oak Island had to contend with.

"I need to wrap a few things up here," Ryan said. "But I'll see you in a couple weeks."

35

IT HAD BEEN FIVE DAYS.

Five days since Erika walked out of Ryan's motel room and the last time he'd seen her.

Five days since Chief Cahill was thrown into a jail cell after being arrested for Lindsey's and Christina's murders with Robert refusing to pay his bail.

And, presumably, five days since Carter had eaten last.

He sat on the cot facing the wall in a position that was becoming very familiar to Ryan after his daily visits. He wouldn't be surprised if Carter slept upright in that same place, never moving, only staring straight ahead.

Outside those walls where Ryan watched Carter, the police worked tirelessly to wrap up the cases and assuage a concerned public. The media blast about the chief of police potentially being a routine murderer of young, beautiful women would kill tourism in the area for at least a year, causing an economic hit the town wasn't sure it could recover from.

Carter had been correct in his guess on the beach, though only Ryan had any idea how. The coroner identified Lindsey Payne as the remains in the cavern. With the time she'd been down there, it was almost impossible to determine the time of death, but the cause hadn't eroded with time.

"Bullet hole at the anterior of her skull," Dr. Ellis explained over the phone to Ryan and Paul. "Execution style. We can't tell specifics after so much decomposition, but the size of the hole indicates a handgun, no bigger than nine-millimeter."

When that information somehow leaked to the press, Ryan didn't envy the position it put Paul in.

The statements from acting Chief Barker said nothing more than that an investigation was ongoing, and a person of interest was being held until all avenues were searched.

For all Paul's professionalism, Ryan had hoped the man would have more faith in his former boss, even if he himself hadn't exhibited any faith in the man a week earlier.

"It's like I predicted: the people are out for blood," Paul explained. "I can't show any preference."

It was unfair for Ryan to judge the other man when he had information that he couldn't share concerning Carter's innocence.

"Seriously, man," he said through the bars as he looked at Carter. He'd slid a prepackaged sandwich into the meal slot hoping to tempt the man into his first hint of sustenance for the week. "If you don't eat that, Barker is going to get a court order to tube feed you."

The justice system won't let you starve yourself to death and avoid prosecution, he thought but didn't add to the previous sentiments.

Carter's head turned towards the sandwich and Ryan could almost swear he heard the man's joints creak with effort. He watched him lean over, not leaving the cot, but reaching for the package slowly before returning to his designated seat.

Neither of them moved or spoke for a moment.

"I'm supposed to watch you eat it," Ryan offered.

Carter glanced down then unfolded the sandwich wrapper. He opened his mouth to speak, then coughed, almost unable to clear it.

"You got water?" he croaked out.

Ryan waved the bottle in his hand for Carter to see before putting it in the meal slot for him. Once the former chief had his beverage, he pulled a piece of the sandwich apart with his hands before eating it.

Ryan waited until he saw the man swallow before trying to pull conversation out of him.

"Why aren't you talking?" Ryan asked. It was a legitimate concern he had. Carter had been as unwise as to deny council last time he was in this predicament, which hurt him. This time, as far as Ryan could tell, talking could only help the man.

Carter shrugged, pulling another piece of sandwich off. "Got nothing to say."

"Bullshit," Ryan replied.

If he heard the expletive, Carter didn't show it. He continued picking at the food and sipping water without reacting to anything.

It was a hard scene to witness. When Ryan met him, Carter Cahill was this huge figure, a man promoted to leadership early in life and physically imposing. Even when what he'd learned about Christina and Carter began to scare him, Ryan still saw him as a great man, if not a good one.

This, his time in the cell, was the first time Ryan saw Carter as small, and to be honest, pathetic, though he felt more empathy than revulsion at the sight.

Ryan tried again. "I know you didn't do it. Either of them."

Carter chewed, Ryan's revelation giving him nothing new. "You don't know that," he said between bites. "I could confess right now. Save everyone the trouble."

"Don't you want to know what happened? At least to Lindsey?"

"It doesn't matter. I could be here, or out there, nothing changes. She's still gone," Carter said.

Ryan changed his mind. His empathy had officially converted to revulsion.

"What changes," Ryan explained to a man who knew better, "is that the murderer answers for their crime. Don't you want that for Lindsey?"

Carter finished his sandwich. "Lindsey's dead."

But she still needs your help, Ryan wanted to say. He wanted to tell Carter that if Erika was to be believed, Lindsey was likely watching, seeing Carter in his cell, waiting for justice before she moved on. Ryan wanted to tell him that his statement mattered in ways that wouldn't be measured by systems built by men on earth, but by something beyond that.

He didn't think Carter would believe him or understand the terms Erika had used, so he spoke with a language to which the other man could relate.

"You have an obligation and a duty to tell the truth. Even though it doesn't bring her back."

Carter tipped the water bottle back, finishing it. He swallowed without commitment, droplets spilling down the sides of his mouth as though he didn't care where it ended up.

Ryan stood with his hands in his pockets, facing the cell. He wasn't on the payroll for Oak Island police, so he didn't have any obligation to stay. Neither did he have any official responsibilities back home, so he could wait there as long as he needed.

Staring at Carter through the bars, Ryan silently begged the man to understand what he couldn't communicate without betraying Erika's trust.

"I didn't realize how much hope I had." Carter's voice cracked as he spoke.

Ryan leaned against his arm and peered through the bars.

"Part of me always thought she was coming back," he continued. "That's the only reason I've been able to keep going since she left. I think I believed, blindly, that she would return to me. Otherwise, I would have descended into this," he motioned to himself half-heartedly, "months ago."

Carter's head turned to the side, facing Ryan for the first time since he'd been visiting him in jail. "So, forgive me," he said, "if I don't give a shit where I spend the rest of my worthless days."

Were it not for the interruption, Ryan would have responded, but he didn't get the chance.

"Gibson," Paul called from the door to the cells. "Swap with Pratt."

Any extended amount of time spent with Tanner was not going to be good for Carter, but Ryan was without options. He didn't exactly work there.

"Sure," he said, not saying goodbye to Carter as he walked behind Officer Barker.

Tanner dipped his head as he passed them before he entered the cell block. Once the door closed behind him, Paul turned.

"There's someone here for you," he said.

Ryan knew not to get his hopes up that it was Erika, but he couldn't help it. "Who?"

"I don't know," Paul replied. "He said he'd only talk to you. We'll give him that, but he said it concerns open cases so you can use the interrogation room while I supervise from the watch area."

"Works for me," Ryan said, not allowing disappointment to flood his voice.

~

THIS WAS THE MOST NERVOUS Ryan had ever seen a man not accused of a crime.

Peter was fidgety to the point of vibrating in his seat. His attire was well-worn but clean, indicating a man without wealth but maintaining a sense of self-respect, including some diligently patched areas on knees and elbows. He didn't seem comfortable around police in general, so putting him in the interrogation room was likely a bad call, but this was the only place a private interview could occur.

Or, at least, an almost private interview. Ryan made sure not to look anywhere near the double-sided mirror.

"It's okay," Ryan tried to calm Peter down. "You're here voluntarily." It was silly to try and comfort someone who came to the station of his own volition, but the man seemed to need it.

Across the table, the man kept his hand on two packages, one a shoe box, the other a small brown shipping sleeve filled to its max.

Ryan avoided looking at them. Peter would tell him why they were there when he was ready.

"Right," Peter said. "I don't know where to start."

Praying for patience, Ryan tried to direct the man. "I was told you have information regarding an open case. You could start by telling me which one."

"Ah. Christina Higgins," Peter said.

Ryan clicked his pen to title his notes, showing no reaction to the name. If he was surprised at all to hear Christina's name, it was only because he'd been expecting Lindsey's. Christina's missing person case had been in the media long enough for most of the voluntary witnesses to have been filtered through already.

Lindsey's name was still fresh to the public.

"Why didn't you come forward when she went missing?"

Peter had settled down and almost appeared more comfortable when Ryan asked the more confrontational question. "Couple reasons," the man admitted. "I try and mind my own business. I don't feel there's any need for me to involve myself unless a crime has been committed."

"You didn't think her being reported missing implied a crime?"

"She could have moved on to another town, not told anyone. Like I said, it's none of my business," he repeated. "When you guys found the body, I thought it might be time to speak my piece."

Ryan pressed the tips of his fingers together and looked across the table. "You waited a few days to come in."

Peter raised an eyebrow. "Do you want to hear my story or not?"

One deep breath later, Ryan nodded. "Go ahead."

"I'm self-employed, and I do a bit of contracting work. Just maintenance stuff here and there, but as I get older, it's harder to do some of the more intense jobs. Last year, I took up ride-share on the weekends as a little bit of supplemental income. It also gives my wife one night a week to play bridge with her friends, which she appreciates."

Ryan didn't interrupt the man or push him to get to the point, but he also had nothing to write down, so he stared across the table without moving.

"A few weeks ago, I had my ride-share branded cab lights on parked near the beach. It wasn't busy, no tourists yet, but I kept myself online just in case. I was going to wait a full hour so Justine could finish her girl's night. As I was pulling away, ready to call it quits, I saw a man running out of the pier. Looked like he'd seen a ghost or something."

"Was he alone?"

"Yeah, or at least I thought he'd been. He definitely left alone, tore outta there real fast. He split in the opposite direction of where I parked."

Ryan made his first line of notes from the meeting. "Could you describe his appearance?"

"Only in the vaguest sense," Peter said. "Definitely Caucasian. He seemed to be a bigger guy with a clean-cut look to him."

"You think you might be able to pull him out of a line-up?"

Peter shook his head. "Not on the record. It was nighttime outside here. Too much mist and shadows and whatnot."

Ryan didn't show any disappointment. Carter had already admitted to being there, so they weren't likely to get an identification on anyone else who might have been there that night and he fit the description.

"Did you see anyone else?"

"After the man left like that, I decided to stay parked another few minutes, maybe see what he was running from. Imagine my surprise when a lady walked across the pier from the same direction."

Adding to his notes, Ryan's curiosity was peaked. "Why would that be surprising? Couples meeting up on the beach at night can't be too uncommon."

"You're not wrong there," Peter replied, settling back in his chair, seemingly having decided he could trust Ryan. "What was surprising was the order they left the beach. You don't see grown men sprinting away from beautiful women like that."

"How did you know she was beautiful?"

"I'm getting to it," Peter chided. "Like I said, the order was weird. You have this grown man running away, and then this tiny thing strutting across the pier like she doesn't have a care in the world. She almost looked like she was skipping along the planks or something. I told myself that whatever happened between her and that guy was none of my business, but I couldn't just leave her there without asking if she needed a ride somewhere. It's why I was there in the first place."

"Right," Ryan responded, needing to see where this went.

"I pulled up to where she's walking, or gliding, or whatever and roll down my window. I asked her if she needed a ride and she grinned through my window at me. She said her destination was pretty far away and asked if I would take cash.

"I said it depends on how far we were going and how much cash she had. These ride-share companies don't pay out like they used to, so anytime I can work out a cash deal with a rider is best for both of us."

Ryan interrupted. "Did you know who she was when you were speaking to her?"

"Not exactly," Peter said. "I didn't ask for her name until we agreed on the terms of her cab fare."

"And what were those?"

"She gave me $1500 cash to drive her two hours away. The address was next to a national forest."

Ryan wrote down the address as Peter recited it, apparently from memory, and was not at all shocked to see that it matched the Cahill Lodge.

"Do you have anyone that can verify what you just told me?"

"Justine will tell you that I was out later than normal that night, but other than that," he spoke as he pulled a sheet of paper out of the top package, "here's my phone's GPS data for that night. It shows a round trip from Oak Island to Croatan with no real stops anywhere along the way."

Peter's hand shook as he passed Ryan the paper, the only indication of his nervousness since he started telling his story. The data looked good, but they would get a warrant for the official records from the phone company when actual evidence was needed.

"Can you describe what she was wearing?"

Ryan listened intently as Peter detailed the same outfit Christina's body was found wearing.

He noted this on the pad before his follow-up. "Anything else identifiable?"

"Yeah," Peter said. "When she leaned into the window to talk to me, I was about blinded by that overpriced trinket on her wrist. I'm lucky my Justine doesn't care about flashy junk like that."

In all caps, Ryan wrote in his notes that Christina was still in possession of the bracelet after Carter left her that night.

That information was more for him than anyone else at the station. It was tangible proof that Christina had lied to Erika since no bracelet was found at the Cahill Lodge and that she was still in possession of it after Carter left that night.

"So, you dropped her off and then went home? Never thought about her again until she went missing?"

"Not exactly," he hedged. "There's more."

"Go ahead," Ryan replied.

The man sighed then ran his hands through what was left of his hair. "For most of the ride, she was quiet in the backseat. I prefer it that way, so it didn't bother me. She can look out her window, I can look out mine. I was getting paid handsomely to get her to this place so if she wanted quiet, she could have it.

"About thirty minutes away, I catch her in my rearview mirror sipping on something. Not the biggest deal in the world, but the open container laws in North Carolina are intense. I could lose my contracts with these online cab companies or in some circumstances lose my license if I get pulled over and one of my passengers is drinking, you know?"

"Sure," Ryan said. "Did you tell her to stop?"

"Absolutely," he replied. "I said if she didn't close it up, I'd pull over and drop her off at the closest stop. She told me it wasn't alcohol, and I didn't smell any, so I dropped it. We were almost there, and it was a lot of money.

"We pulled up to this huge cabin thing, real fancy shit. It didn't seem like the kind of place she'd have access to, and it looked empty, which worried me. I asked her if it was even safe for me to drop her off. She just laughed at me before opening her door. I could hear her muttering to herself at this point, and I figured she'd been lying about the alcohol."

"What was she saying?"

Peter shifted in his seat. "Things like 'I'll show him,' or 'watch him try and get out of this one.' I just hurried her along and once she was out of my vehicle I drove away. Didn't even wait for her to get inside, which is unlike me, but the whole night was starting to feel a little too much like the first scene of a horror movie for me. I got out of there, and that was that."

Ryan scratched the stubble growing on his jaw. He felt like he was getting half a story, one he was never going to get all the answers to, but he might not need all of them to prove Carter didn't kill those women. "Anything else?"

"Yeah," Peter said, pulling a sealed plastic bag out of the top package. "This is what she was drinking in the backseat."

Sitting on the table between them were two empty bottles of liquid NyQuil. Ryan had no idea what the fatal doses were for an over the counter cold and flu sleep aid, but it was reasonable to expect that two full bottles would knock Christina out long enough for her to not care that she was freezing to death.

"You just held on to these for over a month?"

"Well, no," he admitted. "I didn't know they were back there. For my ride-share work, I bought a used EV. Better for taxes and all that, plus it meant I wasn't putting too many miles on Justine and my regular car. The rechargeable car I only use for driving people around for money. I hadn't been inside it since that night. That Christina woman really freaked me out, so I was taking a little hiatus from cab driving until spring break starts up. Anyway, it had gone unused and uncharged until the young woman made me search it."

Ryan paused his note writing. "Young woman?"

"The one who talked me into coming in today," Peter said.

The pulse of his heartbeat echoed in his ears as Ryan fought to stay on topic. "You said you came here to speak to us because Christina's body was found."

Peter had the self-awareness to look guilty for his cowardice but didn't shrink away from Ryan's scrutiny. "That was part of it, sure. But the young woman convinced me that if I didn't come forward, innocent people would suffer. I told her about that night, and we searched the car together."

Clicking his pen, Ryan's eyes drilled into the sealed plastic bag on the table. "We'll keep these as evidence," he said coldly. "Are you comfortable repeating what you've told me under penalty of perjury before a judge?"

"Yes, sir," Peter replied, deferential to Ryan's authority. Without thinking, he glanced at the shoe box still sitting under Peter's hand.

"Ah," the man noticed his gaze. "This is for you, and whoever else," Peter waved his hand around, as if indicating the entirety of the police station, "that it may concern."

He slid the box towards Ryan, who saw his name printed across the lid in clear block letters. Ryan pulled it closer to him, not bothering to cover his hands so they could dust for prints later. He knew it would be a lost cause.

"But this," Peter added, "is just for you."

Peter pulled a small envelope out of his jacket and held it out across the table.

Ryan stared at the note. His gut burned with a desire to know what it said, to get any piece of her that he could. It was like reawakening an exercise habit after a vacation; he knew that he could pore over that note, try to find her, follow her to where she was going next. The habits needed to search for her again were burned into his soul. He'd spent so many months tracking her, what was another few weeks?

But another part of him, the rational one, told him that reading the note wouldn't be another clue.

It would be goodbye.

"Thank you," was all he said to Peter, as he pulled the envelope away and shoved it into his pocket. "Let's get you checked out then you can be on your way."

36

CARTER, SOON TO BE THE FORMER Chief of Police for Oak Island, drove his vehicle carefully down the familiar road.

Less than twenty-four hours ago, he faced a lifetime in prison until Ryan and Paul had walked up to his cell and opened it. He'd been too malnourished to know what was happening, but they pulled him into his own office and sat him behind the desk. After forcing him to eat another sandwich, Ryan placed a shoe box in front of him.

"What's this?"

"Your ticket out of here," Ryan said. Carter looked at the box then up at Detective Gibson and Officer Barker, unable to mask his confusion but not caring if the other men saw it.

Over the next several minutes, Ryan unpacked the box and explained its contents to Carter who stared down at them without blinking. There were photographs of a nine-millimeter pistol being purchased from a pawn shop in South Carolina, along with the GPS coordinates of a cell phone user for the entire week leading up to when he received the break-up note from Lindsey.

A note he had to keep reminding himself was falsified. She didn't leave him, and she wasn't coming back.

Lastly, there was a single leather glove sealed in an evidence bag.

"It was a complete fuck up, losing the glove like that," Paul said as Carter worked his way through the box's contents. He knew what he was seeing, and he understood what it all meant, but the reality of what happened to Lindsey wasn't sinking in for him.

It likely wouldn't until the culprit was brought to justice.

"We're going to run everything we find on it," Ryan continued for Paul. "We expect the blood to come back as a match for Lindsey, and if we're lucky, we'll be able to pull a print or two from inside. While the evidence is processing, the judge will have a search warrant for us in the next hour or two so we can see if there's a matching glove or even a weapon on the property. In the meantime, we're going to ask that you stay here," he finished. "We don't want the perp to know we've exonerated you until after we're able to search the property."

Carter remained quiet as he shuffled through the papers, handing the glove back to Ryan. He turned to Paul when he finally spoke, knowing he was the only one with enough political sway to get him what he was asking for.

"I want to lead this," he implored his former subordinate.

Officer Barker didn't reveal any outward discomfort, though Carter knew he probably felt it. "Chief, I don't know if that's possible. You're really close to this, in more ways than one, so we would need permission from the prosecutor. Not to mention whatever probationary status the mayor needs from you after your involvement with Christina."

Ryan had explained Christina's suicide and attempt to frame him for murder to Carter on the way to the office. It was fantastic in its unbelievability, so much so that Carter found himself believing it right away.

He should never have been involved with her in the first place.

"Tell the prosecutor I just want to be there and make any arrests. I won't touch anything or even lead the forensics teams," Carter said to Paul. "And tell the mayor that if he lets me have this, I'll resign immediately after. He'll be free from having to apologize on my behalf and he can appoint someone else. He can just wash his hands of me publicly."

The silence in the office was so overwhelming that Carter thought the other two men might not be breathing.

Paul cleared his throat, effectively ending the stalemate. "Chief, are you sure about this? Everyone on the force would still support you."

Both of them knew that wasn't entirely true, that there would be no going back to the respect his people had for him before Christina's body was discovered. He believed that they would all very earnestly try, that his men would do their best to see him as they had before, but the reality was that Carter's mistakes would be a shadow over everything they did going forward.

"I'm positive. Let me have this, and I'll walk away," he'd assured them.

Carter parked his vehicle outside the mansion and waited for the rest of the investigative team to pull up behind him. As they parked, he stomped on the steps of the porch, the pink cross necklace slapping against his skin under his uniform where it now hung from his neck.

The morning was bright, sunny in a way that felt like it was mocking him. It should be foggy or rainy or hurricane season. His Lindsey was gone, and Carter wanted nature to grieve her like he was.

He rang the bell, then knocked heavily three times.

It was the middle of the day, so not many people would be home, but a man answered right away.

"Mr. Cahill, to what do I owe—"

"We have a warrant to search the property," Carter interrupted, holding the paper up for the man to read. He didn't waste time waiting for his response but held the door open for the forensics team to enter after him into the foyer. The group spread out rapidly, descending into each room in teams of two.

"I'll need to alert everyone about this, sir," the man holding the warrant up as if Carter wouldn't know what he was talking about.

"You go ahead and do that," he replied, turning and walking farther into the house so the man wouldn't see his smile.

He kept an eye on everyone without interfering, observing quietly while the men and women worked in each room, shuffling through papers and moving photos, digging into every cabinet and pulling up every couch cushion.

"Chief," someone called down the stairs.

"Yes?"

"There's a locked safe in the office. Do you want us to wait for a locksmith?"

"No," Carter replied. "Go ahead and drill it."

"You got it, sir."

A little less than an hour passed during the search before someone found something. Carter had been walking through the upstairs halls, ignoring family portraits hanging up around him when another forensic tech called him into the master bedroom.

"Got something," a woman yelled for him.

With nitrile glove covered hands, she held up a leather glove that easily could have matched the one delivered to Detective Gibson from the cab driver.

"It's the only single glove," she explained.

"Bag it," Carter said. Before he could congratulate the woman on her find, a booming voice hollered throughout the home from the foyer.

"ASHLEY," his father screamed up the stairs at him.

Carter moved towards the voice with no urgency. On his way to the stairwell, the team working in the second-floor office intercepted him.

"Chief," the man spoke from the doorway. "This was in the safe."

He held up a nine-millimeter semi-automatic with the suppressor still attached to the barrel.

"Thank you," Carter said. "I think we have everything we need."

He walked down the stairs, seeing his father barely restrained by two officers.

"What the hell do you think you're doing?" he seethed up at his son.

"Robert Cahill," Carter began the Miranda rights. "You are under arrest for the murder of Lindsey Payne."

"I'll kill you for this, Ashley," the older man spat over his shoulder.

You complete idiot.

"You have the right to remain silent," Carter continued, though he hoped his father wasn't listening. The man could talk himself into a life sentence for all he cared. "Anything you say can and will be used against you in a court of law. You have the right to an attorney. If you cannot afford an attorney, one will be appointed to you."

If there had been anything humorous that came out of the hell that

Carter had lived through the past few months, it would be the image of Max Everitt trying to keep Robert out of prison, fruitlessly begging the proud man to take a plea deal.

He wrapped up the explanation of rights as they exited the home and walked towards a squad car. He passed Robert to another officer, who then placed him in the backseat before starting the car. That would be the last of Chief Cahill's involvement in the case, though he may be required to testify if it made it to trial.

Carter had the privilege of putting hand cuffs on his own father, the man who murdered Lindsey. It wouldn't bring her back, but being able to participate felt like absolution, for failing her while she was alive, for believing that she would leave him in a note.

He should have known better.

The mayor didn't have to let Carter do it. He would have been well within his rights to deny the request, and the chief knew that he didn't have anything to negotiate with besides his own apology. But the men had a trusting, years long relationship, and the mayor had solemnly offered his condolences for Carter's loss and given him the right to arrest Lindsey's murderer as a retirement gift.

That gift might have been the only thing that kept Carter from murdering Robert himself.

He watched the back of his father's head through the rear window of the squad car until it disappeared for a right turn off the property.

For several minutes, Carter stared at nothing until Officer Barker clapped his shoulder and pulled him away from his morbid thoughts. "If I don't get the chance later," Paul began, "it's been an honor working with you."

Carter waited for a group of the forensics team to walk out of earshot before speaking. "I endorsed you to the mayor as the next chief of police," he said.

Surprise erupted unbidden on Officer Barker's face, though he covered it without hesitation. "I don't know what to say, sir."

"You don't have to say anything. You're the right man for the job," Carter replied.

An uncomfortable silence fell over them, and it saddened Carter. He used to be so at ease with his men, his authority unquestioned and his position respected. He didn't know who he was without Lindsey, let alone who he was or what he would do after retiring from his leadership role with the police.

   "You were the right man for the job once, too," Paul offered. "We won't ever forget that."

   Instead of replying, Carter gave Paul a firm handshake and a sad smile that didn't reach his eyes. "You guys go ahead and wrap up, then head back to the station. I have to do something before I hand over my vehicle."

   Paul nodded and returned to the task of cleaning up after the search, while Carter began the drive to the lodge to retrieve Lindsey's engagement ring from his bedside table.

37

A LOCAL NEWS STATION played on the small television in Ryan's motel room as he packed his bags.

It seemed like the entire state of North Carolina was now aware of the deadly drama that had unfurled in Oak Island. Local reporters speculated with almost uncontained glee about the Cahill family dynamics that led their patriarch to murder his son's fiancée. They let their imaginations fly, going on about secret wealth and inheritances that didn't exist, feuds between founding families of the town gone haywire. Never mind that Robert's wealth was accumulated during his lifetime and Oak Island didn't have founding families, the reporters were slaves to an attention economy, and more eyes on them meant renewed contracts with expensive pharmaceutical advertisers.

The coverage of Christina Higgins wasn't much better, though they didn't have to extrapolate far from the truth for that story to be salacious. A woman, driven insane by the romantic scorn of a handsome man, had tried to frame him for murder with her own suicide. No need to add any opinions to that story.

With Robert being held without bail, and Carter remaining silent, Scarlett Cahill became the public face of the Cahill family. As he folded clothes into his duffle, Ryan watched her be interviewed press conference style in front of the Cahill Group offices.

"I can't comment on my father's case," she spoke into a microphone, "but know that our family's hearts are broken for Lindsey. She is missed dearly, and I always considered her to be a sister to me."

Ryan wondered cynically if that could possibly be true, based on Carter's aversion to his own family.

"What will happen to the Cahill Group fortune moving forward? And how do you justify becoming rich with the fortune of an accused murderer?" one particularly bold reporter asked.

"I'm glad you brought that up," Scarlett replied with a smile so convincing many people might actually believe she was grateful to the reporter. "My father has severed all ties to the Cahill Group, wanting what's best for the employees and realtors who are an important driver of the local economy. It would be an unnecessary hardship to layoff so many hard-working citizens of Oak Island because of the alleged actions of one man.

"On that note, I have a community objective update for you all," Scarlett continued, flipping a piece of paper on her podium. "We at Cahill Group saw that our town has a gap between resources and support offered for women in need and the number of people requesting those resources. This is a condemnation of us all, when we fail to take care of those who are weaker than us.

"Cahill Group is partnering with local women's shelters by converting several of our available properties into safe houses for women fleeing violent homes. This unprecedented action will allow more women to be brave enough to walk away from harmful situations and start searching for a better life."

"It's also probably a nice tax break," Ryan scoffed into his empty hotel room. Despite his bitterness, he was suitably impressed. Watching Scarlett turn the crowd around was like watching a public relations magician.

Done with his clothes, Ryan looked across the room at the desk, still covered by the map that had been his guiding force for almost a year.

He didn't need it anymore. He'd already decided before reading Erika's note that he wouldn't try to find her, wouldn't follow her to her next investigations, wherever they took her. Her words had only confirmed that.

"I didn't need your apology," he muttered to himself, though he'd kept the note in his pocket since first reading it.

Ryan didn't feel right leaving the map either, so he folded it away, each familiar crease life a knife taking a little slice of his soul. He knew he wouldn't open it again, but neither could he throw it away. He felt like a religious devotee who had made an impossible pilgrimage, only to discover that his faith was a lie.

The truth changed him, as did confronting his own failures, but he wasn't ready to destroy the holy texts yet.

After one more sweep of the room, ensuring he didn't leave any phone chargers or socks behind, he slid his backpack on, grabbed his duffel, and said goodbye to the motel. It looked different, though he'd obviously not changed anything about it. It was the fact that he arrived there with so much hope and felt like he was leaving having found what he was looking for, before realizing it wasn't what he needed.

Ryan thought that maybe too much of life was spent with unfulfilled expectations.

As the motel door slammed behind him, he clicked his truck's fob to open the doors, only to stop right before he got there.

Carter was leaning against his passenger door with a bag of his own, staring at his feet.

"Where are you going?" Ryan asked.

The other man looked up and shrugged. Seeing Carter before him was not dissimilar to Ryan's view of the motel room. Nothing much about the former chief of police had changed physically since they met, but Ryan's view of the man had shifted so many times it was like looking at a stranger.

"Wherever you're going," he said, and opened the passenger door to let himself inside before Ryan could respond. He followed, throwing all his bags in the back seat before getting behind the wheel and turning on the engine.

"You don't even know if I have a destination in mind," Ryan said to his passenger, though he was misleading him on purpose. He had already decided to go back to Wyoming.

"It doesn't matter," Carter said. "There's nothing left for me here."

That, at least, was something they had in common.

They rode together listening to a local station until a few towns later they lost the signal for it, and another took its place.

"Did you ever find that guy?" Carter asked. "The one with the evidence?"

It wasn't a shock for him to care. Ryan's life had been changed by Erika's help back in Cody, and Carter's had been saved by those same methods recently. If he hadn't been mourning Lindsey and the life they could have had, Ryan guessed that Carter would have developed the same obsession he had, wondering who had swung in heroically and saved his ass with an anonymous tip.

"Not really," Ryan lied. "It wasn't what I thought it was."

"Bummer," Carter said. "I know that was important to you. Sorry, man."

Seaside towns became mountain towns as they moved westward into the state, with views so beautiful they begged drivers to pull over and admire them.

They were parked at a gas station outside Knoxville, Tennessee, when Ryan giggled out of nowhere, then snorted trying to hide the sound.

"Something funny?"

"Yeah." Ryan almost descended into laughter again. "I just realized I'm going to have to go to my brother's wedding."

The two men looked at each other, and Carter cracked his first half smile since the morning Christina's body had been found in his lodge.

"You're right," his smile widened slightly. "That's hilarious."

38

THE LAKELAND SUN BEAT down on Erika with relentless enthusiasm. When she left Oak Island, her intuition drew her south, through Georgia and across the state line into Florida, she assumed she might be working on the coast again. It didn't excite her like it should have. She thought the sounds of the ocean would only sadden her, reminding her of what she left behind in North Carolina.

After landing in the central part of the state, she was rethinking that preference.

"Your generation doesn't understand the evil it's ushering in, voting for all these dagum socialist nutcases," Charles grumbled from his spot next to her on the bench they shared. Lakeland, which Erika resented for its spring heat wave, was at the very least not misnamed, and from their seat they had a view of a mid-sized lake sprinkled with fishing boats.

She wiped a collection of sweat off her forehead and fanned herself with a gas station atlas.

"Do you know what age I was when I learned what socialism really is?"

Erika didn't bother guessing at this point. She would get the story from him anyway. "Let's hear it, Charles," she said.

"I was eleven," he continued. "I took a summer job with some other kids at an orange grove where we were told we'd be paid daily to pick oranges.

We'd get paid twenty-five cents a box. Out of all the kids, I picked the most oranges by far. No one else even came close. I had picked eight boxes that day, thinking I made two dollars, and do you know what happened?

"All of us got paid the same single dollar. It was an outrage. I asked the man in charge where the rest of my money was, and he said that as a group we were paid per box picked, not as individuals, and the average amount picked that day was four boxes, not my eight. That was my first and last day on that farm. I never went back. And that's what socialism does, it punishes the hardworking."

He shuffled in his seat before continuing. "Your socialism cost me a full dollar back in 1938. Still makes my blood boil."

At ninety-seven years old, Charles was by far the oldest ghost Erika had ever seen, much less drawn to work with. She'd been listening to his stories for a week and couldn't begin to figure out why he was the one fate chose for her this time.

"You're a wasteful generation, too. I can't believe the amount of food you all throw away," he continued. "I used to make a Little Caesar's pizza last a week. You can freeze the slices individually, you know. Heat it up and it tastes the same. No need to just toss out what you don't use."

He concluded this particular monologue by explaining that past-ripe, brown bananas are just as delicious as fresh ones.

At first, Erika didn't mind the detour through memory lane with Charles, and it was interesting to hear from someone who had lived during the Great Depression and seen so much that she had only read about. After everything that happened with Christina, she wasn't ready to jump immediately back into her traditional work. She wasn't sure she could trust her instincts anymore, and that scared her. If she couldn't rely on her gut, she had nothing. What if things had been different? What if Carter hadn't saved her from the ocean and she'd been unable to clear his name?

Those questions would keep her up at night for a long time.

But after a few days, she became antsy. There must be a reason she arrived in Lakeland, a reason Charles was still here. In her experience, no one stayed after death without a purpose or something important they left behind. So, amidst his stories, she peppered him with questions that might lead to more information, anything to tell her why he needed her help.

If he spoke about his family, she would ask if there was anyone alive who still needed him.

"Oh, that would be a nice thought," he chuckled. "To still be needed. I'll be missed, but my children are grown and have their own children. I even got to meet several great-grandchildren."

He didn't say as much, but Charles did imply that he had outlived most of his friends his own age.

When he discussed his declining health in his later years, Erika would wonder out loud if there had been any funny business.

Disagreeing, Charles said it had been his time.

"People don't just stay here," she explained. "There must be a reason you're waiting. It's not easy to keep this up," she argued, gesturing towards where he sat.

They were in a safe area, where no one could see them, so Erika didn't need to hide her side of the conversation. As she leaned against the bench and stared at him, he appeared to be taking her question seriously.

"A friend of mine lived to be one-hundred and seven years old," Charles said. "I always wanted to beat him."

Erika blinked twice before responding. "That's it? That's why you think you're still here?"

Charles's laugh was full-throated. "I'm just joking," he chuckled as he talked. "I don't think I'll stay here that long."

They both turned to the lake, watching the small boats anchored in place across the water. He spoke again, less boisterously this time, "I couldn't spend ten years like this. It's too quiet."

Erika almost felt bad for bringing it up. Charles had clearly been social while he was alive, and she resigned herself to being his companion until he moved on. Maybe this was the kind of place she could be useful after her mistakes in Oak Island.

Maybe God or death or the universe didn't trust her with hard cases anymore.

"I've got a tip for you," Charles interrupted her thoughts. "For when it's your turn."

"My turn?"

"To get married," he explained. "If you get married on Easter, the church will already be decorated with spring florals. You can save money on flowers that way."

She withheld a scoff. "People like me don't get married."

"Why not? You're young, pretty, smart. You probably have a boyfriend in every town."

"Because I'm doing this," she pointed back and forth between them. "I talk to ghosts, Charles. I help them move on, to find justice. I can't just drop all of that to play house with someone."

Charles waved her off dismissively. "Sure, you can," he said.

"What I do is significant," she whined.

"It's unique, I suppose."

Erika stood up and glared at him. "Unique? As far as I know, I'm the only one who can do this. No one else is working with these people like I am. They need me."

"That's a mighty self-important take, young lady," Charles countered.

"Maybe because what I'm doing is important!"

"Take a seat, honey."

Charles tone held no invitation to negotiate, so she sat and crossed her arms, refusing to look at him.

"I know about doing important things," he said. "I enlisted in World War II. I solved interstate crimes for the FBI during its genesis. I owned and operated a hardware business, employing people and providing vital necessities to my town. You know what all that pales in comparison to, on the list of things I did that made an impact?"

Still pouting, Erika stared out at the lake, eyes squinting at the sun's reflection off the surface.

It was too hot to have this kind of conversation.

"My family," Charles said. "That was what was most important. That is my real legacy, not the awards or the social clubs. I won't be remembered for the things I did for strangers, who have already forgotten me even if I'm listed in some historical records. It's my children and my children's children who remember me and were most impacted by my time on earth. So, maybe you help people, doing this, I can see that. But I'm already gone, and if you spend your life with people like me, you may as well be gone, too."

Erika swallowed back a pain coming from the back of her throat. She still couldn't look at Charles, and her pride wouldn't let her speak only to hear her voice crack over the words, so they sat quietly for a few minutes.

"I think I figured it out," he said.

"What's that?"

"I'm not still here because I need your help," he explained.

She recrossed her legs, so she could face him more comfortably. He had an elbow relaxed against the back of the bench, still facing the water.

"I'm here because you need mine."

Hoping he didn't see, Erika wiped away a stray tear that had somehow made its way halfway down her cheek.

I don't know who I am anymore.

The sun had finally moved beyond the middle of the sky, but it offered little relief from the heat. Erika used her map fan to dry her face and keep anything else from leaking out of her eyes.

"Okay, Charles," she said after another natural break in their conversation. "Tell me about the FBI."

"You ever been to East St. Louis?"

"Can't say that I have."

"I didn't have the best experience there myself. It was an interstate car parts theft operation that brought me there," Charles began, and Erika listened with renewed interest.

39

RYAN FIRED THE LAST NAIL of the day, then studied it to make sure it was flush with the wood. They still had plenty of light, but the sun was beginning to set earlier than it had a few weeks ago and it was time to call it a day. As he began descending his ladder, he heard Sergeant Vincent's voice from below.

"I always knew you'd come back to work for me, son."

Ryan couldn't resist the small smile as he took each step down, finally on the ground with his former boss. "If you're going to try and tell me this is what you had in mind, I won't believe you," he replied as he folded the ladder to store it for the next workday.

After Carter and Ryan arrived in Wyoming, they found themselves in a similar situation. Neither of them wanted to return to police work, Carter because he couldn't, having violated the law in his last official role, and Ryan because he wasn't ready. He was still on the fence about whether he wanted to work as a detective ever again.

He knew he needed something tangible. He needed to have a task and see it physically completed each day. It was good for his soul to have a project and be able to materially execute it. After Erika, he didn't want to go directly back into a career that relied on instinct.

They were both much older than their other colleagues, but Carter and

Ryan had decided to enter a framing apprenticeship together. It was exactly what Ryan needed, and he could tell Cahill was doing better, too.

Construction was tangible. The lumber beneath his hands in the morning was real. The kickback from the nail gun when he pulled the trigger was real. The weight of a hammer or a tape measure against his palm was real.

Watching a blueprint come to life before his eyes was rewarding in a way that Ryan hadn't anticipated.

"I don't much care how it happened," Vincent said. "We're just glad to have you back home. Loretta, too."

Loretta had given him an earful when he got back to Cody, browbeating Ryan about not keeping in touch when everything happened. She'd had to learn about Robert, Lindsey, and Christina from an internet article while Ryan and Carter were still crossing the country in his truck.

Normally, he would have understood her anger, welcomed it even. He certainly deserved it. But her lecture had come at the reception for Colleen and Travis's wedding, and Ryan hadn't appreciated the additional attention on him during an already weird day.

He and Carter, who he'd brought as his plus one at Colleen's insistence, left early after that episode.

Ryan removed his work gloves and pocketed them. "Not sure why someone your age is expanding," he said, both men facing the framing job.

The sergeant was creating an addition to his home, though all his kids had moved out years ago.

"You haven't heard?"

Ryan shook his head at his former mentor.

"I've got my first grandchild on the way." Vincent grinned, an expression not seen often on his face. "I figure my daughter is likely to bring the little guy around more often if her whole family can fit here."

"Congratulations, sir," Ryan said, offering a handshake with genuine happiness for the older man. "I'm honored you think my work here is good enough for your family."

"Not a lot to choose from around here," Vincent declared, back to his usual gruff demeanor almost as quickly as it had changed to joy. "Do you guys think it'll be done before the first snow?"

It was only August, but weather shifted quickly near the mountains, and the sergeant was probably right to be concerned.

"I think so," Ryan replied. "It probably won't be entirely finished, but it will be insulated and ready for the elements. It's just one suite."

"Good, good," the man stood with his hands clasped behind his back, surveying his property. It wasn't difficult to own land in Wyoming compared to other states, but Vincent had taken care to make sure he left something behind for his family, making him the proud owner of a ranch style house with over twenty acres.

"I'm glad you've found something that suits you for the time being," Vincent continued, "but I don't think avoiding your calling on the police force is a good long-term strategy. Our doors are open when you're ready."

He didn't wait for a reply, leaving Ryan to pack his tools alone before loading his truck. He knew his old sergeant was probably right, but he wasn't ready to even consider it. There was too much left for him to process before he went back to detective work. The job itself was unlikely to change, and he would maintain his commitment to uncovering the truth and demanding justice from the legal system.

Ryan just had to come to terms with the fact that any murder victim he dealt with in the future might be watching him work, unable to communicate their experiences.

The worst part was that he had to process that reality alone. He couldn't share Erika's secret, and who would believe him? It's not like it would help Carter to know that the woman he loved was trapped in some kind of limbo until her murder was solved.

No, he would keep those secrets and find closure in solitude.

Carter's own equipment was nearby, and they boxed everything up together before walking towards the temporary parking area on the edge of Sergeant Vincent's property.

"Want to grab a bite after this?" Ryan asked over the sound of wheels crunching against gravel.

"Can't," Carter replied. "I'm getting dinner at Loretta's."

When they first got to Cody, Ryan anticipated having to drag a morose Carter along with him to social events. After losing Lindsey, then watching the rest of his life fall apart due at least in part to his own actions, as well as those of his father, he would have thought that the former police chief would need time to mourn, that the man would become a recluse in this town he'd never seen before.

The opposite had been true. Carter missed Lindsey deeply and had told Ryan he might never move on from loving her. She had been the one, and he didn't see that changing.

But she was the only thing about his old life he seemed to miss.

"I get a chance to start over," he'd said once over drinks. "How many people get to have that? I'm not going to waste it."

They approached the trucks, lowering the tailgates of their own vehicles. "How come you keep getting all these fancy invites to Loretta's for dinner? I thought she was my friend," Ryan complained.

"Her husband likes me better," Carter joked back. "Plus, I'm helping David prepare for football tryouts. He said there's a lot of competition for Varsity this year, and he's aged out of JV."

Ryan grunted back, both because he didn't have a response and because the act of heaving his toolbox into the truck bed was more effort than he anticipated.

Carter, annoyingly, appeared to lift his tools without effort and shut the tailgate. Something on the other side of his vehicle caught his eye, but Ryan was still loading.

"What's she doing here?" Carter asked.

"What are you talking about?"

Carter's gaze was pinned to something beyond his truck, and Ryan had to shuffle around to his side to see what he was complaining about.

Sitting alone on the hood of her sedan was a small woman with a brunette ponytail.

"Oh," Ryan said. "I think she's here for me."

Carter was silent for a moment before turning around to face him. "She's not Christina's cousin, is she?"

Ryan shook his head but didn't look away from Erika, lest she disappear on him again if he averted his eyes for even a second.

The other man moved towards his driver's seat but stopped to clasp Ryan on the shoulder before leaving.

"Tell her I said thank you," he spoke quietly, neither of the men looking at each other. "For Lindsey."

"Of course."

Ryan listened, rather than watched, as Carter drove his truck off Sergeant Vincent's property.

His pride wanted him to get in his car and leave without speaking to her. If he'd had the strength, if he was a different man, maybe he would have.

But he was Ryan Gibson, and she was Erika Willet, so the only choice was to talk to her.

He walked, crunching the gravel road under his feet, until he reached her front fender.

Ryan had imagined this moment, fantasized about it countless times over the weeks since she left him. He'd practiced monologues berating her for disappearing, picturing her begging him for another chance. In his imagination, he was stoic and emotionless delivering the story of what she'd put him through. He would tell her that she can't run away from the people she cares about without hurting them and she was wasting both their time by showing up again.

But he didn't say any of that. All that came out was, "Why are you here?"

It came out harsher than he intended, but he kept himself from wincing.

Erika's arms were wrapped around her knees, and she kept herself in a tight ball on the hood of her car. She looked at him with an imploring countenance, but apparently didn't see what she wanted, so her attention turned towards the gravel.

"Did you get my note?"

He nodded.

"Well, I meant it. I shouldn't have said those things, and I'm sorry," she said.

Ryan didn't respond. She still hadn't answered his question, and he could wait silently all night until he got one that was adequate.

"It's not the same," she said softly. "I tried to go back to the way I was before but it's all wrong."

He stood over her, unmoving while she continued. "I thought I was

doing something really vital, and in a way, I was. I do think I made a difference, not just for the people who were gone, but for the people left behind."

She coughed to clear her throat, then finally looked back up at him.
"But it's different. They don't seem to need me anymore, or at least not the
way I was going about it. I can still see them, you know? It's just..." she
trailed off, as if not knowing how to explain.

Ryan was in the same boat. He also didn't know what she was talking
about.

"I think I realized that it's time to stop moving. To stop running to the
next place and maybe settle somewhere. Then I remembered one of the
detectives I helped, remembered that I liked the town, and thought I'd ask
him if he wanted my help exclusively. You know, like a consultant or
something."

"A consultant," he deadpanned.

"Or something. Maybe like a team," she replied.

"As you can see," he pointed behind him to the under-construction
portion of Vincent's house, "I'm not working as a detective right now."

He didn't know why he said "right now" and not "anymore," but Erika
didn't miss the implication of his words. Her expression softened into a
look of sincerity and understanding that he wasn't sure he appreciated.

"You'll go back," she responded simply.

Ryan shoved his hands in his pockets, hoping that the action hid his
nerves. "I don't know what you want from me, Erika."

It wasn't unfair of him to ask for clarification. She'd given plenty of
mixed signals before, not to be deliberately manipulative, but because she
hadn't known the answer either.

He hoped, for both their sakes, that she knew it now.

She smiled at him, sad but genuine. "Do you want to grab a drink
with me?"

"What?"

Erika slid off the car and approached him slowly as if he would run
away if she moved too quickly. "Have a drink with me," she said. "I had a
weird day, and I could use the company."

She stood before him, looking up at him. Her face hadn't changed, and
not enough time had gone by to truly alter her appearance, but they were

both different than when they met on Oak Island. His first impression of her had been one of interest, and perhaps a little lust.

Standing over her on the gravel road, Erika's presence almost brought him to his knees.

When she reached into his pocket to pull out his hand, it felt right holding hers, like maybe there were a lot of hurdles ahead, but it would be better to face them with her if she was offering.

And then she smiled, and he realized that was the only option.

Ryan returned her smile tentatively. "I can do one drink."

ACKNOWLEDGMENTS

Thank you, Mom, for being my first editor and biggest cheerleader, and thank you, Dad, for being my best sales rep.

I'd also like to thank my editor, Randall, who played a key role in helping me fine-tune the plot points of this book; your help on this story was immense. Thank you as well to Patricia, my copy editor.

Thank you to Julia and Andrew from the Ten Hut team for all the hard work and support. I truly enjoyed working on these past two books with you guys.

Lastly, thank you, as always, to Russell, my loving husband. You are the best, and I love you more and more every day.

ABOUT THE AUTHOR

Clarice grew up in the American South and now lives in the Midwest with her husband. *The Keepers of Men* is her first novel.

 x.com/authorclaricem

 instagram.com/authorclaricem

 amazon.com/stores/Clarice-Montgomery/author/B0DYQ777J1